THE IRISH COTTAGE

THE IRISH HEART SERIES, BOOK 1

THE IRISH COTTAGE

THE IRISH HEART SERIES, BOOK 1

BY JULIET GAUVIN

JULIET GAUVIN ✦ LOS ANGELES

Scaoil do ghreim agus ar aghaidh leat ag eitilt!

Contents

To my mother—the most interesting, ballsy person I've ever met.

THE IRISH COTTAGE

THE IRISH HEART SERIES, BOOK 1

Prologue: Mags

Dear Lizzie,

If you're reading this, it means I've gone off into the great unknown. My last great adventure. I'm writing this on the first day of the New Year. The doctor said I have a few weeks, maybe.

I suppose I should apologize for not telling you, but you know it isn't in my nature—especially since I'm rarely wrong. And, as usual, you have been incredibly busy; I don't want our remaining time to be spent on specialists and hospitals and you trying to fix everything. I'm just old Lizzie. Almost ninety is, well, almost ninety. We had a good run, kiddo. I could go on and make this a dramatic goodbye, filled with all the horse manure people expect you to put into a goodbye message, but I didn't put pen to paper to communicate pleasantries from beyond the grave.

This letter is for three things: 1) explaining the other letters, 2) kicking your uptight hiney into gear, and 3) apologizing for keeping a promise.

I have written you seventeen letters including this one. You know I was never one to hold anything back—always told you exactly what I was thinking. The thing is, I think I did hold back just a little, either because I didn't think you could hear me or because I thought you would find your own way eventually. But here I am at the end and I honestly don't know if you will find the way out by yourself—while you're still young. So here I am stacking the deck, making sure you do. Think of these letters as guideposts. .

You may not think you're lost, Lizzie, but you are. Winning isn't everything. Living is everything.

I've been disappointed to see all the color drain from your life. You haven't been able to separate who you are from what you do as a divorce lawyer. You used to be so full of life, so vibrant, so . . . fearless. Your opponents might think you're fearless, but I know better, Lizzie. You've been lost and scared for a while now.

Here's the part where I apologize. There were promises I made a long time ago. I swore to keep those secrets from you, against my better judgment, and for that I am truly sorry. Looking back, I think this whole ruthless lawyer thing might be my fault.

Ever since you were a girl, you believed certain things about your parents. You believed that your father divorced your mother and took everything; that she fell apart and left you, and that's why as your great-aunt and only remaining family, I came to raise you when you were four. I think you became such a formidable attorney because of this. You thought your mother was weak and abandoned you. You thought your father was a bastard for ruining your mother and also abandoning you. It doesn't take a genius to see where your issues with men come from, Lizzie.

But none of what you know is strictly the truth.

I promise to tell you how it all happened and the truth behind how you and I became our own unit of two. There's a plan to these letters. I know you must be furious with me for not telling you that I'm sick and for not telling you the truth I've been keeping for the last thirty-five years—and for not just spitting it out in this first letter—but I always did my best by you, so trust in me one last time.

Mags

P.S. Just because I'm dead, it doesn't mean I'm going to take it easy on you. Whether you know it right now or not, you've made quite a mess.

CHAPTER 1: IRELAND

The green was everywhere. The hills, the trees, even the tiny country road appeared to grow grass through the gravel. Ireland seemed intent on washing the black and gray out of her mind and replacing it with green.

There hadn't been a sign in miles. No way to tell if she was lost or going the right way.

"Damn it!" She slammed her hand against the rental car's navigation system. It kept losing its GPS signal.

There was a clearing one hundred feet ahead. She pulled to the side of the road and parked. The car purred to a stop as she turned the key in the ignition. Her knuckles turned bone-white as she gripped the wheel.

"Breathe, Beth, just breathe," she whispered, letting her hands fall from the steering wheel and onto her thighs with a muted thud.

Her head fell backwards against the headrest. Her eyes closed as she focused on the feeling of her chest rising and falling. And the sudden silence.

The light of the day illuminated her closed lids, creating a green screen for the flood of images and memories that crashed into her. Mags lying there looking emaciated, showing every bit of her eighty-nine years. All her vibrancy, her tenacity, her life ending.

And that look she had given Beth—wanting desperately to communicate something vitally important, but no longer having the ability to speak. It was a look of love and hope and something else . . . *pity*.

The tear trailed slowly down her cheek, electrifying her skin as it went. And then another.

The funeral had been bright with color, almost vulgar. Mags hated black and gray; "Anything but that!" she used to say. "Give me red, green, orange, purple—whatever, just give me something I can work with. Something to delight the senses." Her friends had remembered.

She was buried on a Saturday.

By Sunday Beth had received the box. It was blue with a red ribbon and held seventeen letters, each in its own bright envelope. No two were alike save for Mags' ornate writing, which labeled them all. *"Start Here Lizzie"* identified the first. It had left her breathless and reeling—sucker-punched her with no defendant to hold responsible, no legal recourse to make her whole, no escaping the mirror Mags had held up and forced on her.

No one to hold on to as Mags told her that everything she had come to believe about the parents who abandoned her . . . could be wrong.

She hadn't realized it until the letter, but she had become a lawyer to feel strong, unlike her mother. She had become a lawyer to stick it to all the bastards like her asshole father. For the last decade, she had inadvertently based her entire life on a series of assumptions about the two people who had created her. Assumptions which, apparently, were total bullshit.

A path subconsciously chosen because of secrets and lies. And she had no idea how far the rabbit hole went.

She wasn't due back in the office until Wednesday, but she was there on Monday morning resolute in her decision to leave. Bill had tried to convince her to take a couple of weeks. She needed longer.

He had turned almost purple enough to match his silk tie; the firm would sorely miss their lethal shark for however long she would be gone. But what could he do? Nothing. She was the best divorce attorney in San Francisco and she knew it.

The partners at Livingston & Bloom had always had to go along with her decisions. When it came to Beth, they had a proverbial gun to their heads. They were usually happy to oblige since she had made them millions with some of the most difficult and high-profile cases in California.

"How much time do you need?" Bill had prodded, following her into her office.

"I don't know," she huffed as she packed up the few personal items she kept in her desk. She stopped and looked out of corner office, towards the windows that held the perfect view of the Golden Gate Bridge and the bay. "At least a couple of months, maybe more." She returned to the matter of packing up the box she had brought with her. "I'm taking an extended leave."

Bill swayed where he stood, thinking about how to approach her. His potbelly protruded over his five-hundred-dollar belt. "Come on, Elizabeth, you're grieving." He thought some more. "Just don't make any life decisions right now." He held up his hands like he was trying to calm a wild animal. "Take the month. We'll shuffle the clients around temporarily and then get you up to speed when you come back."

She finished retrieving her personals. Her office was massive, but it only took her five minutes. Smoothing her black pencil skirt quickly with her hands, she turned her attention to Bill. "No, assign them permanently to Kayla, Mike, and Ben. They're perfectly capable of handling all of my current cases. It could be an entire year before I'm back."

He opened his mouth to argue. She narrowed her eyes at him. Her contract was ironclad. She didn't need his permission. His job was to keep her happy, keep her with the firm. He quickly composed his features; only the bright magenta color of his skin betrayed his true thoughts. He wasn't happy about losing her for an indefinite period of time, but she had him by the balls.

He relented. "Of course." She could still see through him. He thought her reaction to her great-aunt's death was wildly out of proportion. After all, Magdalen had lived a long and happy life.

It *was* true. More than Bill could know. Mags hadn't wasted a second. But it wasn't about Mags, it was about Beth.

She opened her eyes, leaving the blacks and grays of her life behind, and looked out the window to her right. Ireland was greener than green. She restarted the car—the GPS signal was back.

The trees gave way to a small oval of gravel at the base of the cottage. Beth stopped the car and expelled all the air from her lungs as the silence filled her brain again. For a moment she allowed herself to relish in the arresting of all movement. The stillness. The end of her journey.

She clasped her fingers in her lap as she studied the place she would call home for . . . however long it took. There appeared to be two stories to the little cottage. Double semi-lancet arched windows flanked a bright red front door. The pitched roof was a dark black-gray color with a chimney. She could see a lake peeking out on the right side, behind the house. It was quintessentially Irish.

It looked like a place where peace might be found. Maybe even enlightenment. A few weeks here and she would have her head on straight. Her need to leave, to escape the life she had so carefully crafted over the course of a decade, would be a distant memory, and everything could get back on track.

She would process Mags' death; reaffirm her desire to be the star attorney with the flawless track record; go back to her sleek San Francisco apartment overlooking the Marina; recommit to John . . . well, maybe not *everything* had to go back to the way it was. Mags had never liked John. She thought he was dull and much too dreary for a thirty-five-year-old.

The corners of her mouth turned up slightly as she remembered Mags' disapproving expression.

"Honestly, Lizzie! You've been seeing him for what, a year? It's no wonder you haven't said 'I love you' yet, he's awful! And a total bore; I almost slipped into a coma listening to him. Not bad to look at, BUT *really*. I think you may have gone a little *cray-cray* with this one." Beth laughed out loud at the memory. That was Mags. She loved language, loved knowing what the young people were saying; she even watched The CW Network. An eighty-nine-year-old whose speech patterns oscillated between twenty-two and forty-five, but nothing north of sixty.

She never had any problem being blunt. And John *had* talked about the weather for most of the hour. Beth tried to change the topic more than once, but was more amused by Mags' bewildered expression and his incredible ignorance to her knitted eyebrows and pursed lips. He had spent the rest of their meeting at the café in Union Square talking about eyeglasses.

John was an optometrist.

Beth sat there in front of the cottage trying to remember how she had even come to date him. He was a workaholic, like her, and low maintenance. That was it—he was low maintenance. She liked that she could ignore most of what came out of his mouth and he wouldn't notice. The sex wasn't bad; he took direction well, especially when she compared the sensitivity of the cornea to . . . other parts of the female anatomy.

It had felt good to walk straight past his receptionist, into his office, and say she was leaving and that they were done. There was no screaming, no drama beyond her entrance. No passion. Mostly, he just looked confused.

The wind came to life, making the tall trees on either side of the cottage sway in greeting. The February sky had turned purple with near-certain rain. The amethyst brought out the green that existed everywhere. It was time for Beth to survey her Irish haven.

Her thin T-shirt was less than adequate, ludicrous really for an Irish February. The chill of the air bit into her bare arms and chest, making her feel more than a little topless—and yet, she welcomed the cold, the feeling of being alive.

Leaving the car, she grabbed her high-collar wool cardigan. She drew it around herself and walked towards the right side of the house where she had seen the lake.

Her fingers grazed the house as she passed, taking notice of the windows without looking inside. She would save that, taking in the interiors all at once, like unwrapping a present.

The backyard was simple. There were two white, wooden lawn chairs like those you would expect to come with a quaint cottage. There was a small table too, and a spectacular lake.

Lough Rhiannon was considered a small lake, almost tiny in Ireland, but it was more than enough lake in person. The water was calm. There were cracks in the blue-violet clouds, giving way to golden rays that lit the surface in no particular pattern, setting the waters on fire. The golds, greens, and violets took her breath away.

There was magic here in this beautiful, secluded place. She drew in a deep, cool, healing breath and closed her eyes. The wind rallied and the brisk air brushed her face, refreshing her senses. She was ready for whatever needed to happen here.

Her hands moved to the back pocket of her dark jeans where the next letter waited to be opened. She took it out and inspected the small yellow envelope. Save for the first, each letter had been marked in Mags' elegant script with just a number. This one had a large "*2.*"

It seemed appropriate to open it now, when she had just reached the end of her sixteen-hour journey from San Francisco. But here at the beginning of her own personal quest, her chest tightened and her throat started to constrict as she thought about the next words that Mags would thrust upon her from beyond the grave. Would she tell her the truth about her parents? Doubtful. Was she ready to hear it? No, she was too exhausted. Too drained to deal with . . . *everything.*

She would get settled, shower, and open it with a glass of wine. Her grief at losing Mags and her anger at being lied to her entire life threatened to swallow her whole.

With some effort, she unclenched her jaw and relaxed the fingers that had tightened around the letter.

Her eyes refocused on the lake. It looked to be fairly round-ish, maybe a mile in diameter. Trees bordered the shores, obscuring the view of what lay beyond. She glimpsed part of a stone-colored house farther up the lake. It looked like part of a larger structure, but she couldn't make out much from where she stood.

The decision to vacate her life was only a couple of days old. She had made all the arrangements in a very short period of time, including the cottage. It was the only one that was available on such short notice and would be hers for as long as she wanted.

Others were available today, but were booked in the future, cutting her time into two weeks, a month, and so on. This house didn't have any reservations on the books . . . at all. The contact person she had spoken to yesterday assured her that it was through no fault of the cottage, which was in excellent condition, and only a ten-minute drive to Dingle.

She had believed the man—Shaun Morgan—mainly because of the price. It was nearly five times the price of other comparable houses, situated on similar lakes. The price was so high it was almost as if the owner didn't actually want it to be rented out.

Shaun explained that the cottage had belonged to a woman named Rhia Bannon, the current proprietor's mother, and hadn't been rented since it first came on the market two years before. He had assured her that it was a fully updated, impeccably maintained, fashionable rental. Beth hoped he was right.

She ought to have negotiated the price down, but she just didn't have any fight left in her after the funeral. She'd only seen two pictures of the property and didn't even know if she would have any neighbors. It was the least prepared Elizabeth Lara had ever been in her entire life.

A few drops of rain fell against her cheeks, trailing down her face in much the same way as the tears she'd shed while on the side of the road. It was time to get her things from the car and settle in.

She crossed the length of the yard towards the other side of the house. Carefully, she walked the narrow patch of grass that separated the outside wall from the tall trees, stepping over small fallen branches and piles of compacted leaves. She took notice of the first window as she had before, trying not to look inside and spoil the effect of walking in through the front door.

She was passing the second large window when she caught a flash of movement and instinctively turned to look. A large white bathtub sat in front of the window, a shower was set in the far corner, and a very fit, very *naked* man stood gaping at her. Her eyes found his washboard stomach first, his hands on his hips, partly obscuring the sharp cut of a V beneath his hips, down to his. . . .

It happened so fast that she didn't have time to process what she was seeing in time to look away. Her mouth dropped and for a moment they stood staring at each other.

CHAPTER 2: CONNOR BANNON

Beth collected herself. The attorney in her rose to the surface. She turned and marched towards the front of the house, leaving the naked man staring out the window, still confused.

Just who did he think he was, barging in on her much-needed respite from reality? There was nothing quite as real as a naked man. Gaping. After the most emotionally taxing week of her life.

Why couldn't things just appear to be what they were? She had rented this house, it was hers, and yet there was someone already inside. In that moment she felt *everything*. The lava bubbled up inside her, threatening to burn her—and anyone who stood in her path.

The cheery red front door with its antique handle turned easily. Of course it was open—no need to follow Shaun's instructions to find the key because some interloper had already found it!

Some part of her brain registered that it wasn't the brightest idea to march into a house occupied by an unknown man and so she turned to grab a sturdy-looking umbrella from a round bin by the door. She held it like a player up to bat and walked in slowly.

There was no time to take in her surroundings; she had to deal with this man and call the authorities. Who was she supposed to call in Ireland? Several more thoughts flitted through her brain before she forced herself to focus.

The bathroom would be on the left side of the house. She took a few more steps before the naked man emerged from the bathroom, glistening, a white towel at his waist.

The words tumbled out of her. "Who the hell are you and what are you doing in my house?!" she spat out aggressively. To her own ears her voice was only raised, agitated. To his, she was flat out yelling.

The man's eyebrows drew together in bewilderment. "*Your* house?" His accent was thick, Irish.

"Yes, I've rented it." She shook her head as she spoke and narrowed her eyes, without really seeing him. She averted her gaze from his face and naked chest. "I've paid good money to live here for as long as I like. I'm sure that even under Irish law that means I'm entitled to sole possession of this space—"

"How'd you do that?" He cut her off, his voice lilting upwards. He looked confused rather than angry or embarrassed. Shouldn't he look at least a little embarrassed?

Beth was fuming, her eyes wide. "Do what?!" She shook her head again. She was so very tired. Despite the quick shot of adrenaline, she could feel herself crashing. Even so, she held on to her hostility.

18

"How'd you let the house?" the naked stranger said again. His face remained unmoved, a staunch mask of confusion.

"I found the property listed online and made arrangements through Shaun Morgan yesterday!" Her voice rose in exasperation. "Now who the hell are you and what are you doing here?!"

Why was this happening? It was all too much.

The man looked at her, taking in the umbrella for the first time. His expression had changed slightly with her last statement. His jaw went slack and then, quite suddenly, he burst into laughter. Water from his soaked hair dripped onto the floor as his body shook with the force of it. He put his hands on his knees.

For a second Beth thought the towel might fall. His reaction threw her. Now she was mostly confused. The anger started to melt away, replaced by a sense of not knowing which way was up and which way was down.

"Shaun?" he managed between fits.

"Yes." Her voice had come back into a normal range. Maybe he was crazy. She gripped the umbrella tighter and let her eyes quickly scan the house for a phone.

She didn't see one.

She was just about to turn and make a run for it when he took a final breath and spoke again.

"I'm Connor Bannon, the owner. Shaun is my good friend and property manager. I live just up the lough." He ran his fingers through his wet hair, slicking it back with a raised eyebrow and a boyish grin.

Seriously?

She relaxed a little, dropping the umbrella to her side. Gratefully, she released the tension in her shoulders and took a deep breath.

"Oh. Well, as relieved as I am to know that you aren't some escaped mental patient who broke in, it still isn't OK for you to be here, Mr. Bannon. I've rented the house." She was calm now, but firm. The exhaustion kept whatever fight was left in her at bay.

"Call me Connor. Jaysus, what an impression." He shook his head. "Eh, I apologize for the inconvenience. The work I do, it keeps me traveling. Shaun left me a message, but like an eejit I haven't talked to him."

"Perhaps you should stay on top of your affairs," she said in a deadpan voice, letting her irritation shine through.

"Well now, stop the ball there, Luv." His amusement turned to annoyance at her rebuke. "In my defense, you walked in on *me* in the nip. This is my house and by your own admittance you only made arrangements to let the house yesterday!" He spoke animatedly with his hands; the towel loosened and nearly fell.

He caught it quickly. The corners of his mouth shot up reflexively into an impish grin.

Elizabeth was done.

"Mr. Bannon," she breathed, "I've traveled all the way from San Francisco to find some peace. I'm tired, I'm hungry, and I'm not in the mood to deal with whatever drama I've walked into here." She motioned with her hands. "I get it. You own this house, you didn't know I had rented it, your property manager needs to keep you better informed . . . this is just an ill-fated encounter. What can be done to fix this situation *now*?"

He nodded, following her every word, with a strange glint in his eye.

"Perhaps you would be so kind as to allow me to put on my trousers first." He extended one arm in a mocking bow, the other held the towel to his waist.

Without waiting for a response, he returned to the bathroom and shut the door.

Beth scanned the entry foyer and gratefully fell into a green and ivory over-stuffed armchair.

"You know, in Ireland it's customary to give your name when someone gives you theirs," he said through the wall.

"I'm Elizabeth Lara."

"Well, Miss Lara, what brings you to Ireland?" His voice cut through the banging of cabinet doors and running water.

She opened her mouth to answer and then stopped. It was such a loaded question. She didn't understand it herself. The instant, all-consuming desire that had taken over her life after she'd read Mags' first letter. And why Ireland specifically?

She didn't like not understanding.

"Did you say you live just up the lake?" she sidestepped.

"Yes, I do indeed," he said pleasantly.

She rolled her eyes, annoyed he sounded so cheery after all that had just happened. "Then why were you bathing here?"

"As I said, I travel for work. I've only just gotten back today to find my plumbing in a state. It's a very old house, you see. I've got lads fixing it all now, but I thought I'd get out of their way and come here to have a wash. I redid this place a couple of years ago. You won't have any problems."

"You mean *besides* finding a naked stranger?" she said automatically. The sarcasm in her voice sounded harsh and bitchy, even to her ears, but she didn't have the energy to care. She needed a glass of wine and a nap. "Mr. Bannon, I don't think it's too much to ask for you to bring in someone to tidy the house again, wouldn't you agree?"

"I've really only used the bathroom, but I can have Mrs. Porter come and give it a once-over within the hour. Would this suit you, Miss Lara?" He spoke in an airy, mocking sort of way. She tried not to take offense; he was probably just trying to be funny.

"Yes." Her stomach churned, making her acutely aware of the fact that she hadn't eaten in more than forty-eight hours. "Is there a market nearby? I would really like to pick up some supplies." She threw her voice in his direction. She meant *wine*—lots of wine.

The water stopped running. "If you go back up the road and make a right, you'll find Sullivan's just there. A ten minutes' drive."

She got up and moved to place the umbrella back in its bin. "Thank you. I'll just go do what I need to do, then. . . ." her voice trailed off. "Do you think Mrs. Porter will need more than an hour? It's two-thirty, and I'd like to settle in no later than four." She directed her voice back towards the bathroom so he would hear.

He answered with not a care in the world. "No, that should do just fine."

"Good. I'll just leave you to finish . . . uh . . . getting dressed," she continued awkwardly. She was trying now to sound polite. "If you could please place the key for me under the blue pot where Shaun said it would be, that would be great."

"Yes, that'll be grand," he agreed.

"Thank you," she said stiffly.

She reached the entrance to the cottage just as Connor emerged from the bathroom. The creak of the door caught her attention. She spun around to acknowledge him one last time before leaving, but his reappearance made the words her brain had started to form leave her altogether.

He wore dark jeans and a gray hoodie with the sleeves cut off at the shoulders. His bare arms were defined; a green Celtic cross tattoo adorned his right bicep. He looked like a model on his way to the gym.

She could take in his features now that she wasn't trying to avoid eye contact. He had striking ice blue eyes, a long nose, and full lips. His hair was light brown with a couple of grays. Mid-thirties.

She was surprised she hadn't been immediately struck by his looks before. Elizabeth gaped at him now, completely unaware of what her face was doing.

His lips twitched upwards. "Oh, and Miss Lara?" The amusement colored his voice.

She snapped out of it and cleared her throat. "Yes?"

He flashed her a dazzling smile that did something to her body. "Welcome to Ireland."

The trip to Sullivan's took longer than expected. Connor's directions of "up the road, make a right" turned out to be an oversimplification. There were smaller dirt roads that she hadn't noticed before and no major intersection at which to turn right. She'd taken one of them and ended up at another small lake. And another led to a small shack in the middle of nowhere. The road that actually led to the market was paved, but with the dirt and rain it didn't look much different from the others. She had to get out of the car to check.

The little store was pleasant enough. It was on the outskirts of the small village near Dingle. Green Celtic lettering against a bright yellow background announced "Sullivan's Market & Spirits."

She took her time examining the different packaging of the products on the shelves. There were few recognizable American brands. The complete lack of familiarity was at once alienating and freeing. She was really here. Mags had loved this place. Loved the Irish. Loved the little markets and the different treats.

Even while taking care of Elizabeth, Mags still found time to travel a week here or there, leaving Beth with their neighbor, Mrs. Hollings. Mags had tried to bring her several times, but Beth was stubborn and didn't like to miss school.

Still, Mags found ways to include her in her travels. A trip to the Emerald Isle would mean Hobnobs and Chocolate Fingers and Jammie Dodgers for Beth. She ran her fingers over the Hob Nobs lettering, remembering her excitement as a child.

"But Mags, why do they call them biscuits," she would ask between mouthfuls, "when they are cookies and crackers?"

"Yes, Lizzie, here we would call them that, but in Ireland they have all sorts of names for different things. The important thing is that they taste good, don't they?"

"Mmmhmmm!" Beth would nod emphatically, lips smeared with crumbs, jam, and chocolate.

Beth grabbed several packages of biscuits. Some she had tried while others were new. She filled her cart with supplies for sandwiches, salads, and pasta. Anything that wouldn't require a great deal of time or effort. Carbs be damned. The carts were much smaller than in the States, so when she got to the liquor aisle she found she needed another.

There was no one in the little market except the man at the register. She left her food cart with him and filled her second cart with wine, vodka, whiskey, and some Guinness for good measure.

The round man with thinning hair and red cheeks at the register took in her two piles. He looked from one to the other and then back to Beth's small figure. He blew a low whistle.

"Preparin' for an emergency, Lass?"

"Something like that." There was no returning his smile; the best she could do was give him a friendly nod. She still wasn't in the mood to deal with people. All she could think about was taking a shower—although thanks to her naked stranger, she now had very *different* associations with that particular shower that didn't involve getting clean. She shook her head in an effort to clear Connor from her brain. She closed her eyes and imagined standing beneath the water and then curling up with a glass of wine and some Hobnobs.

Yes.

The man at the register chuckled, but made no further comment.

CHAPTER 3: THE IRISH COTTAGE

Between her luggage and her groceries, Beth's little rental car was bursting at the seams. She would deal with it all later. First, she wanted a second chance at properly unwrapping the cottage. The key was under the blue pot. The bright red door was beautifully painted. A small flower was carved in the middle. She ran her fingers over the design and wondered about the cottage's previous owner, as she often did when entering a space she would live in.

The stories and secret histories to which the walls had borne witness occupied her thoughts briefly. She tried to erase everything she already knew about the cottage before opening the door.

The key turned easily. With a renewed excitement, she stepped inside.

Her eyes found the pristine lake first. Floor-to-ceiling windows occupied the far wall, showing off a spectacular view of Lough Rhiannon. To the right of the door stood a large wooden dining room table next to the first window. A piano was next to the second and a large granite kitchen was next to the third and final window on that side. A set of large French-country-chic cream couches lived in front of the wall of glass.

An enclosed room blocked off a portion of the left side. The bathroom in which she had gotten her first look at Connor was directly adjacent. Two large bookcases framed the first window on the left side with a love seat facing the woods. And finally, the over-stuffed armchair she already knew rounded out her initial inspection. It was lovely. Taking a deep breath, she relaxed. It was more spacious than she had imagined, yet cozy enough that she was instantly at home.

An hour later she was fully unpacked, showered, a glass of sauvignon blanc in hand. It was time to read another letter. She took the blue box with the red ribbon from the coffee table and fingered the painted wood. Mags had probably designed, built, and decorated the box herself. That was the kind of woman she was. No skill was out of her reach. With a bit of practice, an imagination, and YouTube, anything was possible.

Beth couldn't think of the box and the letters without thinking about that first one. The one that had basically said her entire worldview was wrong, the last decade a misguided departure from her true self. Mags' words tugged at her, bit into her heart and that part of her soul that could recognize the truth.

And the tears came again, raw and all-consuming. They dripped down her cheeks and into her wine. She could feel herself collapsing.

No, she wasn't ready for more from Mags. She set the glass down and curled up in the fetal position on the large ivory couch.

It was a good, long cry. She cried for Mags. She cried for herself. She cried because she was tired. She cried because she didn't know why she had come to Ireland. She cried because nothing made sense in her life. She cried because she hated that she needed everything to make sense all the time. She cried because she no longer recognized herself.

She cried because she was alone.

From the couch she had a clear view of the water. Tears blurred her vision. The sunset lit the lake. In that moment, she lived inside a Monet. Beautiful, alive, yet not fully there, not fully knowable.

She'd never purposely shied away from emotion before; she just didn't have time for it. It had been a decade of one case after another. No time—or need—for tears, or daydreaming, or the simple act of . . . *existing*. Being present. And so, Elizabeth dwelled amongst the vibrant colors, letting the tears flow and the thoughts go where they would.

After some time, she peeled herself off of the couch and went to check the windows and doors. It was time to sleep. Perhaps it would be the restful kind she so desperately needed. The kind she hadn't had since the week before Mags had gone to the hospital.

As she made her way back to check the front door, she noticed an envelope on top of the dining room table. The words "Miss Lara" decorated the front.

Inside was a note from Connor.

Elizabeth, A Chara

That is a traditional Irish greeting, meaning "Dear Friend."

I wish to apologize again for our manner of introduction. Jesus only knows what your first impression of me and the Irish people must have been. Rest assured we are not all "naked strangers," as you so fondly referred to me. We are also quite nice, respectable people who enjoy being friendly and having some food and drink with new friends.

I hope you will accept my invitation to dine at O'Leary's Pub tomorrow evening at 6:00. As you are new to our small corner of the world, I would like to take this opportunity to educate you on our ways. It would be quite rude of you not to come. Quite rude indeed. I won't hold it against you, but others might. So come out and have a bit of fun. I daresay it would do you some good, and I'm always in need of good conversation.

Le meas,
Connor

Whether from the lack of food or sleep, the one glass of wine had affected her, and she was not a lightweight. Disconnected from her brain, she was all irrational emotion—another first for Elizabeth Lara.

While the note was left with good intentions, Elizabeth only had eyes for the last line.

"'I daresay it would do you some good'?" she read under her breath. What the hell was *that* supposed to mean? His words sounded arrogant and judgmental in her head.

The room was spinning. She swayed where she stood. "Daresay it would do *me* some good?" she repeated in an Irish accent. It came out sounding British.

She stared down at the note with contempt. After several reads, Connor Bannon's voice had taken on a particularly conceited air in her imagination—nearly ten times the airy, mocking tone he'd used when saying, "Would this suit you, Miss Lara?"

It was like his words were looking up at her, judging her. The last thing she needed was an audience for her international meltdown, or whatever this decidedly ungraceful escape from reality turned out to be. She didn't need to be reminded that she was an uptight mess. There were other letters for that. . . .

She crumpled the note and threw it against the wall.

Who did he think he was? He didn't know her. What the hell did he know about what she needed?

Asshole.

CHAPTER 4: MONA PORTER

The sound of a roaring vacuum woke her. She was face down, her arm draped over the side of the bed, drool on her pillow. The dark navy curtains blocked out the light from the wall of glass completely. If it weren't for the clock next to the bed she would have no idea if it was day or night. Apparently, it was 12:17 p.m.

She'd slept for almost fifteen hours, but it wasn't enough. An entire week wouldn't be enough.

Begrudgingly, she put on her favorite sweater, a black cardigan with a single dolphin embroidered in white on the breast pocket, over her T-shirt and pajama bottoms. Who was in the house now? Angrily, she threw the bedroom door open. A short, chubby woman with aging red hair that was now mostly silver was happily vacuuming the hardwood floors around the couches.

"Hello!" Beth yelled over the noise.

The little woman didn't hear.

Beth moved to stand in front of her, waving her arms. "HELLO!"

The woman looked up.

"Oh, why hallo there!" she said over the vacuum. "Don't cha love these new ones? You can clean everything with them now! It's so clever indeed." She turned the machine off and extended a hand. "It's so lovely to meetcha! I'm Mona Porter; I take care of the house."

"Yes, I see that." It took some effort to stay angry at the cute little woman, but Beth managed. "Mrs. Porter. . . ." She breathed to steady her voice. She spoke slowly, deliberately so that this woman would understand her fully in spite of the cultural difference.

"I'm jet-lagged. I need to rest. I haven't had anything to eat in almost..." Beth tried to remember, "*three* days. It is *not OK*, I repeat *NOT OK* for you to be here intruding on my space while I'm trying to recuperate. Waking up to a vacuum cleaner is *really* very unpleasant." She met the lady's eyes. "Do. You. Understand?"

Mrs. Porter had both hands over her mouth.

"Oh, you poor Dear! Come here, give us a squinch." Before Beth could react, Mrs. Porter had flung her small arms around her with surprising strength and pressed her down into a ferocious hug.

The woman gripped her tightly, leaving Beth stunned.

"Mrs. Porter," she tried to say, "you're hurting me."

Mona released her. Instead, she grabbed her face and smushed her cheeks together. Beth clung to some of the anger she had left and tried to extract herself, until finally the little woman walked away into the kitchen.

Beth no longer knew what was happening. Had she heard her at all? Where did she get off, invading her living and now physical space like that?

"I've made you a proper breakfast. A tomato omelet, some ham, potatoes, and fresh fruit. With some tea, of course." She turned and gestured to the kitchen counter in one fluid movement.

Beth's stomach growled as she registered the smell of the food for the first time.

On the other hand, this small, pushy lady couldn't be all bad. Her total lack of boundaries could be found endearing in some cultures. Probably this one. And with that, Beth gave up being outraged.

She sat down at the kitchen bar to eat. The eggs coated her stomach. The tomatoes provided a kick. The ham and potatoes did something to heal her weary soul. Her facial expressions must have done the talking because Mrs. Porter was silent, delighting in Beth's surrender to the food.

Finally sensing a change in Beth's energy, Mrs. Porter let her curiosity take over.

"So what brings you to Dingle, Miss Lara?"

There it was again. That perfectly cordial question that everyone wanted to know the answer to. *What was she doing in Ireland?*

"Call me Elizabeth or Beth," she managed between mouthfuls, now hyper-aware of just how much not eating had affected her mood, her ability to cope, her *everything*.

She looked down at the remnants of her omelet, and her voice descended an octave. "I just needed to get away."

"And how long are ya stayin' with us?"

She stopped chewing and looked up at Mona, finally forced to face her future, or lack thereof. Her answering lost-girl expression spoke volumes. "I have no idea."

Mrs. Porter's eyes crinkled. "Y'aren't used to not knowin', are you, Elizabeth?"

Beth put her fork down. This tiny woman had gotten to the heart of it in two questions. She was good.

Beth's face stayed frozen as her brain tried to catch up. "No, Mrs. Porter. I don't supposed I am."

"Please, call me Mona, Luv. You just sit right there and let the food give ya strength now," she said kindly.

That was as good a future as any.

And so Elizabeth kept eating, while the nice lady tidied the kitchen and continued the conversation.

Mona asked all the basic questions and, after a few minutes, knew where Beth was from, how old she was, what she did for a living, that she was single, and was grieving the recent passing of her great-aunt who had raised her.

Beth didn't mention the story about her parents or how it could all be one fat, thirty-five-year-old lie.

Although she was interested in learning more about Mona, it was all Beth could do to keep answering the unrelenting woman's questions. So she ate and answered. Answered and ate. After a while, she quite believed that Mona wasn't taking offense to her not posing any questions of her own. In fact, it seemed the woman rejoiced at having an opportunity to have a one-way conversation with her.

Mona motioned out towards the glass wall. "What do you think of the lough?"

"I haven't really had the chance to walk around, but it's undeniably beautiful. The cottage as well. It's all lovely. I'm grateful to have found it on such short notice." The food had done something to her voice, made her sound normal again. Restored her ability to be polite and friendly. An ability she'd been able to go without for far too long.

"Yes, it is a nice place." She looked around lovingly. "It's been completely updated, ya know. It's nice to see someone here again."

Beth took a sip of tea from a giant blue mug. "So it's true then? That I'm the first to rent it since it was made available?"

"Oh yes, you're the first. Connor fixed it up to let after Rhia. . . ." Mona spoke the name with reverence. "His mother, you know yourself. After she passed. Rest her soul." She made the sign of the cross. And then her voice brightened in a decidedly cheery way. "I just don't know how no one's discovered it! Such a treasure, it is that." She motioned to the house.

Beth raised an eyebrow and hid her face in the cup of tea. The king's ransom she was paying to stay there might have something to do with it.

She wondered about Rhia. What she had been like. What her life in the cottage had been. "How long ago did she pass?"

Mona became thoughtful. "Almost two years now."

"It must have been hard on Mr. Bannon." Beth's voice trailed off. Some of the ill will from the previous day turned into empathy as she considered him losing his mother.

"It was indeed. It still is." Mona nodded wisely. And then the woman's expression turned playful. "He said you two met."

Remembering, Beth turned red and hid in the blue mug. She hoped he hadn't told her exactly *how* they'd met. God, it was embarrassing enough. "Mmmhmm," she acknowledged.

"Quite a looker, isn't he?" Mona's eyes glinted with mischief.

"Yup." Her response was clipped, still reliving the first moment she'd laid eyes on *all* of him.

"What a treat, eh? Your first day here and you got to see Connor in the nip!" The tiny woman threw her head back and let out a boisterous laugh.

Oh. God.

"He told you?"

"Oh yes, Luv! The whole town knows. We were all talkin' of it down at the pub."

Beth felt like an embarrassed child again. She let her head fall to her arms. Any moment now she would wake up and realize she was only six, playing a game of Heads-up, seven-up. She couldn't remember the last time she had felt so flustered.

"No need to be shy." Mona patted her on the shoulder. "If I were twenty years younger. . . ." She trailed off and Beth raised her head to look. The woman was lost in some fantasy, one she was sure she didn't want to know about.

"Well, anyway, he's a nice young lad and a fine specimen of a man. Most eligible bachelor around these parts—in the whole of Ireland, Britain and Europe, really," she corrected herself quickly. And then her tone turned serious. "But watch yourself, Luv; he's what you Americans might call emotionally unavailable." She scrunched up her nose at the last part and finished wiping down the counter.

"Oh?" She considered that. "Is he a player?" She wasn't sure why, but the idea amused her.

"No, I can't say that I think he is. He's just . . . *distant.* Wounded, that one. Women have made all manner of advances towards him around here, but no one seems to hold his interest. He does travel quite a bit; perhaps he's different when he's away from home." Mona looked off into the distance as she tried to picture what Connor might be like in a foreign country.

"He's almost never here since Rhia. . . ." She made the sign of the cross again.

Beth looked into the dark depths of her cup and spoke absently. "He seems nice enough. Definitely sure of himself," she said, more to herself than Mona. She caught sight of the crumpled note still on the floor past the kitchen. A thought occurred to her.

"Mrs. Porter," she began, "is it common here to tell complete strangers that a bit of fun would do them some good?"

Mona stopped rearranging the plates in the cupboard, none of which appeared to need rearranging. Mostly she was just taking them out and placing them back in the exact same spot. "Not sure I follow, Luv. Do you mean is there anything improper in it?"

Beth nodded.

"No. Informal, maybe, but then I suppose you were thrown into an unusual situation, weren't you? Bit of an ice breaker, wasn't it?" She laughed again.

"Do you think I look like that?" Beth bit the inside of her lip.

"Like what, Dear?"

"Like a bit of fun would do me some good?"

"Well, a bit of fun always does everyone good, doesn't it?" She smiled briefly, then her thin mouth straightened into a line, and her plump cheeks seemed to rise towards her eyes. After considering for a moment, she answered, "But yes, Elizabeth, since I hope we will be fast friends, I'll answer honestly. I *do* believe your heavy soul could do with a bit."

Maybe she had overreacted? Maybe he *wasn't* judging her?

But then that same pompous tone she had substituted for his voice came back . . . and his words, presuming to know what she needed . . . like he knew her.

"Why'd you ask, Luv?"

Beth just shook her head and drank her tea, deciding right then and there that she'd spent far too much time thinking about Connor Bannon.

They talked for another hour before Beth confiscated Mona's key. She liked her more than she thought possible at 12:17 p.m., but still, she didn't want any more uninvited visitors appearing outside of her bedroom door.

Mona was surprisingly understanding.

"Just give me a ring when you need me to tidy up. It's all taken care of with your rent. Or you could call if you fancy a cup of tea." She picked up her red coat, which was draped over one of the chairs near the door. "And don't hesitate to call if you'd like to go touring. I know all the best spots. Places not to be missed."

Beth almost smiled. "I will. Thank you."

The tiny lady hugged her fiercely again and was out the door.

Chapter 5: The Pub

It was warm for the first week of February. Or at least the sun was bright and the light worked to heat the ground. It was a change from San Francisco, where the sun didn't always do its part to heat anything at all.

Newly fortified by the food and company, Beth was ready to brave another go at the box. She had placed it on the round wooden table between the two lawn chairs outside.

Taking a deep breath, she lifted the lid to find the now-worn letter marked *"2,"* which she had kept in her back pocket during the entirety of her journey. She had put it back in the box after the previous day's failed attempt to open it.

The envelope was a cheery sort of yellow, like the sunshine that was seeping into her pores. She drew her dark gray wool cardigan around her and stared at the letter. It was such a small thing—a piece of paper. A few words. She traced the number with her finger, wondering what Mags had been thinking when she sat down to write it.

"You can do this, Beth." She found the vocal pep talk helpful.

"No big deal, just some more words from Mags . . . life-changing words from Mags. In-your-face, hold-no-prisoners words from the only woman who was ever like a mother to you. She's just looking out for you, even from beyond the grave. Even if she has been lying to you all your life . . . and she basically thinks you've wasted your life as an attorney. . . . Maybe she'll be nicer, more comforting in this one. She probably won't tell you the truth; I mean, there are a lot of letters—"

Abruptly she stopped talking to herself and looked up. First at the calm water in front of her and then at the trees on either side of the lake. She was alone. No one to witness her crazy. And she certainly felt unhinged, sitting in front of a strange lake, outside a strange house, in a strange country she'd only briefly visited in college. Talking to herself. Afraid of a letter.

It was too late to act sane, she decided. Her eyes returned to the smooth yellow envelope; she was now determined to tell herself whatever she needed to in order to get through whatever came next.

"Maybe she'll tell you how much you meant to her and that she was actually proud of you. . . . Yeah. That's it; it will probably be a very nice, loving letter." Her voice was anything but convincing, but Elizabeth was very good at flinging herself head first into the land of denial.

Thoroughly convinced that the bright yellow envelope held only "I love you" and "I'm so proud of you" along with other words of encouragement, she removed the paper. As she did so, some small part of her brain registered that there were fifteen more letters after this one and that flowery platitudes weren't Mags' style.

Nothing prepared her for what was inside.

Dearest Lizzie,

You are too goddamned uptight! For fuck's sake, have a drink. Let your hair down. Open yourself up to new people and experiences— you used to be fearless, full of life. What the hell happened to you?

Do you remember that summer we went to that bar The Nag's Head? You and I had a drinking contest and you outpaced this old lady easily, but then you took on those frat boys. You shamed them, remember? They couldn't figure out how a 5'4" skinny girl like you could throw back so many shots!

I was more proud of you that night—you were so alive, so ballsy—than I was even at your graduation from Yale the week before.

Please find that fearless girl again.

Love,
Mags

She turned the letter over. Was that it? Where was the rest?

Weren't these letters supposed to be *guiding* posts? Yet Mags had basically said, *"Snap the fuck out of it."*

She'd always cursed like a sailor, but seriously? Those were the words of wisdom she had to pass on? Her solution was to have a drink? Find some frat boys and drink them under the table?

Well, at least Beth had been right about her being proud . . . even if it was about something that happened thirteen years ago and was more of a genetic anomaly than an actual accomplishment. Her tolerance for alcohol, with the exception of the night before, was a freakish talent, but one she rather took pleasure in. She'd always been competitive and liked being in control—liked manipulating men. There was no easier way to do all three.

Slowly Beth's confusion over Mags' chosen words gave way to the memory the woman had described.

She did remember that night. It was the summer before she'd started law school. She had been a different person then. She had liked people underestimating her. Thrived on it, even. It had been years. Her reputation as a take-no-prisoners attorney spread quickly and no one had underestimated her in more than a decade.

It was fun to drink grown men under the table. Fun to look so white that people would talk about her in Spanish right in front of her, only to have their jaws drop when she politely bitch-slapped them, fluently. Fun to look so small and have a voice that could fill a room.

She knew how to have fun then. Knew how to be fearless. She wanted to laugh at the irony. The more deadly and fearless she appeared on a daily basis, the more fearful she became of actually living her life.

What had happened to her? She was thirty-five and hadn't had a meaningful relationship since college. And she was including meaningful friendships in that assessment. She didn't keep in touch with *anyone* from her past, and couldn't remember the last time she had actually liked herself. *Really* liked herself.

The sense of pleasure she derived from demolishing her opponents satiated some vicious part of herself, but she certainly couldn't call it fun. And she certainly couldn't say she liked that side.

She took in a deep breath. The weight of Mags' words had taken their toll.

Why hadn't Mags told her this when she was alive? She was always so blunt; why hadn't she said anything?

With a sinking feeling, Beth realized that Mags had said these things before—she just couldn't hear her.

Why couldn't she hear her?

Regret, thick and all-consuming, saturated her body. For several long minutes she leaned back into the white chair and stared out at the water, watching the little ripples and waves created by the breeze. The sun worked its magic, making the ripples glisten and gleam.

How quickly it had all gone.

She wanted to cry or scream . . . or jump into the water. Her chest rose with frustration. She let the tide of regret wash over her. The minutes passed. She focused on her breathing, trying to regain some measure of control.

It was a heavy thing to look back and realize she'd traded ten years of her life for a career she didn't particularly enjoy. Meaningful relationships for empty work connections based on fear and respect. A happy life for a full bank account.

The weight was difficult to take . . . and yet, seeing the choices she'd made so clearly for the first time was a gift.

Finally, she felt completely still.

Calm.

Realizing that she couldn't do anything to change the last decade, she resolved to at least try to change the course of that day. One minute, one day at a time.

She picked up the box and headed towards the French doors that led from the living room to the lake. She needed to get ready.

"I hear you now, Mags. I can hear you now," she said to herself and opened the door.

Her skinny jeans hugged her fit frame. They were a light gray; the style was called "Dublin." Though she doubted very much whether people here actually wore such jeans. Still, they were flattering on her. The tall black boots and royal blue top rounded out her ensemble. She had straightened her long, wavy hair and spent five minutes on her makeup. She hoped the look said *casual and fun.*

She was just about to leave through the front door, when she heard a knock at the French doors leading to the lake. There was no one to see as she had drawn the curtains earlier. Confused, she walked across the cottage to peek through the curtain.

It was Connor.

He saw her look and gave her a boyish grin and a short wave.

Stepping away for a moment, she felt her blood vibrate beneath her skin.

"Can I help you?" she asked as she unlocked the door, trying to sound cool.

He gave her an appraising look. "Actually, I'm here to help you. I've come to take you to dinner," he stated triumphantly.

She narrowed her eyes. "I thought it was an open invitation. I thought you were OK with me not coming?"

"Well I thought about it and I decided that you probably wouldn't show. And even though *I* wouldn't take it personally, other people would call you an uppity American. So the only neighborly thing to do would be to make sure that you came out." His eyes flashed. She could see the dare in them. "Just making sure you don't commit a major social faux pas."

She raised an eyebrow. "*Faux pas?*"

"Shocked, are ya, that we simple Irish country folk could know a bit of French?"

"No. It just sounds amusing when you say it."

"You? Amused? Now I'm shocked." His words were a jab, but his eyes danced with mischief.

She tried not to take the bait.

"You don't know me." She stared at him.

He stared back. "Maybe. But I'd like to."

Was he flirting?

He maneuvered past her, into the cottage. "And owing to the fact that you've seen me naked, how 'bout we just pretend we're already fast friends?"

Beth straightened. "As it happens, I was just about to drive to the pub to meet you."

He gave her a dazzling smile. "Oh, is that right? Is that why you look so fetching? Did you get all dressed up for me?" She flushed as his eyes roamed over her body.

"This isn't dressed up. In California this is casual and fun." She stopped herself from arguing further lest she give herself away.

He wore a white dress shirt, dark worn-in jeans, and stylish brown shoes. The effect was very casual *GQ*. There was a slight wave to his light brown hair, which was combed back in a youthful way.

"Sure, no problem, Luv." He crossed his arms and swayed where he stood. "I understand. You don't want to flaunt your undeniable attraction to me."

She narrowed her eyes and shook her head, looking only slightly scandalized. "Oh, shut up!" She punched him playfully on the shoulder. It felt natural. Definitely how she would have responded to a guy with his bravado in college. She could *do* this.

"Hey now, no touching until *after* you've bought me a drink or two!" he protested.

She shrugged. "You're the one who wanted to be fast friends."

"And that's how you treat your friends?" He tried to look shocked.

"Only the ones with gigantic egos who believe the world revolves around them and that they are God's gift to women."

"Ouch! Well played, Miss Lara." He extended an arm out and bowed like he had the day before.

She bit the inside of her lip. She was very close to smiling. "Call me Elizabeth."

He gave her a wink, then walked across the house towards the front door. "Shall we?"

She looked behind her, back towards the French doors. Didn't he live *that* way? "I thought you came to drive me to the pub?"

"I have. I dropped off my car earlier, then walked to my house, and now I've walked back to collect you and the car. Isn't that clever of me?" He smiled wide, gratified by his own humor.

Elizabeth hadn't considered his proximity. She thought back, suddenly conscious of the possibility that he might live just beyond the trees and would have been within earshot of her very vocal, very crazy pep talk. "Oh. How far away do you live exactly?"

He raised a single eyebrow. "Just three minutes up the lough." It sounded like an invitation.

They rode in comfortable silence. It was nice to be able to look out the window. The sun was setting and casting rays of golden light across the vast, open green fields. It was so much easier to take it all in when she wasn't worried about missing her turn onto the unmarked road.

They pulled into a spot on the small main street, at the entrance to the colorful village.

"Is it far?" Beth asked as they started walking.

"Just a couple of blocks up. Why? Feeling chilly already?"

"No." In truth, she wished she had brought her heavier wool peacoat. "I just like to know how far away we are. You know, get my bearings."

He watched her as she crossed her arms over her chest.

Elizabeth busied herself with the black, old-world street lamps and brightly colored buildings. The streets were filled with people now, some going about their business, others stopping here and there to take a picture.

She remembered Connor's note. "So when you said that other people wouldn't be as understanding if I didn't show up, what did that mean? Are we eating with the whole town?"

"Eh . . . yes and no." He shot his arm out, placing his hand on the small of her back in an effort to maneuver her around a group of children he didn't think she had noticed. She darted to the side just in time.

"We'll get a small table," he continued, "but a lot of people will be in the pub and often we all talk together. We're a very social people."

"Yes, I've noticed," she said under her breath, thrusting her hands in her pockets.

He gave her a sideways glance. "You mean Mona?"

"Well, yes. And you." Two people was a very small sample from which to base a grand sweeping generalization, but she was sure she was right. And then she remembered what Mona had said. "Speaking of which, I have a bone to pick with you." Her voice was full of censure.

He held up his hands defensively. "I didn't do it."

"How do you know what I'm going to say?"

"I don't. Just seemed a prudent way to respond to that accusing tone. You can be very intimidating, you know that?"

"I've been told." She made it a point to let go of the tension that had built up in her body as she remembered her embarrassment during the Mona encounter.

He nudged her with his shoulder. "Go on."

"Did you have to tell Mona and the entire town *exactly* how we met?"

"You mean the naked part?"

"YES!"

Again he held up his hands. She took a deep, cleansing breath. Attack mode was so ingrained in her, she was going to have to make some adjustments if she wanted to communicate like a normal person.

"Because it was funny," he answered. "It made for a grand story. Besides, of the two of us, it should cause me embarrassment, not you."

She thought about that. *He had been the naked one* . . . but then she hadn't exactly been on her best behavior. . . .

His voice broke through her thoughts. "Unless, of course, you were so instantly overcome with lust at seeing me in all my glory—I can understand why you might be embarrassed by that."

"Ha!" She threw her head back and punched him again.

He laughed, gratified by her jab. And then considered her. "If you're concerned that I might have told everyone you were a screaming American, you needn't be. I painted the picture just so. The laughs came from your rightly protecting yourself with an umbrella. You came off as a clever girl and I came off as the blithering eejit for not knowing my own property had been let."

She stopped walking and looked up into his face, opening her mouth to say something, but the words got stuck.

"I'm not a gossip and I'd no intention of coloring the way the village sees you before they've had a chance to make your fine acquaintance," he said kindly.

She was not blind to his gesture. "Thank you,'" she said with true sincerity.

With a nod and a smile he began walking again.

They reached the pub. Dim lights illuminated the gold Celtic lettering that announced "O'Leary's."

A wall of sound hit them as soon as they cracked the door open. It was a fairly big space for a main street that held such cute-looking cottage-like businesses. Nearly one hundred people were comfortably seated, their plates and cups full, their conversations well in hand.

There were very few tables open.

"Connor!" a big man in his fifties called, meeting them at the door. The men exchanged hearty shoulder slaps.

Her guide turned and extended an arm to include her. "Fitz O'Leary, meet Elizabeth Lara."

Beth held out a hand. "Nice to meet you." Her voice rose over the noise.

"Welcome, welcome, Miss Lara." He looked at her with interest and maybe a hint of mischief. Like he knew something she didn't. Or maybe that was just how people in Ireland looked at you if you were a stranger who'd already made the gossip column.

Sure enough, many people stared at her as they made their way to a table for two near the back.

"Why is everyone looking at me like that?" she whispered at Connor.

He laughed. "You've only been here a day and you're already famous. Talk of the town."

Most of the townspeople were giving her the same look Fitz had given her, but she felt some of the women sizing her up—especially the younger ones. They were not, on the whole, unwelcoming expressions, but she couldn't shake the feeling that at least a few of them weren't pleased to see her.

She wondered now whether or not he had *actually* left out how rude she'd been. "What *exactly* did you tell them?" she asked through her teeth.

His voice was calm, serious. "Oh, just the way it happened. You saw me in the buff and then proceeded to jump my bones," he said with a smirk.

"You did *not* say that?" He had to be kidding. It was difficult to tell with him—it had been a long time since anyone had tried to joke with her.

"No, I didn't. But it was worth the look on your face just now." He laughed and she relaxed a little.

He shrugged. "They're just curious about you. Anytime they know more about you than you know about them, you'll get looks like that. And they know that you've seen me naked. Anytime there's nudity involved, it makes for a titillating piece of gossip." He wiggled his eyebrows.

They took their seats at the small table against the wall. He faced the bar and she faced the room. It was a very cheerful atmosphere. Low lighting, lots of laughter, and a band warming up for a set somewhere nearby, fiddles and all. She could hear them but not see them. She was definitely in Ireland.

She looked at the menu and chose quickly.

"I'll have the Homemade Prime Beef Burger with bacon and cheese, please," she told the friendly young woman named Pam taking their orders. Normally she would never order a burger or anything that didn't require a fork in public, but she was turning over a new leaf and the burger sounded like the best decision she'd made in years.

He ordered the cod. "Glad to see you aren't one of those salad women," he said as Pam left.

"What's a salad woman?" She could guess, but she wanted to hear his explanation.

"You know, one of those 'I'm so dainty I need to consume only green things that I can eat with a fork' types." His voice went up a few octaves as he tried to imitate a terrible-sounding woman.

"I could be one of those women. Maybe tonight I just feel like a burger." She was defiant. She didn't know why, but she felt an intense need to go in the opposite direction anytime he assumed something about her. If she thought he expected her to go left, she might have decided to go right.

Picking up on her tone, he raised an eyebrow just as Pam returned to take their drink orders.

Beth looked up at their cheerful server. "I'll have a Guinness, please."

He looked doubtful, which of course secretly gratified her. He ordered the same.

"Do you actually like Guinness?"

"It's one of the only beers I *do* enjoy," she responded.

When his expression remained unchanged, she prodded, "What?"

"Nothing, I just don't know many foreign women who prefer the taste. You know what it's known as here, don't you?"

She clasped her hands on the table and leaned forward. "Many things, I'd imagine, but how about mother's milk?"

He looked impressed.

"So you've been to Ireland before?"

"Briefly. I spent the summer after my junior year in college studying in London. I traveled throughout the south for three days on one of those student-youth tours."

"With your friends?"

"No, I came alone."

"Why?" He continued his rapid-fire questions.

She shrugged. "Because no one else was interested and I really wanted to see Ireland."

"You like travelling alone, then?"

"Not particularly. I don't mind it. It can be more fun sometimes, when you aren't restricted by what others want to do. You can do exactly what you want. You can meet new people and have the time of your life, if you're just open to where the Universe takes you." Her eyes went involuntarily skyward as she imagined the stars above.

She hadn't thought about letting the Universe take her anywhere in years.

Pam arrived with their drinks and quickly scurried away to tend to another table.

"Ahh, now you see, you've made me feel like a real jerk. Here I thought I had you pegged for one of those women who doesn't know how to let their hair down and have some fun."

He took a gulp of his Guinness before continuing, "One of those uptight people who would only be in tune with the Universe if it was a song played in a high-rise elevator on their way to work."

His comment irked her more than she liked. The truth stung.

Elizabeth's shoulders collapsed inward a degree, and her hands enclosed the cold pint glass as she stared down into the foam. "Maybe I forgot for a while along the way," she allowed.

He looked at her appreciatively. "To finding your way back, then." He held up his glass.

She looked up and gave him a hopeful smile. They clinked glasses.

"What about you?" She turned the tables. "What's your story? Mona mentioned you don't spend much time here anymore."

His mood changed instantly. He leaned forward and lowered his voice. "That's true. I've always traveled for work, but I've chosen to stay on the road more since my mother passed two years ago." He lowered his eyes to stare at his hands. The wound rose to the surface.

She was extra sensitive to his pain because of Mags. Her eyes watered reflexively. Pressing her lips together, she tried to stay in one piece.

"It's not that I don't miss this place," he gestured around, waving at a few people as he caught their eye, "just haven't found a reason to stay for very long."

She looked at her own hands. "I'm sorry, and . . . I get it."

"I know." His voice was barely above a whisper. He considered his next words. "Mona told me about your great-aunt. My condolences." She clasped her hands tightly, letting them absorb all the tension and grief she felt every time she thought about Mags.

They let the silence in, only breaking it when Pam asked if they wanted another round.

The energy at the table had turned very somber. She wondered briefly what their grieving party of two looked like to anyone paying attention.

It was a relief when Pam brought their second round. They had both switched from beer to Irish whiskey.

"So where'd you go to school?" she asked to lighten the mood.

"Cambridge." He turned the glass in his hand.

"Really? Not Trinity?"

"See. . . ." He shook his head. "Why does everyone always ask that?"

She ignored his question. "Which college?"

"Are you familiar with Cambridge?"

"A little." She nodded. "I went to Yale; you're our sister university across the pond."

"That's right." He nodded and then narrowed his eyes. "And those pompous blokes at Oxford and Harvard go together, don't they?"

They smiled at each other.

"I was at Magdalene College," he answered her, leaning forward.

She tipped her head to the side. "The Master of Magdalene got me very tipsy once."

"Is that right? You especially? How scandalous." His eyes were wide with humor.

"Yup—well, no, not just me. There was a group of us Yalies. We had one of those big formal dinners where each person gets their own waiter and they stand behind you against the wall? I don't know how many bottles of wine we went through. I just remember it ended with a midnight tour of the college, complete with candelabras."

He chuckled. "Yes, we do enjoy our big, fancy dinner parties." He seemed very amused by the picture she had painted. Then his features changed abruptly. A strange glint of recognition touched his eyes. "When was this?"

"Uh, don't know." She did the math. "Fourteen years ago, maybe?"

"Huh, I was there at the time." He gave her a genuine smile without bravado or teasing. "Did you ever go punting?"

She nodded. "Yup, a couple of times actually. Why?"

He shrugged, hiding his smile in his glass. "No reason."

She took another sip, letting the smoky flavor fill her mouth.

"You know," Connor began, "your speech patterns have changed since you started drinking the whiskey. This is good; much less formal."

"So have yours. You sound less Irish, more British."

"Uh-oh." He chuckled. "It's all this talk of university!" He leaned in to her and lowered his voice conspiratorially. "I'm like a sponge; I adapt to my environment. If you left me in California for a week I would probably start to sound like a Valley girl."

"Oh? And what does a Valley girl sound like?" she teased.

"I've no idea, but I'm sure I would manage it."

They laughed together.

Their food appeared a moment later and they dug in. The whiskey was doing its job; Beth felt less inhibited by the minute.

"Mmmmmm. . . ." She let her food joy be heard. "Oh my God, this is *so* good. I can't remember the last time I had a burger."

When had she stopped going to In-N-Out? Law school? That should have been a red flag right there. A sign that the law would suck all the joy from her life.

Connor finished his bite of cod and surveyed the room. "Yes, well, with all the noises you're making, I think the whole pub knows just how much you're enjoying it."

She looked around and gave the staring faces a wave and a smile. They smiled back and returned to talking amongst themselves.

Connor was thoroughly amused.

"When was the last time you had a meal that inspired strange sounds?" she asked between bites.

"That would be a pizza in Amsterdam last year for one of my mates' stag parties."

"I didn't know Amsterdam had particularly good pizza."

"Oh, they don't; the sounds were inspired by the special brownies we consumed the hour before. They just manifested whilst eating the pizza."

She laughed so hard, she had to bring a hand up to cover her mouth. His answering smile was so pronounced that it physically hurt him.

He liked hearing her laugh.

Pam returned with their third and fourth rounds: a shot on fire of something called a Flaming Jesus, and more whiskey.

"You keep up pretty well for a girl," he said in admiration as they dug into the spicy wedges and butter bread they'd ordered.

She narrowed her eyes at the "for a girl" part. "Thanks?" She tore a spicy wedge in half and took a bite. "Definitely feeling a little tipsy," she observed.

She was feeling great; healthily buzzed, but nowhere near her limit. She was out of practice, but not *that* out of practice.

"I didn't know Americans used the word 'tipsy.'"

She shrugged.

"Is it common?" he wondered.

"I don't know. I've always used it, although now that I think about it, I did pick it up from a group of Irish kids I hung out with when I was eighteen," she mused.

"What were you doing with such a rebellious crowd? I thought the U.S. had rather strict laws on underage drinking."

"Oh, we do. I was studying in France. I befriended a group of Irish kids and only spoke English with them. Which meant that I went to France and came back with an Irish accent."

"Ha!" He shook his head. "You are *not* who I thought you were, Miss Lara." He kept laughing. "Definitely much more interesting than I could have imagined."

She focused on the empty shot glass in front of her and then on him. "I'm pretty boring these days." She placed her hands on the table, palms up. "Most of what you find interesting about me happened a long time ago," she said earnestly.

He gave her an intense look. His voice was a throaty whisper. "I don't know about that." For a moment they stared at each other, neither looking away. The world went out of focus, until only his blue eyes and her green ones remained.

She felt a familiar pull in her abdomen.

He was gorgeous—the kind of gorgeous that made people stare openly. Without breaking the connection, he moved his hand down to the table, lightly brushing the tip of his forefinger against hers. The contact sent an electric shock down her spine and made her blood vibrate.

Whoa.

The intensity scared her. Her chest began to rise and fall quickly. She was only vaguely aware that she'd turned a different color.

She tried to shake her head, but she'd temporarily lost control of her body. With a great deal of effort, she reconnected her brain to the rest of her, slowly coming back down from wherever they'd just gone together. Had he felt the same intensity? He was as still as she was.

No, no, no, her rational brain screamed. The last thing she needed was a romantic complication when she was so lost, so conflicted about . . . absolutely everything.

Ireland was supposed to be her sanctuary.

She was determined to break their connection. "So. . . ." she began, her voice unsteady, "have you lived anywhere besides here and Cambridge?"

It was the first thing that came to mind.

"Yeah. . . ." He shook his head and broke their eye contact. "But what's your definition of living somewhere? One month? Two months?" His voice lightened with every word.

"Hmmm . . . how about a mailing address? And staying with friends doesn't count." She breathed, relieved by their return to the land of normal.

"OK, let's see, I've lived in . . . London, Paris, Rome, New York, Barcelona, I did a stint in Cairo, and there was—"

"Hey, Bannon!" An attractive man in his thirties with curly brown hair cut him off as he approached the table.

Beth was still thinking about all the places he'd just mentioned and wondered how much more there was to Connor Bannon.

"Kil, mate, how are things?" He stood up to clap the man on the shoulder.

"Busy. Like a blue-arsed fly!" He laughed loudly. "What about you, eh? Still runnin' away from the house and the gate lodge? Come on, man, we all miss your ma, but we miss you too."

Connor pressed his lips together and turned an imperceptible shade of red. Then his eyes hooded over into something dark. There was something more than pain in them . . . anger? She was surprised by the sudden intensity of it. Was he angry at this man? He looked to Beth.

"Kilian, this is Elizabeth. She's here from California. Elizabeth, this is Kilian; he's got a lot of opinions and a case of . . . what do you Americans call it?" He snapped his fingers, pointing at Kilian with a smile. "A case of verbal diarrhea." His smile was light, all traces of his previous intensity gone.

"Yeah, yeah, blame the guy who always says what everyone else is thinkin'!" Kilian said pleasantly.

Just then a couple of teenage girls also approached the table. "Excuse us, can we get a pic—" Connor's eyes grew wide and Kilian quickly cut the young girl with brown hair and braces off, steering them both away from the table. He turned his head back towards Connor and Elizabeth for a parting wink as he dropped the sulking girls off at their table, then walked towards the bar.

Connor stared after him with genuine affection.

Beth looked at Connor curiously. "What was that?"

"I told you, Luv. You're the talk of the town. They've probably never met anyone from California before."

She was unconvinced.

"You can go over later and say hallo, then, if you fancy a lengthy conversation about all the movie stars you know," he answered too innocently. His eyes were bright. "I, for one, hope you choose *not* to do that because I would sorely miss your company."

Oh, he was a flirt, all right. The sound of fiddles started up from somewhere behind her. For the first time she noticed there was a whole other section to the pub. There was a second room behind the bar. She craned her neck to see a small stage where the band was playing. The eager audience sat around small tables or stood with their drinks at the bar.

"Can we take our sides and drinks over there?" Beth asked.

"Yes, let me just settle our dinner tab." He looked around for Pam. "So do you mind my asking how you can take such an extended leave from your work?" he said absently.

Ugh. She did mind. But she'd had enough whiskey that there was a good chance she'd be able to skate through the explanation without getting bogged down in the details.

"Exactly how much did Mona tell you?" she wondered.

He turned his palms up apologetically. "Mona tells me everything. She used to be really close with my mum."

Beth nodded. "Well, as Mona told you, I'm an attorney in San Francisco."

"Yes she mentioned as much."

"A really, really good one."

"Modest, are we?" He chuckled.

"It's just a fact," she said seriously, launching in with her monotone elevator pitch voice. "I got my BA at Yale, as you know, then went straight to Stanford Law. I became a top divorce attorney my first year out of the gate. I was at the top firm in the city a couple years later and negotiated a fairly ridiculous employment contract by the time I was thirty. It basically entitles me to all the profits of a partner without the responsibilities of having to bring in clients."

She took a deep breath, feeling the weight of having to recount the last decade of her life. "People come to the firm specifically for me. My track record is flawless. All the top firms wanted me, and as such, I was able to get all of my terms met. My contract explicitly states that I can take as much time off as I want. I'm sure they never dreamed I would actually leave for any length of time. They probably thought I loved it too much."

He searched her face. "And do you? Love it?"

"No. I'm great at it, so there are times when the intoxication of being the best makes it look like I love it, but I don't." She frowned. "Never have."

"Wasn't it hard to leave? I mean, aren't you trying to make, what is it you called it, partner? Or whatever the next step is?"

Her answer came automatically. "You know, I thought it would be difficult to leave, but it just . . . wasn't. It's already starting to feel like another life to me, even though it was just last week. That sounds crazy. . . ."

"Not if you were on the wrong road the whole time. A self-correction when you're on the wrong road will never be difficult. Trust me."

"And as for the other thing, I don't think I've ever wanted to be made partner, which I never thought was strange until now. They offered it to me when I negotiated my contract, but I said no. I didn't see the point then since I was getting just as much money. . . . I don't know, maybe I knew then that I didn't want to marry the law . . . or I'm just a commitment-phobe through and through," she finished with a sad laugh.

"Then why go back at all?" His ice blue eyes bore into her.

She was unnerved by the turn in conversation. She didn't want to think about any of it. Not tonight. Not when she was trying to change.

Elizabeth was suddenly angry with him for bringing it all up. "Connor, I've only just started asking myself these questions. I don't have all the answers and I *hate* not having them," she responded acidly.

He recoiled. "I believe that."

She gripped the glass and downed the last few gulps of whiskey.

After visually locating Pam, they paid the bill and moved to the back room.

As soon as they reached the bar, Beth ordered two more shots. Talking seriously about her job had killed most of her buzz and she was eager to reclaim it. Let the locals think she had a drinking problem. She hadn't come to Ireland to care about such things, and judging by the state of the locals, she'd probably blend right in. She knew how to stay in control and that was all she cared about. After all, she was determined to let her hair down and have some fun, as prescribed by Mags, Mona, and the model standing to her right.

The bartender set the shots down in front of her. Connor thought one was for him, until she shot them both back one after the other and held up another two fingers.

He looked concerned. "I'm not going to have to carry you back to the car, am I?"

She was annoyed at him for forcing her to think about it all again. And annoyed at herself for being annoyed. "No more talking about my job; it's a buzz kill. Deal?"

He held up his hands in surrender. "OK, deal."

"What do you do?" she asked, eager to get out of her own head.

"Oh, my job's not that interesting. I don't want to kill my buzz either, so how 'bout we just table it for tonight—no more job talk."

She nodded and handed him one of the new shots she'd just ordered. They clinked glasses.

That was an excellent plan.

CHAPTER 6: IRISH TRADITIONS

The room was crowded. They stood at the bar with their drinks, listening to the traditional Irish music. It was wonderful. The low light, the music, the pulse of animated chatter around them. Beth hadn't felt this alive in a very long time.

As more people piled in to listen, Connor and Beth were gradually pushed together until they were physically joined by one hip. They existed within each other's space easily. She leaned against the bar and he rested his right arm behind her on the counter.

They continued to talk. Mostly he leaned in to her to explain the background story of each song. Responding in kind, she leaned in to him to ask about the people in the pub. She expected him to answer with, "That's Joe the baker," when referring to the very round man in the corner clapping and hollering with the band, or "Sally the hairdresser," for the woman giving bedroom eyes to a skinny man across the bar. Instead it was, "That's Joe; he has a pet pig named Ruthie, after his ex-wife," and "That's Sally; she makes her own moonshine."

It was light conversation, but the uninterrupted physical contact was making it difficult for Beth to actively listen to his anecdotes. She could feel just how fit he was through his clothes. He extended the arm behind her and started to stroke the outside of her right arm.

The light touch was intoxicating. He could not have had a greater effect if he had touched her in a more intimate place.

The music didn't help. It was upbeat and cheerful, but it had a way of getting in your blood and making you want to feel as alive as humanly possible.

Just as she had seriously started to consider where the night might take them, the song ended and the lead singer of the band, who turned out to be Kilian, spoke into the mic.

"I understand we have a young lass here coming to us all the way from Cali-fornia." He looked out into the crowd. The little spotlight they had rigged to shine onto the stage was suddenly pointed directly into Beth's eyes.

She squinted at Connor suspiciously.

He whispered into her ear, "I had nothin' to do with this."

"Come on up here, Lass." He set down his guitar and came over to them, taking her hand and leading her to the front of the stage. "Now, it's tradition for foreign attractive females to have a dance with a local on their first night here." Kilian turned to look at the crowd; he lifted his hands, egging them on as they whistled and cheered.

"Is that really true?" she asked Kilian. The whiskey allowed her to stand there completely unembarrassed, but had not taken away her aversion to being taken as a fool.

"Yes, it is." Kilian turned to the crowd and made one entire half of his face wink.

OK, they were making it up. A joke at her expense. Yesterday, she would have walked off the stage. Tonight she would play along and see where it took her.

"Tell everyone your name, pretty lady." He gave her a flirtatious wink.

"Elizabeth Lara," she said, speaking into the mic. The crowd answered her with more cheers and whistles.

She was bright red from the heat of the light and the whiskey, but she felt emboldened. Free.

"All right, who will it be?" she asked suggestively, wanting to be a good sport. This would definitely qualify as letting her hair down.

"Me!"

"Over here!"

"Pick me, Luv!"

The men continued to holler, and some of the women too.

"Eh . . . what do you all think?" Kilian worked the crowd. "I think it should be the young, strapping lad you've already seen in the nip!" Kilian declared.

Everyone laughed and jeered animatedly, shouting their agreement.

This made Beth turn a deeper shade of red. She briefly covered her eyes with her hand and then couldn't help but laugh at the situation.

And then Connor was there in front of her.

"Give 'em some room, eh!" Kilian directed the people sitting nearest the stage and they moved the tables against the walls.

The band started playing a jig. Not knowing what to do, Beth played the part by doing a little curtsy. She was laughing with everyone in the room now.

Connor took her hand in his and placed the other on her back. And then they started to move. They were quick, jumping steps that took them all around the little space that had been cleared. People clapped to the beat and yelled every so often. The steps were simple, repetitive, but fun. Connor only took his eyes off of her to maneuver them safely around the floor.

They both smiled so hard, their cheeks were on the verge of cramping by the time the song finished and they broke apart.

Flushed from the dancing and whiskey, they stood staring at each other. Their big goofy grins remained.

Kilian yelled over the roar of the crowd. "Give Miss Lara a hand!"

Beth did a little bow and then Connor wrapped his arm around her waist, pulling her with him. They returned to their spot at the bar, still laughing.

He spoke into her ear. "You are full of surprises, Miss Lara."

The corners of her mouth turned up. It was a relief to know that she could still surprise people, especially herself. "I guess I am."

Several more drinks and a couple of hours later, they were falling out of the pub with everyone else at closing. Lyrics from different songs were being belted into the night air.

"That was *so* much fun!" Beth bounced up and down as they walked up the street towards the car.

He watched her with sheer pleasure. "Yes, it was. Who knew a bit of fun could turn into that!"

"Is it always like that?" she wondered.

"The pub?" He thought about it. "Not for me, not for . . . I can't remember how long."

"God! The music, everyone laughing . . . the whiskey." She flung her hands up over her head in a wild gesture. She was experiencing the perfect level of tipsy, just enough that everything seemed like magic, but not so much that the world was spinning out of control.

She looked over at him as he watched her.

Her face contorted. "Should you be driving?"

"I'm within my limits; plus, it's just up the straight road, but we can walk if you like."

"It took us ten minutes to get here. How long would it take to walk back?"

"Ten minutes."

"How's that possible?"

"There's a shortcut you can only take on foot or by cycling."

She stopped to think about it. When she didn't answer, he decided for them.

"Come on, it'll be fun." He grabbed her hand and pulled her towards a small path through the trees, barely visible from the street. They walked hand in hand for a minute before the energy became too charged and she pulled away using a clearing in the trees and the stars as an excuse.

She looked up.

"Wow," she said under her breath, "the sky in San Francisco mostly looks orange from all the light pollution."

They were like diamonds catching light against a pitch black background. He came to stand next to her. They stood there looking up for an endless, infinite moment.

"When she was sick, my mum used to say, 'Look for me in the stars when I'm gone; I'll be there shining down on you.' I haven't been able to look up since." His voice caught in his throat as he said it.

"Mags used to say the stars were 'our constant reminder of how small and big life can be, how infinite and ephemeral.' She used to take me to the biggest telescopes around when I needed reminding."

He reached out and took her hand. She let him.

They walked that way for a while longer until they found that the path had partially flooded, creating a big pool of water with mud on either side.

"Ah, I can't walk through that!"

"Oh, come on, city gurl, you can do it." His Irish accent was as thick as ever.

"I'm not dainty!" She was defensive. "I just love these boots. Do you have any idea how difficult it is to find tall black boots that I like and are this comfortable? I was a dancer; I have serious foot problems."

"A dancer, eh?" He looked at her suggestively.

"That's a story for another day." She patted him on the shoulder.

"Come 'ere, then." He caught her hand and swung her up onto his back.

"What are you doing? Put me down!" she protested.

"I will, just as soon as we are clear of the mud so we don't sully your precious boots."

"OK." She gave up easily. No one had ever given her a piggyback ride before and it felt good to be off her feet.

He didn't set her down until they reached Lough Rhiannon a couple of minutes later.

She smoothed out her clothing. "Thank you." She reached up to kiss him on the cheek. He was at least six feet tall and it was a stretch even in her three-inch heels.

On her way down, he brought his hands to her lower back, holding her in place and locking their gaze. His arms, his eyes, his wounded heart all worked to trap her in some spell. Her body, her lips, her weary soul worked to trap him in the same spell. They were each trapped by the other, caught in some timeless moment.

Leaning in to her, he took an inch at a time. He was just about to close the distance between them, when her hand moved at the direction of her brain. She placed a finger over his lips.

"Connor, thank you for tonight, but I'm a mess." She paused, wanting to turn her brain off as his gaze intensified, but rational thought persisted. "And you're emotionally unavailable and probably leaving in a few days anyway. Let's not complicate things," she whispered into his face.

He did not release her; instead, he kissed her finger. She felt an overwhelming pull to close the gap; involuntarily she fell back into the moment, letting her finger stroke his lower lip, until again she remembered why she was there. Pressing her hands against his chest, he let her go.

He looked at her seriously. "Maybe that's what we both need: a complication."

She lowered her face. "I'm pretty raw right now." It was all too much. An overload of senses. She had life-changing healing to do.

He could see her vulnerability.

"You're right. I'm sorry; I wasn't thinking." He took a step backwards. "I *am* supposed to leave in a couple of days. And I think we're *both* emotionally unavailable, even for a one-night complication."

She nodded knowingly. Her mind was relieved he agreed, but her body was angry he agreed.

"But listen." He wasn't ready to leave her; he needed more—or at least the possibility of more time. He ran his fingers through his hair, thinking. "How 'bout you come out with me tomorrow? I can take you to the Cliffs of Moher; it'll be a grand drive. Just a bit of Irish fun." He lowered his face so she was forced to look into his eyes.

He was pleading with her.

Beth shook her head. "No, I'm sorry. I have to meditate, heal, or you know, think about my life. Get a handle on what's going on with me. What I want . . . where I'm going . . . where I'm supposed to be. . . ." She shrugged, feeling uncharacteristically helpless.

She was definitely lost and it pained him to see it.

"OK, sure. Well, if you change your mind," he said hopefully, "we can leave by two and still catch some amazing light. I'll keep my day open, all right?"

She tried to smile for his benefit. "I don't think I will, but thanks."

She reached up to hug him, feeling the strength in his shoulders. "Thanks for a grand night, Mr. Bannon," she whispered into his ear, using her best Irish accent.

Reluctantly, he released her.

She started walking towards the cottage. He watched her go. When she turned to look back, he extended an arm and bowed to her for the third time in the last twenty-four hours.

"Miss Lara."

CHAPTER 7: ON THE CLIFFS

She woke the next day feeling better than she had in a long time. Her first thought was of the night before. She smiled to herself as she relived each part bit by bit; she felt a little like a teenager having experienced something for the first time. Silently, she thanked Mags for her not-so-subtle push to get out there and reconnect with that side of herself.

She whipped up a quick omelet and sat at the little round table in the kitchen nook, right by the wall of windows. There had been little time to actually explore the cozy house. The small spiral staircase to the right of the table reminded her that there was a whole other level she hadn't even seen yet. She would save that bit of exploring for another day. Today, she was determined to sit with Mags' words and really think about how she had come to lose herself so completely.

She needed to understand. Beth was a history major and all too familiar with the concept that those who ignore history are doomed to repeat it.

She took the letter outside and re-read it several times, really taking the time to think through all the words. Forcing herself to remember all the times Mags had said these things to her when she was alive, and analyzing every memory. Desperately trying to see where she had gone wrong, and how she could have been so deaf to those words then. All she found in her memories were excuses. She was in the middle of a trial, she had too many cases on her plate, she had to prepare for a speaking engagement at a law school. . . .

Frustrated, she took a different approach. She found a yoga mat in the house and laid it out in front of the lake. She sat there practicing her best *"Ooummm."* Moving from tree pose to downward dog to child's pose, she searched for answers. She tried to figure it out in warrior, in mountain, in reclining hero, in as many yoga poses as she could think of. *The answers must be there.*

When that didn't work, she laid flat on the mat and breathed in and out. Thinking more about the letter, she closed her eyes. More than anything, Beth wished there was some magic reset button that could restore her to her former brain and personality. Some tool you could call upon when you had gotten so disconnected that you remembered your younger self like some mannequin through glass; there was a visual recognition of the memories, but no emotional connection, no road map back. No way to cut through the glass and make the mannequin real again.

After several minutes, she heard Mags' voice yelling at her from inside her head.

"What the hell are you doing?! You think you're going to find answers by lying on a mat and doing *nothing.* Didn't you hear me before? Go out and have more new experiences!"

With that, she sat bolt upright, knowing in that instant that Mags would have actually said those things to her. Well, she probably would have cursed a few more times, but the gist was correct. The realization made her laugh out loud. And then she heard the words again and she began laughing with her whole body, from her belly to her toes.

It was one of those earth-shaking laughs—the kind that come so easily when you're a child, but visit less often as you grow older.

She had to laugh at the idiocy of her approach. The point of the letter was to kick her ass into going out and experiencing new things. Mags had spelled it out for her. It was simple, but she'd made it difficult.

That was probably one of the lessons. *Things don't have to be difficult.*

Still laughing, Beth rolled up the mat and went inside to call Connor.

He was there waiting outside for her, leaning against his sleek black car. Her answering smile was automatic. He didn't even try to hide his enthusiasm, reaching down to scoop her up into a hug as soon as she was near enough to touch.

"It'll be great, you'll see," he said, setting her down.

They spoke animatedly for the first hour as they passed through Tralee and Castleisland. After a while, he started asking more questions about her life in San Francisco; she answered with as few words as possible. He sensed her disinterest and switched to telling her stories about his days at Cambridge. She listened eagerly while staring out the window. There was so much to see.

When he asked her about Mags, she refused to speak.

"I can't . . . not yet. I like hearing your stories; just please keep talking to me while I take all this in." She motioned out the window.

"Deal," he said in response. Satisfied that he wasn't boring her or dominating the conversation, he continued.

For Beth, it was nice getting lost in someone else's life. They passed many small towns on their three-and-a-half-hour drive. Some had names that sounded familiar. She thought Mags might have mentioned them when she recounted her Irish travels. Others were completely new to her.

Connor took great pleasure in telling her stories of how his college mates had come to spend holidays with him and how they had executed various shenanigans in some of those towns.

They laughed openly and pulled over a few times to take pictures of each other with their phones.

It was five by the time they reached the Cliffs. The sun was starting to set and the golden light was spectacular, even from the parking lot. Surprisingly, there was no one else there. It only took a second to find out why. A sign to the right of the lot read, "The Cliffs Are Closed."

"Oh no!" Beth was inexplicably crushed by the idea that she would miss the famed view. Again.

He came around to open her door. "It's OK; just come on."

She looked up at him. "How can the Cliffs close?"

"They rarely do, but there was a bad rainstorm and it made the cliff side really unstable. When it's that bad they don't allow anyone access, they don't want the tourists to kill themselves, you see. The damn fools always get too close to the edge."

"So you knew they were closed?"

"Of course! You didn't think I would drive three and half hours without checking, did you?"

"What am I missing?" She eyed him suspiciously.

"Just come with me, Luv." He took her hand and led her up the path.

"What are we doing? It's all blocked off."

"Not over here." There was a path to the right that veered away from the Cliffs slightly. It led to a tower. "That's O'Brien's Tower; it's the best view of the Cliffs."

"But how. . . ?"

"I know a guy." He gave her his best New York accent.

Just then, a man with a cabbie hat and jeans waved at them from the base of the tower. Connor waved back. "Thanks, Don!"

"Don is your guy?"

"Don is my guy. He manages the place. I just gave him a call and he's letting us up to the top."

Don walked away from the tower, presumably leaving it open for them.

"Cornelius O'Brien built the Tower to harness the best views, you see," Connor explained as they climbed a metal spiral staircase surrounded by dark stone walls. "Don't look out the window; save it."

When they reached the top, she was glad she hadn't looked. The Cliffs were dazzling. The golden sunset rays hit the jagged rocks covered in green. They hit the water and set it on fire in a way she had only ever seen in Ireland. Her sharp intake of breath was audible. She was in awe.

Connor was pleased and a little surprised. "I can't believe I didn't think to ask. Is this your first time here?"

Beth nodded. The tour she had gone on all those years ago had fallen behind schedule thanks to a raucous night of drinking the day before. They'd cut the Cliffs from the itinerary.

Then something clicked inside of her, hitting her with the force of a brick. She remembered that this had been one of Mags' most favorite places in all the world. And she had been everywhere. She would always say that this was where she would want to be proposed to, or die—her dark humor always coming through. Beth had blocked out this small truth. She stood there trying to figure out how she could have forgotten the connection. And then she understood.

It had been years since she'd mentioned the Cliffs of Moher, but it had always been Mags' dream to come here with her. When Beth was a child, Mags would describe them in detail and say, "One day when you're all grown, Lizzie, we'll go together and you'll see, it's a magic place, full of adventure."

"Why do we have to wait?" she would ask.

"Because you won't understand the magic of the Cliffs until you're older. It's a place where things suddenly become clear."

Beth's eight-year-old self thought about that for a second. "Why would they need to get clear? Are things blurry when you get old?"

"Yes, Lizzie, they can get quite blurry when you're an adult," Magdalen answered her with a wise smile.

Mags had tried to get her to come to Ireland after she graduated from law school, when she was twenty-five, twenty-eight, thirty, thirty-three. . . ? How many times had she enthusiastically planned their trip, only to have Beth be too busy to go? Of course they would have come here. To the Cliffs.

Something about this realization caused her to collapse against the wall.

"Elizabeth?" Connor was alarmed. He reached out to hold her up.

The pain ripped her apart from the inside out. Mags had taken care of her, had taught her, had always been there for her. And when it came time to live out one of her dreams for them both, she had been too busy. SHE HAD BEEN TOO BUSY. And now Mags was gone.

Beth doubled over from the weight of her realization. She had come to Ireland not just to grieve Mags, but to make things right with her. Ireland wasn't some random place. It was about so much more than vacating her life. It was about showing up for Mags and showing up for herself.

In the end, Elizabeth hadn't been there for her great-aunt at all. They visited often, but she hadn't paid attention to what mattered most to the person she loved the most.

The sobs came, one wave after another, crushing her body against the rocks of reality.

"I . . . was . . . .too . . . .busy!" she communicated to Connor, who was now holding on to her from behind. She had violently collapsed in on herself and onto the floor. "She . . . just . . . wanted to . . . come here with . . . me. AND I WAS TOO BUSY!!" she shrieked against the old stone.

Beth cried until every muscle in her body had exhausted itself. Time and space ceased to be as she lay broken.

When the sobbing subsided, Connor peeled her off the ancient floor. Her body trembled as she registered the temperature difference between the icy stone and his warm body.

He carried her to the car and drove them silently back to the cottage. She didn't move or speak the entire trip.

He carried her into the house, helped her change into a T-shirt, and put her to bed.

CHAPTER 8: THE FALL

One week went by. And then another. She was so tired. No amount of sleep kept the exhaustion at bay.

On the rare occasion that she felt any amount of hunger, she'd make some pasta. The effort was so great that by the time she finished cooking, she could only manage a few bites.

It tasted like plastic.

The rain in Ireland was unlike anything she had ever experienced. There was no respite. The sky opened to weep and never stopped.

There were many calls from the office. From the few voice mails she checked, they all involved some unpleasant reality of a case. The wife cheated, there's a prenup with a clause, how do we get around it, and so on. She turned her phone off and buried it beneath her sweaters in the bottom drawer of the mahogany dresser that stood opposite the bed.

By the second week she had animated herself enough to explore the house a degree. She walked to the two bookcases that flanked the first window on the left side of the house. Her eyes didn't get past the middle shelf in front of her. The first book she picked up was *The Three Musketeers* by Alexandre Dumas. She took it back to her room, collapsed onto the bed, and began reading the seven hundred-odd pages.

Escaping into a book seemed to work better than sleeping. She always had to wake up to reality with the latter. And every time she woke, there it was again. The grief of losing Mags, the guilt of having failed her, the gut-wrenching realization that she was now alone in the world.

Her mother had abandoned her when she was only four and she had never known her grandmother, so it was left to Mags. They had been a family, through and through. Until Beth changed—*devolved,* really.

The tears came sometimes. When they did, she let her entire body erupt with the violence of them. They left her feeling raw, not unlike being hung-over. Still, there was the smallest change with every spell. Like the three G-words loosened their iron grip over her heart one agonizing moment at a time.

After Dumas, she read Hugo, Binchy, Tolkien— usually the first book she noticed. She thought it a sign from somewhere else. If something caught her eye, she devoured it. Someone else had to be showing her the way, right? She couldn't really be alone.

And so she continued into the fourth week, hungrily inhaling the words and worlds of others. The reading had made her feel the beginnings of true hunger again. But she didn't cook. Sometime during the third week, food just started appearing in the fridge.

There were casseroles and pasta dishes and enchiladas and all manner of different cuisines to choose from. She didn't know how Mrs. Porter was doing it, and for the moment, she didn't care. She couldn't even feel gratitude for the woman who had taken it upon herself to keep Beth alive. That would have been a fourth G, an emotion outside grief, guilt, and gut-wrenching sadness—and she was still incapable of it.

Mona had also left a stuffed bear. It had dark fur and a thick cream sweater with a big green shamrock on its chest. It fit perfectly in Beth's arms. And so for that last week she took to keeping it close by or in her arms at all times. When sleep did happen, it would be with Beth curled up in the fetal position, clutching the bear.

Until one morning, near the end of her four-week hibernation, the rain stopped. She knew it as soon as she opened her eyes. The endless pounding of water just wasn't there. Birds chirped animatedly from somewhere nearby.

Like a child who had been cooped up because of the rain or an illness, Beth jumped off of her bed and went to the French doors. Without a moment's thought to the three G-words, she cast the curtains open. They swayed from the intensity of her assault. The light welcomed her with a warm hug as she stepped outside.

The water washed away the remnants of the three Gs. It was nice to have it cascading down her body instead of pounding on her house or gushing up from inside of her. She stayed in the shower until the water turned ice cold. It was at once invigorating and shocking.

She quickly jumped out and grabbed her towel, smiling to herself as she remembered the plumbing of the old house in Berkeley. They had moved there when she was ten. The tank of their hot-water heater was tiny and Mags loved her long showers. As a child she was conditioned to get clean quickly or risk the torrent of arctic water that would come for her. It became harder to go faster as she grew older, and by her teens, the cold water was expected. Naturally, she complained. And Mags would be Mags.

"It's just a little reminder from the Universe, Lizzie . . . that you're alive." With that, she would give her a pat on the shoulder, her not-so-subtle way of saying *buck up and get over it*.

She settled on a quiche from the magic food fridge and sat down to eat in the kitchen nook. It had spinach and basil and tomato with something else that gave it a kick. It tasted like the Mediterranean. Each mouthful fortified her body and continued to heal her soul. Finally, she was overwhelmed with gratitude for the tiny lady who had silently looked out for her.

She looked out at the lake and the green and the sunshine, and felt the color finally permeate her brain. Ireland was her very own green grass road and it was there to take her where she needed to go.

The third letter was housed in a blue envelope. Beth didn't pause to brace herself before opening it. Whatever Mags had to say, it couldn't be worse than the month she had just survived. No longer filled with anxiety at the thought of a thirty-five-year-old secret about her parents or Mags' blunt statements about Beth's life choices, she dove in.

Dearest Lizzie,

I want to thank you for being my family. You were my second chance after losing Elsa so young. I'm sorry you never got to know your grandmother Aurora, or grow up with Carolina. Both were loving and kind. I know you think Carolina was weak and abandoned you, but she didn't, Lizzie—not really. But this isn't THAT letter—I just wanted to tell you that I am grateful we were brought together to make our little clan, even though it was through the cruelty of life.

You never really understand how important family is until it is taken from you. I was so happy when Elsa was born. Our little unit was everything to me. There were many people and places that helped bring me back to life after. Twenty years of people and places before life brought me to you. Each had their own hand in helping me heal, but you were the one to put the final missing piece together. And for that, my dearest, I am grateful.

I hope you've been taking my words to heart. And that you are currently surrounded by people and places to help you now that I'm gone.

I honestly believed that you had been spared any childhood trauma from losing your parents the way you did. You were so open to life—all the way through your college years. And then you found the law and suddenly it was like all the issues I was afraid you would have just consumed you through your work.

You need people, Lizzie. You can't go through life the way you have because sooner or later you will wake up and realize that you've wasted it. Demolishing your opponents, as you once described it—and always winning—aren't substitutes for having true friends and lovers and LIVING.

Love,
Mags

P.S. Just because I got a little sentimental in this one, don't think that I'm not going to kick your ass in the ones to come. You're welcome.

She read the postscript with a smirk. It was like Mags was standing there speaking to her.

Somehow Beth *had* managed to find people to help, in spite of herself. Connor had been there to remind her of who she could be, who she had been for most of her life. He had been there to peel her off of the cold stone floor and heroically carry her from O'Brien's Tower.

Their night at the pub and walk back to the lake had awakened something inside of her. She was sorry that he was gone. Sorry that she had used her finger instead of her lips, her brain instead of her body.

And then there was Mona Porter. Beth had been so rude at their first meeting and the woman's only response was to hug her fiercely and feed her.

She could only remedy one of those relationships. It was time to thank the bubbly Mona for her kindness. An invitation to lunch was in order.

CHAPTER 9: IN TOWN

Café Shannon was about halfway up the main street. Beth sat at a little table for two located in the large front window. From what she could tell, it was more upscale than the rest of the restaurants and pubs in town. Although she'd only passed a few on her way there.

The tables were covered in long white linen tablecloths, each with a single fresh flower in an elegant vase in the middle. Hers was pink.

The servers were dressed like traditional French waiters. Black suit vest over a white shirt, bow tie, black pants, with a white server's apron on top. Two medium-sized chandeliers hung from the ceiling and light classical music played in the background.

It was a bit much for the little village, but she'd asked to take Mona to the nicest place in town. Looking around at the sparsely occupied tables, she rightly supposed that the townsfolk dined here only as a special treat.

There was a well-dressed family with two school-aged children sitting at a table closer to the kitchen; they admonished the little girl when she slouched in her chair, and fiddled with the boy's collar. Three older women in pearls talked animatedly over some brochures against the far wall. A young couple holding hands at the large window on the other side of the main door rounded out the patrons. All tourists.

Mona walked in. She was wearing a light blue dress with a Jackie O, sixties neckline. It set off what was left of the red in her hair, which was carefully secured in a bun. She carried a small matching blue purse. Her cheeks were bright pink from the walk. She looked overjoyed to see Beth.

"Hallo there!" She walked over to the table.

Beth stood to give her a hug. Again, she was surprised by the sheer physical force that Mona put into the embrace.

She smoothed her dress self-consciously before she sat down opposite Beth.

Looking around, Mona took in the simple elegance of the café. "Isn't this just lovely!" she exclaimed.

"Oh, is this your first time?"

"No, but I've only been a precious few times. It's so kind of you to invite me. I just can't thank you enough."

Beth opened her mouth to express her gratitude for what Mona had done over the course of the last two weeks, but found that she couldn't speak fast enough. Mona was in fine form.

"Isn't that just beau-tiful the way they place one flower at each table just so. And tha boys wear those fancy suits, such a fine place." She took the briefest of sips from the water goblet in front of her before continuing.

"Oh, and the food is divine. Such tiny portions, but quite delectable, if I do say so myself." Taking a breath she looked at the menu. "Jaysus, Mary and Joseph! I'd forgot how way outta that the viddles are here! And me in such a state, I'd ate the arse off of a baby elephant!" She threw her head back and laughed from her belly.

The tourists turned to look to see what was so funny. Beth didn't know either. She could only guess that Mona meant the food was expensive and she was hungry.

"Please, order whatever you like. If you want to order three plates, then do," Beth said earnestly. "I don't care if they have to bring us a second table. It's my way of thanking—"

"Oh, what a kindness!" Mona raised her voice and clasped her tiny hands together in complete excitement. "Now you're not just saying that, are ya?"

"No, no, please, I'm not just being polite. It would bring me great pleasure." Beth studied the menu. The omelet she'd had that morning hit the spot, but after barely eating for a month, she was starving again. An audible grumble from her stomach confirmed it. "In fact, I think I'll order a few things myself." She gave the woman an encouraging smile that she hoped said *really, let's go for it.*

Mona was bouncing with excitement. They ordered eight entrées between the pair of them. Their waiter, Mickey, raised a judgmental eyebrow, but otherwise remained silent.

Beth narrowed her eyes at him, having a temporary lapse as she envisioned speaking to the owner or manager about their waiter's expression. Or better yet, giving him one of her renowned polite verbal bitch slaps. But he had access to their food.

Still, waiters shouldn't be judgmental, especially when faced with a woman as tiny and cute as Mona, whose overt pleasure at placing the order could only be taken as delightful.

Mona's wonderfully thick Irish accent snapped Beth out of it. "Can you believe that the good Lord finally delivered us the sun? What a storm that was! There was just no stoppin' it, was there?" Mona shook her head sagely. "I haven't seen that kind of relentless downpour since the Return of the Westerlies when I was in France some years ago." Her eyes widened at the memory.

France? Beth was suddenly curious about the kind woman sitting opposite her. Where had she traveled to, and who had she met? She wished for one more opportunity to speak to Mags about the people and places of her life, as she had referred to them in the letter.

"Have you always lived here, Mona?" She took a sip of her orange juice.

"Yes, I have. Born and raised!" she declared cheerfully. Then she stopped, and added, "Although I did leave for a time, but I didn't exactly live anywhere else." She narrowed her eyes as she thought about whether her past situation qualified.

"Well, why did you leave?" Beth prodded.

"Oh, I was a dancer. Well, more acrobat, really. I loved to dance, but I was always such a tiny thing that I was mostly stuck doing the acrobat work."

Whatever Beth had expected to hear from this tiny round lady, it hadn't been a revelation of a past as a professional dancer or circus performer.

"You worked as an acrobat?"

"I was part of a dance troupe. We were very famous for a time. Toured all over," she remembered proudly. "We'd be gone for months and months at a time, you see."

"How long did you dance professionally?"

"Five years." Mona stared out the window, clearly somewhere else. "It was a grand time. Lovely." Her voice dripped with longing.

Beth's curiosity stirred. "Why'd you stop?" She needed to hear about other people. About their lives. She was sick of being limited to her thoughts, her memories. It was too narrow a space to occupy for as long she had.

With a look that was sad, proud, happy, and wistful all at once, Mona returned to the table. "I met my Richard and got married." Her face hadn't settled on an emotion. "I never danced again. But I had my family."

"You miss it," Beth observed.

Mona glowed as she nodded. Some secret memory danced behind her eyes.

The food arrived all at once. They hadn't needed to add a second table; they'd needed to add a second *and* a third. Beth didn't think Mona could have gotten more excited after ordering the smorgasbord. She was wrong.

Everyone in the café now turned to watch her clasp her hands and squeal in delight. The children giggled. The adults gave them appreciative looks colored by a touch of envy. Envy that the two women by the window had the balls to be exactly who they wanted to be in a stuffy place like this.

Amazingly, Mona was quiet as they ate. At least for a time. She took small bites of her risotto and salmon and filet mignon and crab cakes and so on, relishing every flavor. It was Beth who broke Mona's food reverie.

"Tell me about your family. Do you have kids, grandkids...?"

"I have two children. My boy, Sam, lives in Dublin. He's a banker," she answered proudly. "And my girl, Mollie, lives in Killarney. She's the head of a school there, you see. They're both very clever."

Mona spoke animatedly about her children for a spell. About how they had always been smart and how she had pushed them to be diligent in their studies. How she'd wanted Mollie to be a dancer, but it turned out that Sam had the greater talent for it. She spoke of her husband, Richard, as well and explained that they were as happy as they'd ever been, although it varied widely from day to day after thirty years of marriage.

"So where did you travel to when you danced?"

"All over Ireland, of course. We went to London, Edinburgh, Paris, Lyon, Nice, Barcelona, Rome...," she took a breath, "Brazil, Argentina, Sweden... we went everywhere. We were a group of fifteen and we would get into so many shenanigans after the shows!" She laughed heartily.

"Oh, I wish you could've seen us. We were something to behold."

She launched into a story about how a group of them had tricked several businessmen into buying them thousands of dollars in jewelry in a single night, only to walk away leaving them hot and bothered. The next day the girls were on a plane to Barcelona.

"Although, mind you, I was secretly terrified. I didn't know if we would get away with it. But we did! Oh, the thrill!" Mona shook with the excitement of it.

Beth tried to picture it. "Did you think they were violent?"

Mona gave it some thought. "Oh, I don't think so, but then we didn't really know them, did we? You can never really tell with a man—especially when you've made him look the fool."

Beth considered that. She took a bite of her filet, again trying to imagine a young Mona, and what it must have been like to feel terrified. "That's true. Did any of you know how to defend yourselves?"

"No, no, we didn't. It just wasn't done then." She looked curiously at Beth. "Do you know how to . . . you know, give it back to 'em?"

Beth nodded. "Yes. I'm not a black belt or anything, but I've taken a lot of self-defense and different martial arts classes. And I'm pretty good at throwing knives."

Mona looked impressed.

At that Beth just shrugged. "You've got to be able to take care of yourself. Otherwise, who will?"

Mags had ingrained that in her early on.

"So wise, so wise." Mona nodded.

"Did any of the other girls come back to live here?"

"Well, we weren't all from here exactly. Some were from farther south and we even had a couple of girls from Dublin. There were three of us from here. Myself, Cailin, and Rhia."

"Are you still close?"

"I see Cailin a few times a week. Out and about or when we go catch a show together. She's still one of my best friends." She took a bite of her crab cakes, turning somber. "And then, well, you know what happened to Rhia."

Beth shook her head slowly. She'd only been told about one Rhia; Mona hadn't mentioned a second until now.

Mona's eye grew small. Did she mean . . . ? "Wait. Rhia *Bannon*?"

"Yes, Connor's mother. It was a blow when the good Lord took her from us." She made the sign of the cross. "He hasn't been the same."

"I'm sorry," was all Beth could say.

Mona's expression turned sympathetic. "Well, you know all about grief, don't you? I'm very glad to see that you're doing better."

Beth nodded, lost in thought. "You know the Bannons well." It wasn't a question.

"Yes, Rhia and I were friends since we were wee ones, and then, of course, I worked for Connor's father at the house for a . . . *time*." She stopped abruptly.

"So you've been taking care of the cottage for a while, then?"

Mona bit her lip and was about to answer when Mickey asked if they were interested in dessert.

Beth insisted they have some even though they had now consumed more than Beth had eaten in the past month. Mona was more than happy to oblige.

"Connor mentioned that you had a healthy appetite. I'm glad to see it. Too many young women don't know how to eat and enjoy."

Beth's eyes widened. "Well, I've definitely been one of those women," she admitted. "And I certainly haven't eaten much in the last month. Maybe I'm just catching up."

Her eyes had been bigger than her stomach. She'd definitely overdone it, but it was worth it to have a front-row seat to the Mona show.

"Speaking of which," Elizabeth began, her voice serious, her eyes earnest, "I can't thank you enough for making all those dishes. It was the nicest thing anyone has ever done for me." She hoped that Mona could really feel her gratitude.

The blood rose to her cheeks. "It was nothin', Luv." She was pleased.

"It was . . . a lot." Beth's voice broke. "I'm just sorry it took me so long to thank you. I was . . . in a very bad place."

She wiped a single tear from her eye discreetly before it could fall.

Mona reached out across the table and patted her hand affectionately.

"I don't know how you knew or how you did it, but I'm grateful," Beth finished.

Mona looked taken aback. Surprise colored her cheeks. "Well, Connor, of course."

Right. Connor had told her about the Cliffs.

Beth was suddenly self-conscious. She hated to think she'd had an audience for her global meltdown. It was already too much that Connor had witnessed part of it. "Oh no, does everyone know?"

"No, no, Luv. He just told me."

She nodded, feeling more gratitude at not having the whole town know what a wreck she'd been.

"How'd you get into the house?"

"Connor."

"He gave you a key?"

"No, he let me in each time," she answered absently as she dug into her crème brûlée.

Beth stopped.

Food had been appearing for the last two weeks.

She didn't know why, but her heart pounded loudly in her ears. "But . . . I thought he left?" She tried not to sound too interested.

"Oh, he did. He was gone for a couple of days about a month ago and then came right back. I can't remember the last time he went on such a short trip. Or came to stay for so long." She quickly returned to her dessert.

He was still here. And he had been watching out for her.

She was suddenly hyper-aware of herself. She tried to think back, to remember if she'd heard anyone. "You don't think he saw me when you came by to drop off the food, do you?" She had avoided mirrors.

"Oh, no, darlin'. We came in the wee hours to make sure we didn't disturb you. The door to the bedroom was shut," Mona assured her happily, now moving on to a piece of chocolate cake. "What sinful indulgence," she said under her breath. "Lord forgive me." Her voice was full of reverence as her eyes widened, taking in the layers of cake.

Beth was lost in thought. "Well, that was very kind of him. I've never seen such thoughtful behavior in a man. His mother must have raised him well."

"Yes, she did. But I've never seen Connor take such care with anyone. You must have made an impression." Her voice was still as light as a cool breeze as she floated on her cloud of chocolate.

Beth paid the bill, which was considerable, but nothing she wasn't used to spending at a good restaurant in the city. She tipped Mickey fairly; pity for him, as she was used to tipping very generously. That raised eyebrow had cost him. *A lot.*

Mona was all hugs and thanks. She'd never been treated to such a meal. Beth watched her as she trotted down the street, moving quite fast for someone who had just consumed so much.

She didn't want to go back to the car just yet. There was so much to see on the little main street.

The businesses were straight out of a storybook. Some were painted in bright colors while others were made of stone. She passed by the bakery and made a mental note to come back to stock up her kitchen with some fresh treats. Then did the same for the chocolate shop across the street. It was a surprise that she could still be so attracted to food after everything she had just eaten.

She felt different as well. She was still raw, but before her month-long fall off the deep end she had felt raw in a crumbling, poisoned kind of way. Now she felt raw in a shiny and new kind of way. Like the difference between a dying phoenix and one who'd newly risen.

A shop called Beverly's Irish Treasures caught her eye. There were several ornate crystals with dragons and wizards on top of each at the window. The smell of incense hit her as she stepped inside.

"Good day to you," a twenty-something girl with hot pink fingernails called from the register of the small shop.

"Hello."

"Were you lookin' for anything in particular? A genuine Irish souvenir, perhaps?" she asked, clearly hoping to make an instant sale.

"I'm just looking, thanks."

The girl's face fell quickly.

Elizabeth noticed a carousel of necklaces next to the dragons and wizards at the front. The pendants were traditional Celtic symbols. Some she recognized, and others were new.

A poster on the wall explained. In a large Celtic-looking font it declared, "Legends of Rhiannon: A Unique Collection of Celtic Charms & Enchanted Jewellery." She wondered if they spelled jewelry differently in Ireland or if it was just a typo. There were at least fifteen pendants.

They had names like Wheel of Arianrod, which was for good luck and fortune, or the Sword of Nuadha, for winning and success. Her eyes fell on the High Celtic Cross, which was for guidance and protection, and instantly remembered Connor's tattoo. She had never liked tattoos on herself or found them attractive on men, but there was something about its placement on Connor's well-defined bicep. . . .

She shook her head and turned to a more rational state, resolving to thank him for his kindness as soon as possible. The thought of seeing him did something to her stomach. It was a strange feeling—like being fifteen instead of thirty-five; she was excited and nervous and maybe a little queasy. It hadn't even occurred to her that she might be able to see him again. Finding out that he was still in town felt like a gift from the Universe. At least she'd be able to leave things in a better place with him.

It bothered her, thinking that he might leave again still believing that she was some crazed weepy American who needed to be carried from a tower.

She picked up the Celtic cross and paid for it at the register, much to the pink-nailed girl's delight.

There was a small farmers' market up the street. It was tiny compared to the markets that could be found throughout San Francisco on Wednesdays or Fridays, or Saturdays and Sundays for that matter.

As she smelled the fresh basil, she thought of how she would contact Connor. Should she call him? He lived up the lake; maybe she should drop by his house to thank him? Maybe with some food? What did they do in Ireland?

If he were American, she could just buy him some beer and call it a day. Then again, if he were American he wouldn't have broken tenant laws to enter the house without giving her notice. Hell, he wouldn't have even *thought* to be thoughtful enough to break the rules.

Tenant laws? She shook her head, hoping all remnants of the law would fall out.

Mollie's Chocolates was next. She bought a box of assorted chocolates and several more colorful-looking sweets she was sure would lead to a sugar binge.

She was arranging the box in her bag with one hand and reaching for the door with the other when she noticed a small magazine rack off the entrance. Some of the rags faced the shoppers as they left and others faced the street. A picture of a very familiar face adorned the cover. He was gorgeous and photogenic to boot.

Stunned, she was still looking at the photo as she exited the shop. Her eyes travelled to the other side of the rack as she moved onto the street, her feet moved her farther away from the magazine, but her gaze remained trained on the picture behind her. She'd just started to read the headline—"IRISH NO"—when she collided with someone walking at full speed.

He caught her before she could fall to the ground.

It would have looked like a dip if they had been dancing. She clutched the arms of her assailant and savior, all at once recognizing the sapphire eyes she'd just been examining in detail . . . the eyes of Connor Bannon.

CHAPTER 10: UNEXPECTED ENCOUNTERS

He looked down at her for an extended moment. The corners of his mouth turned up into a boyish grin.

Although he was fully supporting her weight, it wasn't a comfortable position. "OK, you can let me up now, thanks." Her voice was strained from holding up her neck.

"Oh, sure, sorry there." He placed her back on her feet.

"Hi," they both said at the same time.

"Oh, sorry."

"No, what were you going to say?"

They continued awkwardly.

He ran a hand through his hair. "Well, this is ridiculous. No need for things to be so . . . yeah, well," he started. He remembered something and chuckled. "I mean, you've seen me naked," he joked, stuffing his hands into the pockets of his gray pants.

"And you've seen me naked," she blurted out without thinking and with all the grace of a gawky teenager. Oh, God.

She'd been so out of it, she'd forgotten about how he'd helped her into a T-shirt after the Cliffs.

"That's right. Well, technically you had your underthings on, so it doesn't count," he said, putting her at ease. And then quickly ruining it. "So technically, I haven't seen you naked. *Yet.*"

She turned red and punched him.

"What did I say about the drinks and the touching?" He acted offended.

"Well, you're the one who rammed straight into me and almost rendered *me* unconscious. And you did *that* without buying me a drink."

"Stop the ball. It was *you* who ran into *me*," he bantered back.

They smiled at each other. Finally on the other side of awkward.

He was staring into the sun; it made the ice of his eyes look electric. "I was just coming to find you, actually."

"Really? I was just staring at your face on the—" she motioned with her arm behind her and then realized she didn't know how to explain why she'd been staring at a picture of him. "Never mind." She shook her head as he raised an eyebrow.

"Read anything of note?" His expression changed; he looked suddenly guarded.

"No, there was a picture on a magazine, nothing. I didn't even get a chance to look at it really." She waved the whole thing off.

"Oh? What did the headline say? Did it tell you anything interesting?" He shoved his hands further into his pockets and swayed where he stood.

He looked like he was bracing himself for something. "No." She scrunched her eyes together, "I didn't even get a chance to read the headline; it just said 'Irish'—which was, you know terribly telling. If I didn't know you were Irish before, the magazine definitely helped fill me in," she teased.

His face relaxed. "Oh, so you're witty, are you? Full of surprises."

She smiled up at him. "How'd you even know I was—" She stopped herself.

"Mona," they both said together.

Beth nodded, understanding completely.

"I just spoke with her. She couldn't stop talkin' about how you'd treated her to the meal of her life. The whole town will know by now." He smiled cheerfully. "And she mentioned that you were on the mend. I thought you would be back at the house by now."

"We had so much food, I wanted to walk." She shrugged. "And I wanted to explore a little. I am in Ireland, after all."

"You don't say?" he teased, turning his body to nudge her with his shoulder. "Would you mind some company?"

This was her chance to thank him. "What did you have in mind?"

He pointed towards the sea. "It's just a block in that direction."

She squinted into the sun and started walking in silent acceptance.

They sat on a bench overlooking the Dingle Harbour.

For several minutes they didn't say anything; they just sat and looked out at the water, letting the ocean breeze whip their hair in wildly unpredictable ways.

Until Connor angled his body to face her. "I'm really glad you're doing better."

It was as serious as she had ever heard him.

She mirrored his body. "Mona told me that you were the one who let her in so she could leave the food." She looked down at her clasped hands. "That was really kind."

He nodded, sensing she had more to say.

She looked up into his face and worked to keep her voice level. "And, you know, thanks for that other thing."

His lips twitched. "What other thing?" He was all mischief.

"The whole. . ." she took in a breath and said it as quickly as she could before the ridiculous nature of the statement stopped her, ". . . peeling me off the stone floor after I freaked out, carrying me from a tower, and putting me to bed . . . *without looking* . . . thing."

She tried to make it sound like it was no big deal, but she was clearly flustered by the rescue.

He searched her face, taking in every detail. "Who said I didn't look?"

Again she couldn't tell if he was kidding.

"I just assumed you were being a gentleman and didn't look." She wasn't sure why she'd assumed as much, but the whole chivalric rescue might have had something to do with it. Surely a man who carried you from a tower could get you into a T-shirt without examining your bra and panties. "Was I wrong?" It was her turn to study him.

His eyes were dark and his smile suggestive. "Oh, I definitely looked," he finished with a wicked smile.

The blood rose to her face.

Seeing her embarrassment, he let her off the hook. "Relax. Like I said, you were in your underthings. I didn't see more than if you'd been on a beach in a bikini."

She could feel the flush calming. "I guess that's OK, then." She kicked his foot lightly and shook her head.

He had a way of making her feel like a teenager—the good parts and the bad. Remembering that she was actually a fully functioning grown ass woman, she returned to the matter at hand. "Seriously, though. Thanks. I've never fallen apart like that. Ever." She looked into his eyes trying to communicate her thanks, breaking through their juvenile banter.

His gaze grew intense, intimate. It did something to her heart and made her feel uneasy.

She turned to look at the Atlantic. "And I've certainly never been rescued before. So that was new."

"Well, that's good, because I've never rescued anyone before." He was light and serious at the same time.

"How did you even know I was still having a hard time, weeks after you saw me? Didn't you leave?" She already knew he'd only left for a couple of days, but she wanted him to tell her.

This time when he looked at her, she felt like he was looking straight into her soul. "I did leave, but I found myself missing home." His eyes cut through the face she put out to the world. Through the face she'd fooled herself into believing was hers—for a decade. It was unnerving. A chill ran up her spine.

Elizabeth Lara was as sharp as they come, but she'd always been emotionally immature. His unwavering intensity made her hair stand on end, made the cells in her body dance to life, connected her to something outside of herself . . . and she was completely terrified.

She leaned back against the bench, facing the ocean, focusing on something else, *anything* else. "How did you know I was still having a hard time?" she repeated in a controlled voice.

Connor wanted her to look at him. He wanted to see her reaction as he explained. Elizabeth was unlike anyone he'd ever met and he was starting to understand that he would have to be careful in his approach.

He started with the truth. "I went to Paris on business for a couple of days. I cut things short and found myself walking across the lough the same day I returned. I was just about to knock on the French doors when I heard you crying." He stopped for a moment.

Elizabeth ventured a sideways glance. The memory seemed to pain him.

"You were sobbing just like at the Cliffs and I couldn't help you. I sat outside just listening until you stopped."

She tried to picture him—the emotional voyeur, listening. To her surprise, she was more curious than mortified. "Why would you do that? Listen, I mean?"

He clasped his hands in front of him and turned his palms up, keeping his fingers laced together. "Because I understand that pain. Believe me, I do, but I don't cry. I haven't even since my mum. . . ." He stopped.

For someone who'd proven to be so considerate, that surprised her. He was thoughtful, sensitive, but he didn't cry when his mother died? She considered the man sitting next to her; she wanted to understand. "Is it a guy thing? Stay strong?"

"No. . . ."

"It isn't for lack of emotion; I can hear it in your voice," she observed.

"No, I never said I can't cry. I said I don't." He held her gaze, searching for the words to explain. "These last two years, I've felt that if I let it go, then I'd fall apart. I wouldn't be able to put the pieces back together. I'd just stay . . . *broken*."

Beth nodded, understanding. "But if you don't let it go and fall apart, how will you ever heal?"

He looked out at the water. Slowly he shook his head and shrugged his shoulders. "I don't know. But that's why I listened to you. It was like you were crying for the both of us."

That made more sense to Beth than anything she had experienced since coming to Ireland.

"I came back the next day and the day after that. Every day I made the walk in the rain, hoping you had opened the curtains. Then I'd know you were OK."

"And that you'd be OK too," she finished for him.

He nodded. For a moment she stared into his blue eyes and imagined that she, too, could see into his soul. He was the one to break away.

"But you didn't, and so a couple of weeks later, I used my key to get into the house to make sure you were OK." The distress in his voice was plain. Realizing this, he made an effort to lighten his tone. "You know, just to make sure I didn't have a dead body on my hands. Nothing devalues a property faster than a corpse." He flashed a half smile before continuing.

"I found you in the bedroom, asleep, but alive. Then I went to the kitchen to make sure you'd been eating. From what I could tell, you hadn't, so I told Mona what you'd been going through. She made the food and I let her in."

Beth was overwhelmed listening to the lengths to which this stranger had gone to help her.

Then he remembered, "Well, almost all of the food. Did you eat the enchiladas?"

She shook her head.

"I made those," he announced proudly. "I'd never tried to really cook before, but I found a recipe online, so if they're terrible. . . ," he turned towards her again, "don't tell me."

She laughed at this admission. She'd thought they looked different from the other plates. Like a present wrapped by a child next to the handiwork of Martha Stewart.

And then she remembered something else she had forgotten to tell Mona. "I didn't thank Mona for the stuffed bear. It was . . . it really helped me there in the end."

"Oh, well, then thank me. I got it for you." He beamed like a little boy who'd just received a gold star.

Her mouth went slack, she was floored.

"That was . . . I don't even know how to. . . ." She struggled for the words. She settled for, "Thank you," again. "You Irish sure are friendly. I've never experienced such selfless, caring behavior from virtual strangers in all my life." She said it more to herself than him.

"Well, I don't know about selfless. I think I've made it pretty clear that I have less than pure intentions," he wiggled his eyebrows suggestively, "and we definitely aren't strangers. We've danced, you've cried, I've rescued."

She rolled her eyes. "Yes, well, there's that."

"That's already more than most relationships I've had." He said it more to himself than her.

She looked at him with mock pity and then turned away. "That's kind of sad." She tried to lighten the mood. "But I don't think this qualifies as a relationship."

123

"Well, no, you won't even let me kiss you, for Christ's sake."

Right. The almost kiss.

"It made perfect sense at the time," she argued. "Still, that's sad." There was true pity in her expression now.

"Oh, don't look at me like that, Luv. From what I know about you, I'd wager that you haven't exactly found yourself in any emotionally mature relationships either. Probably kept the poor lads at arm's length."

"Oh, like you've gone on more than . . . five dates with the same woman?" She threw a random number out there. For some reason, she was sure it was more or less the truth. "At least I was in a relationship," she said defensively.

"Uh-huh, for how long?"

"Over a year."

He looked at her appraisingly. "No, I'm still not buyin' it. You probably didn't even love him."

She gave him a withering look. How could he know that?

His eyes grew wide. "Oh, I'm right! There you have it. Of the two of us, who is more dysfunctional? The person who cuts things off before they become serious because he doesn't see a future there," he jabs at his chest with his thumbs, "or the person who stays in a relationship for *a year* when they aren't even in love!" He threw up his hands like he had just won the match. Case closed.

Elizabeth could see what he wanted and where this was heading. She couldn't resist using her talents. "Well, by that same token, how dysfunctional would I be if I became involved with someone who lives sixteen hours away? Furthermore, my instincts were *starting* to tell me that I should kiss you. So if you've just proven that I'm the more dysfunctional one, then we shouldn't trust my instincts."

She said the next part extra-slowly for effect. "I guess you're right, Connor."

She won the argument like she won most things: by being the first one to understand what they were really talking about. Keeping her eyes firmly on what the person actually wanted instead of getting caught up in the particulars of a smaller conflict. If she knew what they were ultimately after before they had worked it out themselves, then she could beat them there by purposely losing the battle and instantly winning the war.

His jaw dropped and for several seconds he couldn't speak. Realizing that he'd just talked himself out of going further with her, he closed his mouth and sat back against the bench.

"Well, Jaysus, woman, that was feckin' brilliant."

She rolled her eyes and smiled.

He sighed and then tried again. "But you didn't mean it, did you? About setting your mind against snogging me?"

She remembered the feeling of his lower lip against her finger. Surely she could have a bit of fun while she worked through her own mess. She'd just spent the last month alone. Perhaps she had done all she could do in isolation. And there was no denying the electricity that often flowed between them. She knew was she *wanted* to do. It was just a question of allowing herself to have it.

"The jury's still out," she answered casually.

His expression was hopeful, but calculated. "Well, while they're out decidin', how 'bout you come with me to the Food & Drink Festival tonight?"

There was a festival? She looked behind her towards the town. Maybe they used the word "festival" differently in Ireland. "Aren't festivals like that usually an all-day or all-weekend event?"

"Well, our main festival is in October. This one is a single evening. Brings people together, allows local business to showcase new ideas so they don't have to wait an entire year."

Her stomach did a little flip at the idea of spending the evening with him. *Oh, geez. Get a grip.* She would play it cool. Even though he'd seen her at her worst, she was determined to hold on to whatever shreds of dignity she had left.

She squinted, bringing her lips together as if considering. She hoped her face said *it's an interesting idea, but. . . .*

When she didn't say anything, he nudged her foot with his, playfully. "I've been asked to judge one of the blind dessert contests, so I have to go, but it would definitely be more fun with you there."

Still she said nothing.

Connor could see her stubbornness. He thought it was very Irish of her. "Oh, come on now, I know you have a sweet tooth. Don't think I didn't notice all those chocolates in your sack."

She gave him a look that said *eh* and shrugged.

"Jaysus, Mary, and Joseph, it'll be a craic!" He threw up his hands. "You know how last time we aimed for a bit of fun and it turned into that? Well, tonight is *guaranteed* to be a craic and that means a lot of fun to start."

It wasn't that she was trying to frustrate him; rather, it was that she quite enjoyed listening to him try to convince her.

He smiled hopefully. "Just think; we'll be passed out from joy by the end of the night."

She thought about where she wanted her night to end, and it definitely involved him. But he didn't need to know that. She would wait and see. This time she wouldn't choose her brain over her body.

"Yeah, OK," she relented, gratified by how casual it sounded.

He sat up and narrowed his eyes. "OK, you'll come, or OK, you're open to this?" He motioned with his hands to indicate the two of them together.

She wasn't sure what he meant by the gesture. All she had in mind was a bit of fun. A bit of *don't think too hard* fun. Beyond that she couldn't process. Currently, she was an emotionally immature mess and he was an emotionally unavailable bachelor; surely a bit of fun was all they could manage together. She was counting on it.

"How about OK to tonight?" she clarified.

He gave her his biggest smile. The one that said *I won.* "I'll take it."

CHAPTER 11: THE IRISH FESTIVAL

She looked in the mirror. The day had been unseasonably warm since the rain had stopped, especially for the last day of February.

Connor had wanted to stay with her, to show her the sights, but she didn't have time. Of course, she hadn't told him why.

She hadn't exactly packed light, but the few dresses she did have with her were more elegant, sophisticated, and now as she looked at them again, more appropriate for a funeral than a festival. Beth's wardrobe was mostly black and gray, like her life. There was nothing in her closet in San Francisco that wouldn't look out of place in Ireland.

The only solution was to go shopping. The colorful boutiques in the village were filled with European styles and had so many beautiful pieces; she'd had a very good time putting together a small new wardrobe.

She enjoyed the frivolity of buying things just as much as the next person, but she hadn't gone shopping for fun since she'd become an attorney. Which meant that the second she could afford to shop freely, all the joy had gone. She only bought work clothes, casual wear, and designer dresses for black-tie fundraisers.

The red dress fit her perfectly. The neckline showed off just enough, including her favorite platinum pendant, a tiny dolphin she never got to wear. She put on a warm white cardigan, and buttoned it strategically. This time she was going for alluring.

She made an effort with her makeup and pinned her hair up casually in something that resembled a French twist. Her eyes looked greener than she had ever seen them before. The overall effect made her look and feel ten years younger.

The bed was covered in new clothing. There were a few more dresses, several colorful tops, and she had even purchased some lingerie. Getting intimate with anyone was literally the last thing on her mind when she had packed her bags and vacated her life. Her bras were all black or blush and practical.

They held up the girls and couldn't be seen through clothing. It had worked just fine with John. But Connor did something to her. He made her *want* to explore that part of herself. To look the part.

Like her appetite, everything else inside of her was waking up.

Carefully she put her purchases away and went into the bathroom using the connecting door from the bedroom. She had discovered the bathroom had two doors: the one Connor had used to greet her in his towel that led out to the living area, and one that connected it to the bedroom. She surveyed the area. Everything was in its place.

She checked the kitchen and living room as well, tucking Mags' letter box into one of the cabinets along the wall.

She put on warm stockings and located her black jacket. She would probably still be cold, but between New Haven and San Francisco, she'd come to accept it.

Her two-inch black booties covered her feet. These were comfortable, but not as painless as the boots she normally wore. If she could have gotten away with it, she would have worn the tall black boots that came to her knees.

When it came to heels, she only wore boots if she could help it. She reserved her uncomfortable but gorgeous heels for certain events where walking was absolutely guaranteed to be kept at a minimum. And they didn't make it out of her closet if the event was longer than three hours, either.

She went back to the mirror. She didn't look anything like herself and yet . . . it had been years since she had looked this much like herself.

The desire to look different was as new as everything else in her life. She hoped the look said *fun and flirty*. She was OK if it said *sexy and stunning* as well.

The curtains were open. It was evening, but the light from the sun remained. Connor was already walking along the lake.

Beth had an overwhelming desire to watch him without being seen. She hid in the bedroom and peeked out over the ledge to the wall of windows.

His stride was masculine, but there was something else there . . . raw power? It was the kind of walk that would have looked appropriate on a country lane or on the catwalk at Paris Fashion Week.

There was something about the way he moved. Confident and sexual, but heavy. Weighed down by the world. Or grief. Or something else entirely. There was a darkness in his expression. His eyes hooded over the way they had that first night when Kilian had said something about running away from home.

As he drew closer, she could see he was still in the pair of gray form-fitting slacks from earlier, but had changed into a black dress shirt. It hugged his arms and chest.

He reached the French doors and was about to knock when he caught his own reflection in the glass. He ran his fingers through his hair, checked his collar, and then smiled to check his teeth. Beth was amused and gratified that she wasn't the only one making an extra effort tonight.

He knocked and scanned the room for her. She hadn't moved from her hiding place beneath the frame of the bedroom door; only her head and shoulders were visible from where he stood. He found her then and gave her a dazzling smile. His features transformed. He was lighter; the heaviness that he carried when he walked alone was all but gone.

When she stepped into full view, his smile vanished and his jaw dropped involuntarily. He recovered quickly, fixing his face into a pleased expression. But his eyes. He couldn't banish the hunger.

"Hello," she said as she opened the door, returning his smile.

"You look feckin' amazin'." He reached down to give her a hug. It wasn't a playful embrace like the one they'd shared outside his car the day of the Cliffs. Their bodies were completely pressed together. He smelled of rich oak and sandalwood.

Reluctantly, they broke apart.

"Eh, we should go," he said, nervously walking past her, towards the front door.

She bit the inside of her lip, again gratified by the crack in his composure.

"You dropped the car off earlier." It wasn't a question. She followed him out.

Like the previous ride they had shared into town, they were silent. Unlike the previous drive, it was *not* a comfortable silence. She looked out the window trying to see the scene in front of her. She couldn't. The trees and hills and vast fields were there, but her vision was colored by Connor's presence beside her. The air was so charged, she wondered how they would get through the evening.

He gripped the steering wheel with excessive force, resisting the urge to reach over and touch her.

They parked in a small lot farther up the main street, directly opposite the harbour. In the few hours since they had been there, the lower part of the street had been transformed. There were food vendor booths along the walk that ran parallel to the water. Café lights were strung across the entire area, their glow becoming more pronounced as the sun set over the Atlantic. The golden rays created an undulating line of fire, splitting the ocean in half.

The crowd buzzed with excitement. She was glad for it. Glad for the distraction the scene provided.

"How many people are expected?"

He shrugged absently. "Depends. Anywhere from a few hundred to as many as a thousand."

She took in the people milling about from vendor to vendor, blue bands around their wrists, samples in hand. There were those who walked methodically trying each in turn, down the line, while others made a beeline straight for specific restaurant booths. There were little Irish children speaking with their delectable accents, stuffing their faces happily and reaching for seconds of their favorites. She tried to listen to a conversation between a boy and a girl who looked about six or seven.

"I wan' sum mo' of the green mushy thing," the boy said to the girl with his mouth full of something. She couldn't understand what the girl said in response.

Suddenly, Connor was in front of her. In his hand was a small black velvet box.

"Elizabeth Lara, would you do me the honor of. . . ."

What the hell. . . ?

He lifted the lid of the box. Inside was a blue plastic bracelet, like the ones she'd seen everyone else wearing. "Of accompanying me to the Food & Drink Festival?" he finished with a devilish smile.

She slapped his chest.

"Jewelry would be a bit much for our first date, don't you think?" His mischievous bravado was on full display.

"Is this a date? I thought I was still thinking it over and in the meantime I would come with you to this." She motioned at the scene in front of them.

He arranged his features into a ridiculous-looking pout. "So Fonzi didn't win you over?"

She stared at him blankly.

"You know, the bear I got you?" He was suddenly unsure of himself.

She wasn't aware it had a name. "Why'd you name him Fonzi?" she asked, confused. He seemed to think that should mean something to her.

"Fonzi the bear." He frowned. He'd thought he was being clever; now they were on completely different pages. "I thought *Sesame Street* was American?"

Oh. "It is," she confirmed, "but there is no bear named Fonzi."

For the first time since they'd met, he looked embarrassed.

But he would not be deterred. "Yes there is," he insisted, convinced she was just forgetting, "He's brown? He says some line like 'Waka!' all the time?" He was floundering. "Waka! Waka!" He tried again, imitating a character.

Then she understood.

"You mean. . . ," she half-chuckled, "Fozzie Bear!" She laughed a little more. "He's from *The Muppets*, not *Sesame Street*."

She looked at him again. He was the color of her dress, which took her chuckle to a laugh, and her laugh to an unabashed fit of laughter. Of all the things they'd already experienced together, and it took mislabeling a Muppet to embarrass him?

She reached for his arm as she doubled over in hysterics. He supported her while she let it out. People were looking at her with interest. The words "crazy American" lived in many of their thoughts.

It was better than her full-body laugh on the yoga mat nearly a month ago. Of all the physical releases she'd expected Connor to provide that night, she hadn't expected this.

He wasn't amused. "OK, OK. Haha, the Irish guy is an eejit for fumbling an American pop culture reference. Yes, yes get it out." He gestured with his free hand.

Her laughter slowed bit by bit until finally she was able to stop. Beth straightened, looking at him with a smile that actually hurt her face a little.

"Feel better?" he asked curtly.

"Mmmmhmm," she answered simply.

He couldn't hold on to his straight face as he took in her smile and lightened mood. He was glad she was laughing now, instead of crying. He broke into a smile. "Oh, come on, then!" He took her hand and slipped the plastic bracelet onto her wrist.

They went down the line trying each vendor, one after the next. There were crab cakes and ceviche and mini burgers and gourmet pizza. They tried something called a Dublin Coddle, which had sausage, bacon, onions, and potatoes. They tried colcannon and soda bread and corned beef and several stews. There was an entire section dedicated to food concocted with heavy amounts of Guinness, Bailey's, and Jameson whiskey. The steak drizzled in whiskey sauce was amazing. Of the desserts, the Guinness cake was the best, closely followed by the Bailey's Cheesecake.

"Can you get all of these here in the village?" she asked him between seconds of Guinness cake.

"No, some of these restaurants are located as far away as Killarney."

"Is that far?" She had been to Killarney, of course; she just didn't have any concept of how far it was from Dingle.

"About sixty-five kilometers."

She smiled bashfully. "Is that far?" she repeated.

"Oh, eh, I don't know the U.S. conversion. . . ." He trailed off, trying to work it out for her.

"No, I know that's about forty miles," she waved him off, "I mean how *far* is it? How long does it take to get there?" she clarified.

"An hour or so." He thought through her question. "Is that an American thing? You ask how far and you mean how long it takes?"

"No," she considered between cake bites. "It's a California thing. It's such a big state we don't measure distances in miles. We measure how long it takes to get there. Forty miles could mean thirty minutes, or in L.A. it could mean three hours."

He nodded, understanding, and then bit his lip in an effort to hide his smile.

"What?" she asked. She couldn't imagine what could be so amusing about discussing distances.

He just shook his head.

"Oh, come on, what were you thinking?"

"Something naughty in reference to what you just said. Well, it's more of a chat-up line."

She was overtly happy and especially playful from all the sugar. She lowered her voice seductively. "Let's hear it."

"Twist my arm, why dontcha," he said, and then he stopped himself. "But I warn you—it's terrible."

Beth waved her hand in a *just say it* gesture.

"OK, here goes: Hey girl," he modulated his tone to sound huskier, "I'll take you as far as you want. . . ," he paused for effect, "and I'll take the *long* way round." Then he wiggled his eyebrows and made a *Zoolander* pouty face.

She covered her eyes, "That *is* terrible." She shook her head. Unscripted Connor was more witty than whatever that was. "Sorry, but I don't think you have a career as a professional pick-up artist," she teased.

"No?" he scrunched up his nose. "Are you sure? I think I could kill with that line."

She shook her head again.

"Well, you did ask. A guy can't be expected to produce quality material off the cuff!" He was full of mock indignity.

And then his look turned dark with the same expression he'd carried when he had walked alone by the lake. The intensity surprised her. "Despite what you might think, I'm not that type of bloke. I'm not a smooth, silver-tongued liar."

She wondered what was behind it, but then his expression changed quickly and another thought won out. "What is your day job exactly?" It had come up in conversation before, but they'd quickly moved on and she hadn't pressed it.

He shrugged.

"Is it a secret?" Now she was curious. "You've managed to artfully escape telling me a couple of times now."

He turned his palms up in front of him. "No, it just isn't that interesting. You Americans are always defining yourself by your professions. You're a lawyer, a doctor, a teacher. As if all that you are could be summed up in a word or two. Your job is your label."

Beth was intimately aware of how right he was.

He considered his words. "I don't have a day job per se. I work for myself. Most of the time I like it very much. I'm in acquisitions."

Huh. "The way you say that sounds very . . . *sketchy*. You're not some kind of smuggler or thief, are you?" Her eyes widened as she looked at him, full of jest, but slightly serious. "Are you a fence? Come on, you can tell me." Could he? She wasn't actually sure she wanted to know if it was shady.

"Ha! Witty *and* a healthy imagination. . . ." He ran his fingers through his hair. "No, nothing like that. It's all very legal. I do work with expensive collections—"

"Well if it isn't his Lordship!" a man called out from behind them.

Connor whirled around with wide eyes and an annoyed expression. "Feck you, you bloody bollix! Ya know better than that!" he answered in retaliation.

Two very attractive people with brilliant red hair approached. The woman had a Jessica Rabbit-type figure and the man had the build of a superhero, like Connor.

The man's eyes narrowed at Connor's words; a fighting expression claimed his features. He closed the distance deliberately. Connor was equally serious and measured in his actions. For a brief moment, Beth wondered if a brawl was about to break out. And then the two men's faces broke into huge grins, and they threw their arms around each other heartily.

The trio embraced eagerly, their pleasure plain. "Hey Connor!" the woman said brightly.

"Bram! Bree! Feckin' A! It's been an age!" Connor grinned from ear to ear.

Bram smiled at his old friend. "More than a year, Ban," he said, looking over at Beth appreciatively.

Bree did the same.

Connor put a hand on the small of Beth's back, bringing her into their circle. "Guys, this is Elizabeth Lara from California. And these are the Wilde twins, Bram and Bree. We all grew up together," he explained.

Bram nodded. "We did that. Don't be taken in by his charms or his money, Beth. He farts just like the rest of us!"

"Don't be crude," Bree swatted him, "you'll scare her away."

"It's all right; I don't scare easily," Elizabeth answered with a laugh, enjoying how they'd skipped the polite part and gone straight to including her.

Bree gave her an approving smile. There was something else behind her light blue eyes. She looked more than a little interested in Beth.

Bram turned to her. "Apologies, only coddin'; he's a good lad. A bit too noble for my taste, but a good lad." He winked at Connor. "And you are *quite* fetchin', aren't ya?" His gaze roamed freely over her body. If he hadn't been extremely good-looking and radiating good humor, it would have been creepy. He turned his attention back to his friend. "I'm still as rough as a bear's arse, but it's not going to stop me from getting off me face!" He laughed.

She looked at Connor for a translation.

"Eh, he thinks you're gorgeous, 'cause you are." He gave her an earnest smile. "He's still hung-over from last night, but it isn't going to stop him from getting flat-out pissed tonight."

"And he's well on his way," Bree confirmed.

As if on cue, Bree's twin planted his feet and had the look of a man who'd just had a splendid idea. "Ban!"

Connor leaned forward, recognizing his friend's tone. "Yes, Bram?"

"I challenge you." Bram raised an arm like it was a flag about to drop, signaling the start of a race.

Bree shook her head. "Oh, geez."

"The terms?" Connor asked with unnatural severity.

"Down that way," he pointed and swayed a little, "is a booth where you can try the hottest chili on the planet, the bhut jolokia chili. I challenge you to a single bite. Whoever can stand the fire the longest without needin' milk wins."

"The prize?" Connor raised his head, answering the call.

Bram thought for a moment and then looked at Beth. "A kiss from the lovely Elizabeth."

They all looked at her now. Three sets of inquiring blue eyes. She hadn't had enough Guinness cake for this.

What was it Mags had said? New experiences. . . . She could think of worse things than snogging either of the two men standing in front of her. Although she had an obvious preference.

"You don't have to—" Connor began.

"Sure, I'll do it," Beth said in a rush, cutting Connor off before she changed her mind. She searched the booths ahead of them. "But first, let's have a few drinks."

Bram looked eager, Bree looked impressed, and Connor looked . . . *determined*. They all nodded in agreement.

They bypassed the liquor sample area and went straight for the cash bar. After knocking back two shots of whiskey, they were all in good spirits.

When the three friends were caught up in a conversation that involved the latest gossip about someone named Barry the Baker who was having an affair with Susan the Postmistress, Beth ordered a third shot.

She held it up and spoke to herself quietly, "Here's to you, Mags. And letting my hair down."

"What was that?" Connor had noticed her absence and was now at her side.

"Nothing." She waved it off.

"We're headin' over now. All right?"

"Lead the way," she answered.

The chili stand was set up as a challenge booth. There were two men in the middle of a contest as they approached. One fell to his knee and the other was doubled over with both hands on the booth table for support. They both raised their hands at roughly the same time and were handed glasses of milk.

Beth and Bree stood a couple of feet away on Connor's side.

"Do they do this a lot?" Beth asked her.

"Oh, yes. Since we were kids. Feckin' eejits. They're always good-natured contests, but they are pissing contests nonetheless." She met Beth's eyes. "What is it with men? Always busting them out to measure?"

Beth wanted to laugh, but Bree seemed genuinely perturbed.

"Jaysus, I hope it's safe. I'm not dealing with Bram if he hurls. I refuse." Bree put her hands in the back pockets of her jeans and shook her head disapprovingly while Connor and Bram spoke with the officials.

There were two men in white chef aprons behind the booth. They cut and measured a piece of one of the chilis and placed the bites in front of the challengers.

"They'll be fine," Beth assured her. "The bhut jolokia isn't even the hottest chili anymore. It hasn't been for years. It isn't even the *second* hottest chili."

Bree looked impressed. "How'd you know that? Are you a chili aficionado?" She touched Beth's arm.

"No, I had a case last year. A husband and wife were getting divorced. They developed a new chili that made the top ten hottest in the world according to Guinness World Records. It was listed as an asset. They fought tooth and nail for it."

"And who won?"

"My client, of course," Beth answered with a smile. Like it was the most obvious thing in the world. She managed to sound confident instead of smug.

Bree's smile widened. She enjoyed Beth's certainty. It was something they had in common, other than Connor.

"And what is the hottest chili in the world currently?"

Elizabeth answered automatically, "The Carolina Reaper. It's made in the U.S. by The PuckerButt Pepper Company."

Bree pursed her lips together, trying to stifle a laugh. She failed. Beth had been matter-of-fact; she hadn't considered how it would sound coming out of her mouth. She fought it for a second and then cracked with Bree and the two women laughed together while the men prepared for battle.

"Ready, lads?" one of the officials called. The contestants nodded. "And GO!"

They each took the spoon that contained the bite and off they went. There was a digital stopwatch displayed on the booth so onlookers could see how long the contestants had gone without the milk. After twenty seconds, Bram was purple and holding on to the booth for support. Connor got to forty seconds before he extended an arm out to his left, where Beth stood. She took his hand and helped him stay mostly upright.

At a minute, Bram raised his hand in surrender. The official handed him his milk. Connor tried to smile through the tears in his eyes. He was a reddish sort of puce. The milk disappeared within seconds.

The party of four moved to a round park table nearby while the men recovered from their exploits.

"All right, take your prize then." Bram motioned to Beth across the table, who was sitting next to Connor.

They looked at each other. There it was. That feeling of being in high school. Sitting at a red In-N-Out table at night, feeling like anything was possible.

Beth was ready. Connor searched her face, gauging. He still looked unsure as he leaned forward. When he was just about to close the gap, he changed course and planted a soft, lingering kiss on her cheek. His breath was warm against her skin, his lips firm. Her lids half-closed involuntarily.

He pulled away reluctantly and gave her a small smile. She couldn't see anything past the sapphire orbs staring back at her. Her cheek tingled like he'd sent an electric current through her skin. Surely a residual effect from the capsaicin of the chili on his lips.

Bree narrowed her eyes, looking from one to the other.

"Ahhhh . . . cheat! Cheat!" Bram jabbed him.

They were roused from their trance. "Hey now! I'm an honorable man," Connor protested.

"Only in title, lad!" Bram laughed heartily.

Connor looked down at his phone, quickly changing the subject. "I've got somewhere to be." It was time for the blind dessert contest.

They walked farther down the harbour where a small stage had been set up.

"Ah, I see our last judge has arrived!" a man with no hair save for a big mustache straight out of a Western film declared.

Connor walked up to the man on the stage and whispered something. A few seconds later he was back at Beth's side, wearing his mischievous smile.

"Eh, it seems there's been a change," the mustache man said into the mic. "One of our judges has ruined his buds in a chili-eating contest and will not be able to taste the masterful flavors. In his place we have Miss Elizabeth Lara from Cali-fornia. Put your hands together for her."

People clapped over the buzz the announcement had created. It seemed everyone was interested in the newcomer. She felt like a spotlight was suddenly trained on her. Hundreds of brains were now actively engaged in examining everything about her, including her comfortable proximity to Connor.

She turned to him, speechless. He was very pleased with himself.

Acutely conscious of the glass fishbowl she was in, Beth looked out into the crowd as she climbed the stairs to the stage. She recognized many faces, all merry or tipsy or both. It was about that time that her brain registered a pair of cold, dark eyes. They belonged to a pretty woman with spiky black hair that stopped at her shoulders. Her mouth was set in a line, her expression full of loathing. Beth wondered who she was staring at.

Shaken out of the thought by the mustached man who touched her elbow, she was steered quickly to her seat next to the other two tasters. Her first co-judge was a round man who looked like a baker. Perhaps this was Barry the Baker, famed lover of the postmistress. And beside him was a silver-haired woman in her sixties, with a thin face and a shrewd but pleasant expression. They all nodded to each other in greeting before donning the blindfolds set out for them on the table.

There were three desserts to taste. The first was some sort of cheesecake. It was made with a lot of alcohol. She could taste whiskey, maybe some Bailey's and some other liquor she couldn't place. It was just slightly out of balance; the liquor overpowered the sugar a little too much.

The second was a type of German chocolate. The darker flavor was paired with again more alcohol. The flavors did not complement each other.

The third and final dessert was some kind of chocolate carrot cake hybrid; she tasted Guinness and whiskey. It was in perfect balance. They took the desserts away and, after removing their blindfolds, the judges filled out their ballots. All three had chosen the last dessert.

Everyone clapped as the winning dessert chef came up to receive a small trophy and a check for one thousand euros. The judges were excused and the crowd dispersed with a renewed level of boisterous clamor. Beth rejoined her group happily, only to find them all with their backs to the stage, preoccupied.

Connor's stance was wide, his arms in fists at his side. He seemed to be leaning forward towards someone. Bram had a large hand on his shoulder, holding him back.

Bree was standing behind them, arms crossed, brows drawn together. She looked concerned and confused.

Beth came up beside her. "What's happening?" She tried looking around Connor's considerable frame. His superhero body was on full display. He looked about five inches taller than normal.

"Leave it, mate; it isn't worth it," Bram warned, his voice suddenly sober.

The crowds had moved along. Whatever was happening, they didn't have an audience. She stepped closer so she could see. Connor was fuming, staring daggers at a preppy-looking twenty-something with shaggy brown hair and bloodshot eyes. He was flanked by two tall and equally lanky companions. They were much smaller than Connor and Bram.

No one was speaking, but Connor was visibly vibrating. The strangers must have been daft because they didn't even have the decency to look scared, just defiant.

"Bree, what's going on?" she repeated.

"The one in the middle there," Bree motioned with her head, before continuing in a low voice, "he said something about you."

"Me?" What could he say that would warrant such a response?

She opened her mouth to ask for more when Bree continued, "I've never seen him like this." Her expression was thoughtful, perplexed.

Beth kept her eyes trained on Connor. "Like what?" she whispered.

"Like. . . ," Bree started, "like," she lowered her voice to match Beth's, "like his father."

Elizabeth considered that. She didn't know anything about Connor's father. The only parent that had ever come up was Rhia.

Connor's intensity was disconcerting. "You mean he doesn't usually get into brawls and have an anger management problem?"

Bree shook her head. "Never. Always keeps his cool. There was only once, when he was a teen. . . ." She trailed off.

"Bree, what was said?" Her imagination was now running wild. If Connor was so level-headed, what had the man said about her?

"They're just drunk tourists in from Cork or Killarney. They were standing behind us; the eejit in the middle was running his mouth saying how much he'd like to slip it to you and how you'd love it," Bree explained. "Connor turned around and told them to shut it, which they did at first, and then the moron said something he probably thought we couldn't hear, otherwise . . . Jaysus, they're feckin' gobshites."

Beth shook her head and motioned for her to finish.

"He was whispering to his mate about how he was going to get you alone and then slip something in your drink or corner you someplace quiet."

At that Beth rolled her eyes. She looked at the boy again, taking his measure. Connor was overreacting. She could take care of herself. Although the boys were clearly scum.

The lead maggot caught her eye. Connor followed his gaze and took a threatening step forward.

"Leeeave it, mate," Bram said more forcefully. "He's a gombeen, bloody langer he is and high as a kite. Look at the boy, for Christ's sake." He jerked his head towards the infants. "Move along, ya maggots; go back to your town if you know what's good for ya."

The boys sneered then backed away and Beth stepped forward to cover Connor's balled-up fist with her hand. He released the tension in his body almost instantly.

As they left, the shaggy-haired idiot muttered, "He's only a fuckin' bastard, doesn't deserve. . . ," before they were out of earshot.

"Are you OK?" She squeezed his hand.

He opened his palm, grasping her fingers. His face was completely normal, devoid of any care. "Absolutely fine, why?"

"Umm. . . ." Seriously? Her eyes grew wide. "That was a little intense."

"Was it?" He looked surprised.

"Well, yeah. It looked like you were going to hit him." She turned back towards where Bree and Bram were standing. He was so blasé she wondered if they had just experienced the same event. Bree shook her head and shrugged in an "I have no idea what just happened" gesture.

"Nah," he frowned and considered it, "I was just trying to scare 'em a little." He stopped. "I mean, I wanted to hit him—and I haven't wanted to hit anyone in decades!" He stared off towards the water as he sorted through his thoughts.

"OK, good." She was weary. "So you *don't* have an anger management problem?" She scrunched up her face.

"Not at all." The idea seemed to amuse him. "Why would you say that?"

Her mouth dropped. "Intense. You. Just now. About to pop a guy for being an idiot?"

"Was it really that bad?" He narrowed his eyes.

Her face remained unchanged. He looked back towards his friends. Their eyes were wide, confirming what Beth had just explained.

Bree's arms were still crossed. "Like your bleedin' father you were!"

At that Connor, snapped back, letting go of Beth's hand. It was like he'd just been hit.

"Now, hey, there! That's a low blow." He was more confused than angry as he considered how it all must have looked.

When Bree didn't budge, he held up his hands in surrender. "All right, all right, I hear you. I was a little off my rocker. But those feckin' langers! Could you believe his plan?" He was looking for some validation from his friends. He turned to Beth. "Did they tell you?"

She nodded.

His face changed again as he remembered what was said. There was a darkness there. "I should have hit him, I should. I should bloody find out who he is and ruin the bastard!"

She'd had enough. "No, you shouldn't. Revenge is never the answer. Now are you all done or do you want to pound your chest some more?" She caught Bree's appreciative smile with her peripheral vision.

His eyes changed with her reproach, and his humor returned. "I find I like you scolding me." He took her hand and smiled, completely returned to himself.

"Good, because you definitely deserved it. Now, what next?" she asked, eager to move on.

The Wilde twins led the way back towards the rest of the booths. Connor kept her hand as they walked.

His voice was pensive. "Jaysus, what are you doin' to me, woman?" His free hand came up to his hair.

Her mouth dropped. "Uh-uh, nope. I'm not doing anything. It's on you."

He looked up towards the sky. "That's . . . fair. It's just that you're waking something up in me."

It was difficult to focus on the busy scene of people and food around them. Her stomach dropped with his words. "Something bad?" she wondered.

He shrugged. "No, it's all feckin' fantastic . . . except, sometimes—I feel . . . not like myself. A wee bit out of control?" he said, more to himself than her. "Like I don't know what I'd do if someone hurt you." He looked down and away, shaking his head as his eyes hooded over. His voice dropped. "Is that barmy? Do you think me a mental case for thinking such things?"

She surprised herself. His intensity should have scared her. Her logical brain ought to have warned her that it meant he cared more for her than an emotionally unavailable bachelor ought to care for someone who could only be a fling. But instead, she found comfort in his words. His confession made her feel less alone.

"No, I appreciate your concern." She was sincere. "But you don't have to worry about me. I can take care of myself." She lightened, flashing him a smile.

He read the confidence there. The certainty. It was his turn to take comfort in her words. "I don't doubt it." His dazzling smile returned as he took in her matter-of-fact tone and set features. "I pity the man who stands against you."

She nodded as they stopped at a booth with small blue bowls filled with thick soup, set out in neat rows. "As well you should."

She released his hand to try some Irish stew. The four of them stood together in a circle, happily eating their festival fare. All the light camaraderie returned as they joked about what Bram would have done if Connor had thrown a punch. "I would have tackled the other two lads in one Herculean move. It would have been epic."

They laughed as the tense encounter was quickly turned into an Irish story, the kind they'd tell a year from now, the details augmented and changed to suit a more dramatic tale. Connor would surely be able to shoot lightning from his eyes and Bram fire from his hands by the time they were through.

After the stew they tried the liquor samples. There was an expert for Scotch, whiskey, vodka, and rum. Each station provided a series of small shots and then described the difference in taste between each. It was an education in locally-made liquor.

By midnight they were all quite merry.

They gravitated towards the main stage and the live entertainment. The lofty, joyous sounds of Irish music had filled the air for most of the night.

The party of four caught the tail end of a jig. The people in the middle were engaged in a choreographed set of group dances—like an Irish version of an Austen novel.

When the music changed to slow lyrical melodies with heavy fiddles, the twins excused themselves. They were in town for their mother's birthday, which was the following day, and even though they were thirty-six, she'd box their ears if they showed up still drunk from the night before.

Beth watched them go. "Nice people," she said.

"Yeah, they're a good lot," Connor acknowledged, taking her by the hand and back out to the floor. He pulled her into him, placing her arms around his neck. "They both thought you were grand."

"It's nice to be liked," she answered tipsily and looked up. The sky was partially obscured by the café lights strung across the floor. It reminded her of a film with a country dance scene set in the South.

"Yes, it is, but I think they liked you a little too much," he mused, narrowing his eyes at her.

"Is that possible? To be liked too much?"

"I mean they *liked* you, Beth. As in they would have been over the moon if you had chosen to go home with either of them."

"Ohhh . . . oh!" she understood.

He nodded.

"Bree goes both ways, but she usually prefers women. She *really* fancied you."

Beth's smile widened. She was flattered.

"Well, she is beautiful. Maybe I should go find her." She moved to walk off the floor.

"Come 'ere, Luv." He pulled her back into him. Closer this time.

The softness of her body melted against the hardness of his. The charge that had existed between them all night was suddenly concentrated in that moment.

"Why didn't you kiss me?" Her voice faltered. It was difficult to form words when her body could feel every line of his.

He leaned in, whispering into her ear. His lips grazed her skin, and his breath sent chills down her spine. "Because the first time I kiss you, I won't be able to stop."

CHAPTER 12: UNIVERSE KISSES

The song ended, but they were still swaying.

A disembodied voice came over the speakers. "Thank you for coming out to the Food & Drink Festival! It was a gas craic altogether. Goodnight, ladies and lads."

"I guess we should go now," Beth whispered.

"That we should," Connor breathed back.

His ice blue eyes bore into hers. She wanted to reach up and close the narrow distance between their lips.

Someone clapped Connor on the shoulder, shaking them both out of their trance. He turned to wave as the man left the floor.

"Fancy a walk back?" He released her and shoved his hands into the pockets of his gray pants.

"Sure." She looked down, feeling a little like a giddy teenager.

"Come on, then." He took her hand.

They walked in a charged silence until they reached the shortcut back to the lake.

As she thought about where she wanted the night to end, she remembered a question that had lingered in her subconscious after that first conversation with Mona.

"May I ask you something?" Beth ventured cautiously as they stepped through the trees that framed the entrance to the shortcut.

"Eh . . . sure. You sound a little nervous."

So far she'd only seen the good in him—even his almost-brawl had been to protect her—but there had to be a reason Mona had described him the way she did that first morning at the cottage. She was counting on her being right. He had to be emotionally unavailable for this to work. But she also needed to know why. "Nervous, no. Not sure I want to know the answer, maybe."

She needed to be careful, even if it was just for the night.

He turned her so she was facing him. She'd made him anxious.

"Mona mentioned that a lot of women around here have made . . . *advances* towards you."

"Yes." His face mirrored her hesitancy.

She wasn't naive. There was no Prince-Charming-at-the-end-of-a-rainbow fantasy secretly lurking in her psyche. She just wanted to know what she was getting into. Connor was a person who had already helped heal a piece of her in a way. She would open herself up to him for tonight, but would take care not to fall. She didn't want him to be something else she'd have to heal from. "Well, why haven't any of them held your interest?"

"Oh." He let out a breath. His face relaxed as they started walking again. "That's easy. People around here, they know my story. They know my family. How I grew up." His eyes hooded over with the darkness. The same intensity she had seen before. "They have their own preconceived notions about who I am, who I should be, and what they can get from me."

"That sounds a little paranoid."

"Maybe. It's not like I think everyone wants something from me. Or that all women here just want to land me—although I'm fairly certain that part is true; I *am* such a catch." He glanced at her with a smile. "It's just that I would never really know if they were interested in me . . . for me."

Paranoid . . . and cryptic. "As opposed to—?"

"And then there's the Universe." He cut her off.

"What about the Universe?" She tried to make all the pieces fit.

"I believe in it. I think there's a plan in everything. I think we attract the people who are supposed to be in our lives. I believe in timing." They reached the clearing where they'd previously looked up at the stars. He pulled her to face him again.

"This might sound corny—that's a word you use in America, right? Corny?" She nodded. "But," he continued, "I believe in a grand love. I believe in soul mates, in magic, and all the rest of that bullshit that men aren't supposed to admit to. And I know when it isn't there. So, I don't lead women on. I cut things off." His expression was hard with some unknown resolve. Like he was swearing an oath. "It might paint me as a commitment-phobe like you, but it's really just that I know what I want."

He stood staring at her, his expression softening. Some part of her brain wanted to protest to his calling her out on her commitment issues. But the ice of his eyes melted; they expressed a raw hunger that made her stomach drop. Desire filled her body. She stopped breathing as he pulled her towards him, closing the gap inch by inch until his hands were on her waist. The thin fabric of her red dress bunched slightly as he held her firmly in place.

She could hear her heart pounding in her ears. He took one hand from her waist and tipped her chin up towards him, moving it to cup her face as he closed the final inch.

And then he was on her. Their lips moved together with all the hunger they had kept at bay. His tongue parted her lips as he deepened the kiss, moving his arms to encircle her. He crushed her to him. Beth moved her arms around his neck. Her hands clasped his hair as she brought him down on her harder. They were lost in the moment.

His lips were soft and firm. It was a passion she hadn't felt in more than a decade. She wanted to melt into his hard body as he broke the kiss to run his lips down to her neck, using his tongue to make her go weak at the knees. She moved his head back to hers and their kiss cooled slowly into something sweeter. Beth pulled away, placing her hands on his shoulders as she caught her breath.

"Wow," he breathed. His breath tickled her nose. "Thank you, Universe," he said to himself so Beth couldn't hear.

She heard him say something about the Universe, but couldn't make out his exact words over the sound of the blood rushing through her brain and body.

Connor looked up at the stars as Beth gathered her breath.

"Look, look." He gestured with his head, still holding her.

She looked up just in time to see a shooting star. Its trail was the longest she'd ever seen. Something about the spectacle caused butterflies to rise up in her stomach and a delicious chill to run down her spine. It felt . . . divine.

He noticed her shiver and put his arm around her shoulders as they began to walk again. She smiled at him and his return expression was dazzling. They talked of Guinness cake and which local whiskey they each liked. Connor told her about the full festival that happened in October.

"It's three days of nonstop eating and drinking. Really a craic. Bram and I used to fast for a couple of days beforehand to train."

She grinned. "Kind of like an American Thanksgiving."

He nodded.

The ground started to soften beneath them. They had reached the muddy stretch where he had given her a piggyback ride. The month-long torrent had made it less of a muddy patch and more of a lake. It was made especially precarious by the dark.

"Of course! Ah, eejit, I should have known it would have flooded over like this." He put his hands on his hips and squinted. He fished his cell phone out of his pocket and cast a light over the scene, trying to find a way through. There was a narrow strip of mud that seemed passable on the left.

Beth wondered if she should take her heels off and try to go through barefoot.

Without warning Connor swung her up into his arms, placing a light kiss on her lips before she even knew what was happening. He walked to the strip and carefully balanced his way through.

"I've never been carried so much in my life. Admit it—you have a hero complex," she teased.

"Ahh, no. Never been very interested in playin' the hero. I do like carrying you, though," he said, paying more attention to her than his feet. He stepped a little too freely and began to slide. His leg slid out and stopped abruptly. They narrowly escaped a fall into the muddy water.

Connor forcibly expelled the air out of his lungs. "Sorry about that." He readjusted her, bringing her into his chest more tightly. "Now keep quiet. I need to concentrate, unless you want to go swimming in this very fetching red dress of yours."

She pressed her lips together and shook her head, focusing instead on the tall trees that framed a path of stars. She liked how it felt to be pressed into his chest. Liked the feeling of his hand on her bare thigh. She tried not to think further than tonight. Her brain wasn't going to get in the way again—it was time to do some living.

When she thought he had left, she had regretted not having at least one night with him. Regretted not allowing the passion she felt to take over and further banish the blacks and grays from her life.

They were only a couple of steps from clearing the water when she decided she didn't want to wait any longer. Still in his arms, she grabbed his face and brought him down on her, kissing him hard.

Connor was taken by surprise, but responded immediately, using his tongue against hers. Quickly, the desire consumed him and he forgot his feet. This time he couldn't stop them from falling. He managed to place Beth vertically, inches from the mud bath, before he hit the ground. His torso got the worst of it, landing in a couple inches of water.

Beth brought her hands to her face. "I'm so sorry!" Her voice rose in shock before moving to help him up.

The muddy water had soaked the back of his dress shirt, and dirt clung to his trousers, but the rest of him remained dry.

"Jaysus, woman! If you wanted to get me shirt off you just had to say so." He started unbuttoning.

The moon was nearly half full. Light reflected off the lake and onto his smooth skin. His muscles rippled as he quickly extricated himself from the wet garment.

Her mouth watered as she watched, feeling everything all at once.

He looked at her as he pulled the final sleeve off and registered the desire in her eyes, instantly returning it. In one movement he threw the shirt to the ground and moved towards her, grabbing her face with both of his hands and kissing her deeply.

After a few seconds or a few minutes, he picked her up so she was straddling him.

He walked in the direction of the cottage, still wrapped in their kiss. He didn't need to look where he was going.

Beth clung to Connor's bare shoulders, clasping onto his smooth muscles as they surged with excitement.

She could sense his need for her growing. Her dress had ridden up and she could feel *all* of him through his gray pants.

When they reached the French doors, he pulled away.

His breathing was out of control, and his voice was strained. "Are you sure?"

She didn't hesitate. "Yes." She kissed him again.

He tried to speak. "Because we don't have to—"

"Shut up." She ran her tongue along his lip.

He smiled. "Yes, Miss Lara."

He carried her into the bedroom and threw her down on top of the purple comforter. She reached for his belt and undid his pants, leaving him in only his black boxer-briefs.

Pulling her up to stand on the bed, he moved his hands up her thighs, to her dress, until he had access to her stomach.

166

He kissed up from her belly button to the edge of her bra, then brought her to her knees so that he could unzip the red garment that kept him from seeing all of her. Slowly, he removed her dress until only her matching red lace bra and panties remained.

She was still kneeling; her breasts spilled over her bra as her chest rose and fell quickly.

He reached into her hair, taking the clip that held it in place and threw it against the wall with a *clack*; her long brown waves spilled wildly to her shoulders and breasts. He took his time, watching her. His expression evolved, from hungry to ravenous. With his hand on her chest, he pushed her backwards.

He moved onto his hands and knees, stalking her until he was directly above. He allowed some of his body weight to press into her exposed flesh.

She gasped as her body registered his need. He came down on her again, kissing her with more fervor than before, forcibly parting her mouth and delving deeper inside of her. A low moan escaped her lips as he kissed her long and hard, moving his hips into her as he went.

His hand moved down to her waist, to her thigh, and finally to her knee. He hitched it up around his hip and let more of his weight come down on her.

Beth was on fire. She had no frame of reference, nothing to compare the passion to, the sense of being alive, the connection of the moment. All previous interactions could be described as a demure pink compared to the shade of fire engine red she was living—and they still had their clothes on.

Connor pulled away, his face hovering over hers. His voice was a low growl. "Are you still sure, Luv? Because it's going to become impossible to stop if you don't say something."

She'd never been more certain of anything. "Connor, it's just for tonight." She reached up to kiss him. "A one-time thing." She pulled away so she could look into his eyes. "No need to analyze." It served as a reminder for her as well.

He smiled down at her like he knew something she didn't. "Whatever you say, Luv."

He moved to kiss her neck, sending vibrations down her body, to her sex. Desire pooled in her lower abdomen. Hot and heavy. She moved the other leg around his hip as he moved his tongue down to her breasts.

Connor brought her up to a sitting position so that he could undo her bra. Once her breasts were free, he took one in his hand and massaged her, running his thumb over her nipple.

His other hand reached for something he'd taken out of his wallet earlier. He pushed her away for a second while he took off his boxer-briefs and then ran his fingers slowly up her thighs, giving Beth goose bumps as he found the waistband of her panties and pulled them off.

There was nothing left between them. They were both vibrating with intensity, excitement, and a deep, deep longing that only the other could satisfy.

He sat on his knees and brought her closer until she was straddling him. He took one of her breasts into his mouth as he grabbed her hips and brought her down onto him.

She gasped, letting her head fall back, as she felt him possess her inch by agonizing inch. When he'd filled her completely, he flexed his hips until he could feel her body relax. He held her there in place, looking up into her eyes, trying to convey something to her.

It was an emotion Beth didn't recognize. It was earnest and fierce and piercing and . . . devoted? After a long moment of unspoken communication, he began to move, driving into her. She cried out as she accepted him further and further into her body. Moving with an intensity that left no room for deliberate thought, she collided with him again and again. He groaned as her wild possession threatened to unhinge him.

They moved together, hips in perfect rhythm. His arms wrapped around her lower waist, moving her body roughly with his.

Their passion rose further up and past their corporeal forms. They were bound together in an endless moment of exquisitely eternal ecstasy, until finally, they found release and collapsed into each other.

Connor moved Beth into his chest, wrapping his arm around her shoulder. He looked down into her face with an expression that closely resembled awe.

"You're amazin', that was. . . ." Words failed him. He leaned in to kiss her.

She gave him a youthful, carefree smile. "Thanks; you're not bad yourself."

He rolled his eyes. "Woman, please. You practically touched heaven."

"So did you." She tapped a finger to his nose. He moved it to his lips.

"That I did." He kissed her again.

CHAPTER 13: LOUGH RHIANNON

Beth woke to the sound of birds chirping happily outside of her window. A crack of sunlight spilled through the dark curtains. She stretched her arms overhead, feeling completely relaxed and satiated. She turned to find a note in place of Connor.

Elizabeth, A Cuisle

I had an early morning call. I haven't forgotten what you said about wanting last night to be an isolated encounter, but I do hope that you will join me for lunch. I'm thinking a picnic by the lough.

Since you've only just rejoined the land of the living, I trust you don't already have plans. Therefore, I will be outside waiting for you at 1:00. It would be quite rude if you declined my invitation. Quite rude indeed. Especially after last night. It would make me feel cheap, like you just used me for my body.

Le meas,
Connor

She grinned so hard her face hurt as she remembered their night together.

It was mind-blowing.

Perhaps it didn't *have* to be an isolated incident. They were genuine friends. Maybe they could keep their physical relationship going. It didn't mean she had to fall for him. She wasn't about to risk getting attached to a man. Especially one who'd been labeled "distant" and "wounded" by Mona. And who lived on the other side of the world.

There were too many unknowns in her life without adding a doomed love affair. A sex affair, on the other hand. . . .

The clock read 11:38. She would have just enough time to shower and get ready.

By 12:45 she was outside. She hadn't explored the area around the lake at all. Perhaps she would surprise him by showing up on *his* doorstep. She walked in the direction she'd seen him coming from, stopping to stare at the lake for a few minutes.

The day was warm for March, or maybe it was in keeping with regular temperatures; she didn't know. She had expected it to be colder, but was delighted to leave her jacket behind, wearing only a long-sleeved dolman top, skinny jeans, and ballet flats.

She moved her white, oversized sunglasses from her face to the top of her head, wearing them like a headband. It was cooler in the shade, especially as a light breeze picked up across the water and caressed her skin. She hugged herself and started to walk again.

A minute later she approached a small bronze statue. It was of a young woman with long hair, wearing a sundress and carrying a basket. She was balancing on one foot, wistfully gazing up at the sky. She reminded Beth of a fairy in human form. Beneath the statute was a plaque.

It read simply: *For Rhia.*

Running her fingers over the raised letters of the name, she wondered what the fairy woman had been like.

She hadn't gone ten steps beyond the statue before Connor emerged from the trees.

The dazzling smile that transformed his features was blinding. It stirred something inside of her. This smile was more carefree, happy—like waking up on Christmas morning.

A goofy grin claimed her own features, in spite of herself.

He carried a large picnic basket straight out of a storybook. The tight-black-T-shirt-and-jeans look really worked for him. She could see part of his Celtic cross tattoo protruding from the fabric covering his bicep.

He set the basket down and took her in his arms, sweeping her off her feet and spinning them both around in a ridiculous gesture.

She wasn't sure why, but she blushed like he had done it in the middle of a crowded street with people watching.

"Hi there," she said a little awkwardly as he set her down.

He tipped her chin and placed a light kiss on her lips. She instantly wanted more, but he pulled away.

"Is that OK?" He looked unsure. "I know you wanted it to be a one-off, but I really wanted to kiss you." His boyish grin tore at her insides, making something crack open.

She was more pleased than she wanted to admit. Speaking would give that fact away, and the last thing she wanted was for him to think she was falling for him. "Uh-huh." It would have to do. She pressed her lips together, the corners of her mouth turning up a degree.

He gave her a suspicious look, like he could see through her.

They moved to a large oak tree that was at least one hundred feet tall. Its shade was expansive, but hazy rays of light still poured through in certain spots. The effect was mystical.

Connor opened the blanket he had stored in the basket and set it out on the lush green grass.

She felt her stomach growl. "I hoped you packed well, Mr. Bannon, because I'm starving." Their romantic encounter was more physically demanding than anything she'd done in weeks. Remembering Mona's expression at Café Shannon, Beth tried for her first Irish saying. "I'd ate the arse off of a baby elephant!" she repeated.

He stopped setting the food out and gave her a strange half-smile. He chuckled. "Where'd you hear that?"

Had she misunderstood the expression? "It means I'm starving, right?"

"Yes, but where'd you hear it?" he pressed.

She shrugged. "Mona."

He nodded. Of course. "My mum used to say that all the time," he remembered with a wistful smile, not unlike the expression on the statue.

"Tell me about her."

"I will, but first I think I ought to get some food in you. I wouldn't want you to go after any baby elephants." He winked.

"All right," he said, reviewing his handiwork, "we have a green chili bisque, a salad with grilled chicken, a baguette, some white wine," he dove into the basket one last time, waiting until her eyes had made their way through the food and back to him, "and I grabbed you some Guinness cake since I know how partial you are to it." He extricated the dessert. "This one has an orange frosting drizzled on it. You'll thank me," he finished, clearly very pleased with himself.

Beth ate her food eagerly as they looked out over the lake. The water was calm, but a strong breeze picked up every so often and set the waters in motion.

"It's so beautiful." She turned to look at him. "What was it like to grow up here?"

He looked down at his hands as he tore his baguette into smaller pieces, then at the lake.

He weighed his answer, unsure. "It was fun . . . sometimes." And there it was: the darkness.

Something was preventing him from saying more. It frustrated Beth more than she liked. She wanted to understand. "That's it? That's all I get? Everyone's childhood is fun . . . sometimes."

"It's home." He shrugged. "Home can be complicated. There was a lot of love, my mum made sure of that. I was well cared for, the lake was fun to be near, you know." The weight he sometimes carried settled firmly on his shoulders, and he shrugged again.

Beth was on high alert. They'd already been through so much; why couldn't he tell her what it was like to grow up in such a place? What had made his beautiful home so complicated? "Why are you being so evasive? If we were in San Francisco I would have put you on the witness stand by now and wrangled the answers out of you," she challenged.

He'd already seen her at her worst, he knew her grief, but she knew so little about him. He'd spoken of losing his mother, of not crying, but she couldn't explain the darkness. An anger she couldn't account for bubbled up. It wasn't clear if she was angry at him for forcing her to ask so many questions or angry at herself for allowing herself to feel anything at all for someone who she didn't really know.

He was surprised by the fierceness in her voice. Suddenly, he realized how it all must look to her. "Sorry, I don't mean to be shifty. It's just that I grew up in kind of an odd way." His eyes hooded over with intensity. His eyebrows knitted together, and his entire body language changed. He took a deep breath like he was gearing up to go through an ordeal.

It was unnerving. She was suddenly sorry she had pressed him for answers. What had happened to him? "I didn't mean to take you to some dark place."

"No, no, it's nothing like that. I wasn't abused. I didn't experience a sinister childhood trauma." He gave her a sad smile. "It's just that I have issues with my father and how he treated my mum."

"Oh." She didn't know what to say.

His jaw tightened as he remembered. "Yeah, he was a real piece of work. I hated him, the feckin' bastard." The depth of his anger was palpable.

"You don't have to talk about it if you don't want to." Beth looked away from him, not wanting to see the pain she had caused him to remember.

"No, it's good. I never talk about it. People around here have known the story my whole life, and people out there," he motioned to indicate the people he met when he traveled, "don't know or don't care."

He rested his arms on top of his knees as he brought them closer to his chest. He'd made himself smaller. Beth wondered what he looked like as a boy.

"The story goes like this," he said, expelling the air from his lungs. "My father was already married when he met my mum. It's a big house; she was part of the staff. She was a dancer, my mum. She was part of a dance troupe that traveled all over." He looked at her. "Did Mona tell you that?"

Beth nodded.

"When the troupe disbanded, she took a job as a live-in tutor for my father's son. She was young and believed that people were basically good. He told her that he and his wife were both unhappy, that his wife had already found another relationship—she had been away for months so at the time it was believable—and that they were looking for a way to get divorced, even though it really wasn't done around here.

"So she allowed him to court her. He proposed. I was conceived. The lying bastard failed to mention that his wife was away because she had cancer and was being treated by several specialists in Switzerland. It was a great secret. No one knew she was sick; the rumor in town actually supported the lie he told my mum.

"He also failed to mention that he was the only one looking to get out of their marriage. And on top of that, my mum later found out that he never had any intention of getting divorced or marrying her, but by then she was pregnant with me."

He looked at Beth. She was careful to keep her expression under control, even though his story was reinforcing her own issues with the father who abandoned her.

"It was a real scandal. Fueled the gossip for years. He set up my mum here at the gate lodge," he flicked his head in the direction of the cottage, "which she was initially grateful for since she didn't know how she would raise me alone."

Connor took another piece of bread in his hands, moving his fingers back and forth until it crumbled to the blanket. "He was a great manipulator, that one." The anger rolled off of him in waves. He was shaking with it. "He lied to her and then when she was at his mercy, he twisted things so she felt like she should feel grateful." He let out a sound like a laugh. It was full of acid.

Taking a deep breath, he tried to calm down. "After a few years, she wanted to move away and make a home for us somewhere else, but he was a powerful man. He kept her here, tortured her with the idea of the family living in the big house just up the lough, which she could never have. Tortured his wife with the presence of a woman with whom he'd had an affair and the bastard they had created. He wanted control over everyone, you see?"

It physically hurt Beth to hear him talk about himself in that way. She moved closer to him and took his hand, giving it a gentle squeeze. She could tell he wasn't finished.

He continued to look out at the water. "I grew up wanting his approval until I was about ten. My mum, she managed to be a happy person in spite of it all, and she created a happy home for me." His face was full of love as he remembered his mother. "But there were times when I'd hear her crying or talking to Mona about the situation. And so I started to hate him.

"We kept our distance as much as possible, but it followed me wherever I went. I was known as 'the bastard' until I was about thirteen. I had some good friends, like Bram, Bree . . . Kilian and a few others, but it wasn't until I was thirteen that I started to make a name for myself through sport.

"That's when the old man wanted to be a part of my life. I told him to fuck off and boxed him in the face. For all the power he had, he never had to resort to getting physical. He staggered away, not being able to really do anything to me without bringing shame on himself—I was the bastard, you see, but I was a well-liked bastard. He never bothered me again." There was real satisfaction in his expression.

Connor turned his eyes to her, showing the vulnerability of a boy, and the determination of a man. "That's why I don't want to be anything like the power-hungry, manipulative, lying, deceptive little fecker, you see? The way he threw around his power? The way he got even with those he thought had wronged him? Beth, he was disgusting."

In that moment she understood the darkness, understood the intensity and loathing he sometimes showed when he thought no one could see.

She wanted him to keep talking. She wanted to keep drawing out the poison. "What happened to your half-brother?"

"He was eight when I was born. There was something wrong with his heart. That's why they hired my mum in the first place—because he couldn't go to a normal school. He died a few years after I was born.

"My father's wife died of cancer when I was seven. My feckin' arsehole of a father died when I was twenty-two. I inherited the big house, the money, all that rubbish. I fixed up the cottage for my mum and renamed the lough after her. My way of reclaiming this place and making it what it always should have been."

A weight had been lifted. A small smile formed as his sapphire eyes found her emerald ones.

"And that, dear Elizabeth, is my sad story. Aren't you glad you asked?"

"I am, actually. I didn't enjoy watching you relive that kind of pain, but I'm glad to know you better."

His gaze turned serious, intimate. "I want you to know me better." He leaned in to kiss her softly. She could taste the wine on his lips. "I want to know you better." He pulled away. "What's your sad story, Beth? I know you have one. I knew it the first time we met."

"About losing Mags?"

"No." He stroked her fingers. "What happened to your parents? It isn't typical to be raised by a great-aunt, is it?"

She took a bite of cake, giving her more time to answer, like one of those candy-bar commercials. He was right; the orange frosting added another dimension to the sugary goodness.

She'd only opened three letters. What happened to her parents was still a mystery. She didn't want to lie to him, but she didn't want to admit the truth: that she didn't really know. And she didn't want to tell him about the letters. No one knew about the letters. No one needed to know—they were between her and Mags.

She settled on a half-truth. The lawyer in her chose her answer carefully. "I didn't really know my parents. I grew up thinking that my father divorced my mother, leaving her penniless and abandoning us. She fell apart. My grandmother died the year I was born so her sister, Mags, came to help raise me when I was almost four.

"My mother was such a wreck after my father left that she ended up leaving me with Mags. I don't know what she did or how she lived; I know she was homeless for a while, even though Mags tried to get her help." Her shoulders rose in a little shrug. "She died when I was ten." Beth looked down into her wine glass, watching her own reflection.

"Did you ever wonder what happened to her or your father?" he asked gently.

She shook her head. "I was a pretty curious child, but I managed to block out any curiosity I felt about the situation. I didn't ask Mags about my mother and I never thought to track down the asshole who was essentially just a sperm donor."

They were silent for a couple of minutes. Beth was grateful. She, too, had never laid out her history like that. The calm waters of the lake helped bring her some peace. Some perspective. "I think . . . I didn't want to know. It would hurt too much." She paused. "Does that make sense?"

A sad smile formed on her lips, tearing at his insides.

She looked down and continued. "When both your parents abandon you like that . . . they weren't dead, they weren't being shipped off to war, they just chose to leave. . . ."

She shook her head slowly before collecting herself. "I focused on Mags and the family we made. We had a great life together.

"She was the most interesting, ballsy person I'd ever met. She loved me and challenged me and always supported me." It was still difficult to remember without breaking.

He'd watched and listened faithfully, giving her the space she'd needed to let him in, but now he couldn't stop himself from holding her. He drew her in to him, placing his arm around her shoulder, the way he'd wanted to when he'd listened to her sob outside the cottage after the Cliffs.

She wiped a tear from her cheek, turning her face so he wouldn't see.

They held each other for several minutes before Connor resolved to change the mood. "Let's relive some happy memories, eh? What's one of your favorites of your life with Mags?"

The question had the desired effect. Her thoughts shifted. There were so many. She'd really had a happy life. It astounded Beth that her childhood issues had risen to the surface in spite of the life Magdalen had provided her.

How she relished crushing every husband when she represented the wife, like she was getting to lash out at her father, and relished crushing every wife when she represented the husband, like she was punishing her mother. It wasn't quite revenge. She didn't believe in revenge. It was like justice. A subconscious justice she never even knew she was pursuing.

How she'd never really trusted men or allowed herself to fall in love and let anyone truly see her. . . . She shook her head, choosing to refocus on the question.

She settled on a memory she often turned to. "It was December. I was eleven. We read a book in school—I can't even remember the name, but it had this scene where the girl goes outside at night because it's just started to snow. She catches snowflakes with her tongue. She looks up into the sky and describes how the white specks just appear out of nowhere.

"I was obsessed with the idea of snow falling because I'd never seen it fall. We'd always lived in San Francisco or Berkeley. I mean, I'd seen snow—Mags loved to travel so I got to see a lot—but I'd never seen snow *fall*. It bothered me that I couldn't imagine it."

Beth continued, speaking animatedly. "So one night Mags wakes me up out of nowhere. It must have been midnight or something. We get in the car and drive three hours to Yosemite. She had checked the weather report and knew snow would be falling in the park, so we spent a couple of hours before sunrise just looking up at the white specks appearing out of nowhere, against the pitch black sky." She smiled to herself and then at him. She liked telling Connor. It made her feel better to share some of Mags with him.

"I take it she was spontaneous like that, your Mags."

Elizabeth nodded.

"Mags . . . is that short for anything? Margaret, maybe?"

184

"Magdalen." She moved away so she could look at him. He dropped his arm from her shoulder, taking her hand instead.

"Like my college at Cambridge?"

"Yes, only without the 'E' at the end. And you all don't pronounce the 'G' so it sounds like maudlin, which . . . I never really understood." She raised an eyebrow thinking about the strange pronunciation for the first time in fourteen years.

"That is true. The English are bizarre creatures, I'll give you that. Thank *God* I'm Irish." He sighed with mock relief.

"Your turn. Give me a happy memory of you and Rhia together." She nudged him with her shoulder and then stopped him before he could answer her. "Wait. Your mother's full name is Rhiannon?" She remembered the detail about renaming the lake. It hadn't occurred to her that Rhia was short for something.

He nodded, clearly perplexed by the obvious nature of her question.

"So your grandparents named her Rhiannon Bannon?" She raised her eyebrows.

He chuckled and then nodded.

She smiled back. "Wow. It's a gorgeous name, but. . . ." She trailed off, not wanting to offend him or Rhia.

He laughed hard as he took in her guarded expression. "Yes, let it never be said that we Irish do not have a sense of humor."

"Rhiannon," she said under her breath. It really was a gorgeous name. He was still showing his amusement. "All right, all right, your memory, please, Mr. Bannon."

He looked out at the water again, quickly calming his laughter, losing himself in thought. "Does a memory of her slapping my father count?" His smile was wide.

Beth pursed her lips and shook her head. "I said happy, not gratifying." Her voice was all light teasing.

"Oh, apologies. My mistake." His joking bravado resurfaced for a moment. "We used to go traipsing through these woods." He motioned to the trees behind them and on the other side of the lake. "We'd play hide-and-seek and she'd let me climb every tree I fancied.

"It was always great fun, but one day when I was eight I found an old-looking map buried beneath the fallen leaves just outside one of the paths that run through the woods. It was a treasure map, you see. All day it led me to different parts of the forest, where I found old-looking things like fossils and arrowheads and crystals." His face lit up at the memory.

"My mum knew I had been having a rough week at school and so she created the map and buried the treasures for me to find. I knew she had done it because I recognized one of the crystals. It was an old bauble, fairly worthless in terms of money, but I had seen it in her wardrobe the year before.

"The thing is, it wasn't any less fun because I had figured out it wasn't real. It just made me feel special and loved. After I found the crystal, I came home and told her about all the treasures, asking her to come help me find the rest. We didn't finish until the following day because we kept thinking up stories about what each item was and how it came to be there."

Beth looked at Connor, seeing the happy little boy he must have been on that day. Physically, he was gorgeous, but she correctly divined that his worth extended far beyond what the world could see.

For a moment she imagined herself falling for him. Imagined that he wasn't an emotionally unavailable bachelor. Imagined that she wasn't an emotionally immature commitment-phobe. Imagined that the practical differences in their lives could work to create some magical recipe for lifelong happiness.

She didn't notice him staring at her. Or the depth of feeling in his eyes.

He drew soft circles on the back of her hand with his thumb. "So what should we do for our sixth date?" he asked cheerfully.

"Sixth? How do you even know we'll get to six?"

He was unconcerned. "Because six comes after five. This is our fifth date," he answered simply.

"Does math work differently in Ireland? Because if the festival counts as a date, then this would be our second."

"Well, let's see. What constitutes a date? Is it a date if there is flirting, food, nudity, and/or sex?"

She indulged him. "I suppose some of those are likely to happen on a date."

"All right, then. Well, the first day we met you saw me naked. So nudity check. Date number one."

She waited for more of his sound logic.

"The day after that we flirted, there was food, and you definitely wanted to get me naked. Date number two.

"The day after that we went to the Cliffs, and there was flirting and nudity, remember? I saw you in your underthings. Date number three." He held up three fingers as a visual cue, just in case she wasn't following. "Yesterday we flirted when we ran into each other on Main Street. We ate at the festival. We definitely got naked and had sex. So check, check, check, and check.

"In fact," he continued confidently, "there is an argument to be made that those were all actually separate dates, but let's be conservative and count them all as one. Date number four. And here we are on date number five. Do you accept my logic?"

"Do you mean do I accept the notion that our first date was you standing in a towel while I yelled at you and threatened you with an umbrella? Shockingly, I don't."

He was laughing now. "I stand by my calculations."

"Well, then by your logic, you should be running for the hills right about now. You don't go on more than five dates with the same woman, remember?"

He narrowed his eyes. "That was the number *you* guessed. It's usually more like two dates. So really I crossed my threshold a month ago."

She continued their light banter. "Well, good, because I'm not sure I want you to run for the hills just now."

He turned serious in an instant. He gave her his dazzling smile mixed with something resembling hope. "You don't?"

She blanched. They'd just been teasing each other, right? That was their thing—light banter. "Well, no. Not just now." She was hesitant. For someone who'd been labeled emotionally unavailable, he sure was making himself *appear* available. And open.

She started to second-guess their physical relationship. Would she have gotten involved with him if she hadn't believed Mona's label? She thought she would be safe. With him being unavailable and her being commitment-phobic, she'd liked those odds. Now she wasn't so sure.

He could read the thoughts as they crossed her face. "Do you remember what I said last night when we were walking back from the festival? About the Universe? About not leading women on? That was my father and I hate everything about that man; that's why I cut things off. Do you remember what I said about knowing what I want?" His gaze was intense, full of meaning she wasn't ready for.

Butterflies rose up in her stomach. She was nervous now. "Connor . . . what are you saying?"

"You're so smart; deduce what you will." His expression transformed from smoldering intensity to mischief. "Don't look so terrified. Come 'ere." He pulled her in to him, capturing her mouth with his like she was his dessert.

Beth forgot why she had been nervous a moment before as he deepened the kiss and pushed her down onto the blanket. He pressed into her, moving his hands freely over her body. She pulled him down onto her, meeting his tongue at every turn. He groaned with desire.

"Jaysus, woman!" he managed between kisses. He moved his head so that he hovered an inch above her. "We're only snoggin', but I could let go right here. Do you know what you do to me?" He kissed her once more, softly, and then fell onto his back, breathing heavily.

"Maybe we should go back to talking," Beth panted, "because I am not having sex in front of the lake in broad daylight."

He hadn't caught his breath. "OK, I'm open to suggestions."

"Uh . . . what's your favorite sport?" Beth asked, going with the first thing that popped into her head since their breathing sounded like they'd just finished a sprint.

"To watch or play?"

"Play," she responded.

"Rugby. Good. This is good. What's your favorite book?" Connor countered.

"*To Kill a Mockingbird*," she answered.

"What's your *real* favorite book? The one you would never admit to but makes you giddy every time you read it?" he tried again.

"The entire Harry Potter series," she blurted out without thinking.

"Reaaally?" He turned on his side to stare at her. "So you're really a romantic at heart?"

"What makes you say that?" She mirrored his movement.

"Harry Potter is all about magic, about adventure, friendship, love, possibility—you know what type of person is attracted to that kind of story?" He stroked the length of her nose with his index finger. "A romantic."

"I don't know about that. Maybe it just says I'm a child at heart, not a romantic."

"Either way, there's hope for you yet."

CHAPTER 14: LETTER #4

After the picnic they went their separate ways, but not before Connor asked Elizabeth for a sixth date. He'd invited her to dinner that same night, and out of some lust-filled haze, she'd said yes.

Now, as she sat on the large sofa opposite the wall of glass, looking out onto the lake, she was rethinking everything. Connor had been nothing but open and affectionate with her. Which ironically made her feel like she didn't know where she stood with him.

Had Mona been wrong in her assessment? Her head was screaming at her, flashing red lights. She was in real danger with him. John had been an ideal mate. She was secure in the knowledge that when it ended, it wouldn't hurt, wouldn't reach her. But Connor. . . .

It was just supposed to be a one-time thing. A way of living a little by putting her body ahead of her brain. The realities of the situation were too obvious to ignore.

She lived in California; he lived in Ireland. He was a serial bachelor; she was a serious commitment-phobe. She was in the middle of a midlife crisis or whatever a thirty-five-year-old mess was supposed to be called. She was feeling better, but she still had no idea what she was going to do about her job in San Francisco or where she would even be for the next year. He traveled a lot for work and could be gone again at any moment.

People left, abandoned you, that's just what they did—better to not get too invested. In what Universe could this possibly end well? End without her getting hurt, if they continued this level of real intimacy.

Memories of the night they'd spent together came rushing back. The blood rose to her face again as she remembered what it had felt like to experience so much passion and pleasure that it felt like she was leaving her body.

On the other hand, her brain had been in complete control these last ten years. That was ten years of never experiencing that kind of ecstasy. Hell, forget the last ten years—she'd never experienced anything like that *ever*.

Beth continued in this way, trying to see all possible sides to the situation. The bottom line remained: she didn't want to get hurt. It wasn't smart to continue setting herself up for something else to get over. *She'd just lost Mags.*

Her thoughts turned completely to her great-aunt—and the truth she had kept secret. How was she supposed to understand or decide anything when she didn't even know the truth about her parents? All of her frustration surrounding the Connor situation was now laser-focused on Mags and her thirty-five-year-old surprise.

She crossed the living room to the cabinet that held the box in five quick strides. She took it to the round dining nook and didn't stop to think about what Mags would say next. She just wanted the truth. She needed answers.

The envelope was pink, and there were tiny brown diamonds on it. The number "4" was written in blue ink.

Dearest Lizzie,

I know you must be getting really impatient by now so I'll start off by saying that this isn't THAT letter.

Beth stopped reading. She gripped the paper, almost tearing it. She dropped her head onto the table with a smack.

It hurt. "Ugh!" She brought the palm of her right hand up to massage her forehead. She looked back into the open box of letters, dangerously close to ripping them all open until she found the truth.

Sorry, honey. Just stay with me. I don't need to be especially intuitive to know that you are going cray-cray right now. It's my fault, I know, but just stay with me.

Beth smiled a little. She'd always admonished Mags for saying words like *cray-cray*; it sounded so ridiculous coming from someone in her eighties. Like a girl embarrassed of her mother, she'd always apologize for her if they were in anyone else's presence. Mags retaliated by using it again, in combination with other teen expressions like "totes adorb."

This letter is for sharing a story with you. You were always so curious about Elsa, but I don't think we ever talked about her father, Matthieu. The year was 1957. I was 33.

Beth suddenly thought of Sophia from *The Golden Girls.*

I was living in a small city, Verneuil-sur-Avre, about an hour or so outside of Paris. I had a little pâtisserie in town. My pastry chef and I used to have a table at the Saturday morning market where we greeted the people from the village and introduced ourselves to tourists with samples.

It was raining and even though we were under a tarp, the ground was already slick. Michelle, my chef, was setting out the éclairs when her foot slipped. Instead of falling onto the table and our colorful display of treats, she managed to throw her weight backwards, almost knocking a man over.

It was the butcher. He was an awful man with a big belly and the worst anger issues I'd ever seen. She apologized over and over again, but he wouldn't stop screaming in her face.

A visitor from Paris, a young man of twenty-six, started to defend her. He was very calmly trying to reason with the man, who wouldn't be reasoned with. Poor Michelle; she was a small woman and almost fifty at the time. I don't know how any human being could yell at her, especially with such body-shaking fervor.

The butcher was none too pleased to be called out like that by the visitor in front of everyone—even though he was such an ass, everyone was thinking the same thing. They wanted to help, but didn't want to lose their access to meat. The man wasn't dissuaded; he just kept calmly talking to the butcher like he was a wild animal—which, believe me, he was.

The butcher had enough and punched the poor guy right in the stomach, causing him to double over. He was about to hit him again when I got between them with my sturdy umbrella. They don't make them like that anymore; I could have done some serious damage. In his rage, he almost lost control and hit me, but at the last second realized what he was doing and that hitting a woman in front of everyone at the Saturday morning market would be tantamount to walking into the local cathedral and pissing on the altar. He stalked away from us, still fuming.

I helped our brave visitor to his feet and asked him to come by the shop around lunchtime so that we could thank him with a meal. He was there at one. We ended up talking for hours. His name was Matthieu Fleury, a grad student living in Paris who was on a mini holiday.

One week turned into two, two into three. He spent the entire summer with me in Verneuil and then every weekend until Christmas. It was around that time he asked me to move with him to Rome, where he needed to do the next leg of his studies. I declined. I loved him, but I had my own path to follow. Don't ignore that inner voice, Lizzie. The one that tells you where to go next. It's your most important guide in this life—your direct connection to the Universe.

Anyway, the adventurer in me was ready to take off again and try my hand in another foreign place. I sold the pâtisserie to Michelle and set off for Madrid in January. A new year, a fresh start.

I found out I was pregnant with Elsa that March. In her short eight years of life, she and I lived in Madrid, Barcelona, and Málaga. It was one big adventure after another.

Matthieu and I reconnected thrice more in my lifetime. I don't think we spent more than two years total together, but he was my great love. I don't regret a second of it.

Now for the not-holding-back part, which I know you love so well: I hope by now you've dumped that loser John and at least opened yourself up to the possibility of finding someone with whom you can find true passion. Fall in love, Lizzie; let go of your brain and just fall in love as often as possible. There's nothing like it on Earth. Even if sometimes it hurts. Let love affairs be what they are meant to be. A week, a year, a lifetime. When you're on your deathbed, it won't be one of the things you regret. Trust me.

Love,
Mags

After re-reading the last paragraph, Beth stood up to look around her.

"Mags, did you fake your death so you could send me off on a quest? Are you watching me right now?" She did a quick visual check for cameras, then continued out loud, "Are you just watching this whole thing play out and then sneaking in here to deposit the next letter because you know it's what I need right then and there?"

She was acutely aware of how crazy she sounded. Mags had always had a heightened sense of intuition, but this?

Or maybe Beth had just chosen a highly predictable path, the unraveling of which was easily foreseeable.

She went back to the couch. Connor made her feel alive. He could really see her, and she, him. Maybe it was worth it to have a week together, a month, whatever.

At a time when she was questioning every decision she'd ever made, Elizabeth Lara did the bravest thing she'd ever done—she listened to her heart.

She knew she was already starting to fall; she would let herself. Because when someone who really loved you gave you deathbed advice about falling in love, you owed it to them and yourself to listen.

Chapter 15: A Noble Surprise

The blue dress set off her porcelain skin and pink lips. She wore her hair down without straightening it, letting the natural wave be. The tall black boots weren't an obvious choice, but they felt right and since she was all about going with what felt right, she trusted the decision.

Connor knocked on the French doors at seven sharp. He wore a loose-fitting white shirt, unbuttoned a couple inches at the collar, and khakis. He didn't hesitate when he saw Beth, grabbing her around the waist and kissing her enthusiastically.

"Hi there, gorgeous," he said without withdrawing his face more than an inch.

"Hi," she replied happily. She'd made her decision and would now give herself permission to feel as giddy as she pleased.

They stood in the back entry, embracing each other for several moments. It felt good to surrender.

"Shall we?" He released her and took her hand instead, pulling her back out towards the lake.

"We're walking there? I'd rather drive to the restaurant; these are my comfy boots, but still." She looked down at her feet.

"We can't drive there, Luv. There isn't a paved road between here and there," he answered with his devilish grin.

She narrowed her eyes and smiled. "What do you mean?"

"Just that. There isn't a road to drive on." When her expression didn't change, he added, "Don't fret. It's only a three minutes' walk." He put his arm around her shoulders as she locked the door.

"Did you make me dinner?" She reached up and kissed his neck as they walked. He turned his head and intercepted her lips.

"No, that wouldn't have worked well for either of us. I had a chef prepare something."

"Wow, slick move. Very classy, hiring a private chef just for dinner." She nodded slowly, impressed. "Your other sixth dates would have approved," she teased.

"You mean if I'd had any?" He kissed the top of her head.

They walked past the statue of Rhia and went into the forest.

The sky was mostly dark now, but she could see a trace of lights through the trees up ahead.

He led her into the woods, towards the light. They reached a clearing and then a curved path with hedges on either side. The path led directly to a massive ancient structure. It could only be described as . . . a castle.

"And I didn't exactly hire a chef just for tonight." His voice was low, deliberate. "*Tech*nically, he's on staff year-round. Although I rarely use him," he finished slowly, carefully examining her expression.

Beth's jaw had dropped. The structure was so big, she couldn't even take it all in. She realized she must have caught sight of it that first time she'd looked out at the lake and never given it a second thought. He said he'd inherited a *big house*?

She pulled away and turned to face him. "Umm . . . Connor? Could you possibly, maybe, have left—" She paused, crossing her arms. "I don't know—*something* out of the life story you told me earlier?"

He was genuinely concerned, almost fearful. "Are you cross?"

"I don't know." She was confused. "I pegged you for an authentic, direct kind of guy. Care to tell me about this?" She waved her hands at the castle and waited.

"I absolutely am that guy. Truly. I'm nothing but upfront with people. I think it's the only way to be, especially since my father was . . . who he was." He took a deep breath, trying to find the words that would keep her from running away.

"I won't even use the fact that I did tell you about a big house—I realize that using that vague truth as a technicality is completely deceptive. Something *he* would have done. This is obviously substantially more than a big house. I'm guilty. I purposely didn't tell you about Castle Bannon."

She was so beyond her depth. "It has a name?"

"Well, yes, most *do*. I renamed it after the vermin died to carry mine and my mother's surname in place of his."

She had nothing.

He was weary. "Say somethin' . . . please?" His accent thickened with his anxiety.

"Why did you keep this a secret from me?" The idea made her feel uneasy. Did he think she was some gold digger? That couldn't be right.

"That first day we met. You were so angry I had intruded on your day—and rightfully so, even if it was a misunderstanding. I'd be pretty annoyed if I found someone else in the place I had let as well." He looked into her eyes with a smile. "Although if it had been you naked in the bathroom, it would have been a very lovely surprise."

Soft lights spilled out from the castle, illuminating his face. He looked towards the house.

"The thing is, I hadn't been spoken to so balls-out, so honestly, since before the old man died. After I inherited the house and title, everyone became so polite. My friends treated me more or less the same, but I didn't get that same reckless truth from them anymore. Sure, they'd tell me when I was being an ass hat, but you know, they wouldn't say, 'Mate, you're being an ass hat,' anymore. Sometimes you just want people to say what they are thinking *without* a filter.

"Then you came along. I enjoyed your open temperament. I told myself I was inviting you to dinner at the pub to be polite and apologize for my intrusion, but I also really wanted to keep talking to you. You didn't have an agenda or a filter. It was refreshing." His smile was apologetic and pleading. "I knew I couldn't control what people said in front of you that night, but I hoped we could have a nice evening without *this* coming up." He nodded his head towards his inheritance.

"I liked you more and more as the evening went on. I thought you were gorgeous and refreshing from the start, but I didn't think we'd have so much fun together." He paused, like he was carefully constructing the next part. "Or have so much in common. Our grief, the Universe, your knowing Cambridge and all that." He watched her expression carefully. "Like it was . . . *fate*."

He waited for something to click. When she didn't say anything, he continued. "Or that you would be as interesting as you are. From then on, I didn't purposely keep it from you. I just steered the conversation when I thought it might come up." He breathed in sharply; another admission was coming. "Except I did ask one person not to tell you. . . ." He looked at her, hesitant again.

Beth didn't need to guess. "Mona."

He nodded, pleading. "I just didn't want anything to change."

"Why did you assume it would?"

205

"I didn't. I just didn't want to risk it. I felt a very strong connection to you and I was afraid that something like this would alter the careful relationship we were building."

She was annoyed and hurt by his assumption. "Well, I guess you don't know Americans very well. Or lawyers. Or me. I wouldn't have spoken to you differently."

"Would you have allowed yourself to keep seeing me, though?" He brought his eyes down to her so she couldn't look away. "Be honest. Your head and your heart have been waging a not-so-secret war behind that beautiful exterior."

She looked away from him. Away from Castle Bannon, back towards the trees and lake. Would she even have allowed herself to get this far? Far enough to have to decide whether she would let this romance be whatever it was meant to be? Connor had turned out to be quite the romantic ideal. Gorgeous, thoughtful, smart, funny, capable of seeing through her and helping her to remember who she'd been for most of her life.

She'd known she was in danger with him from the start. Throw in a castle and her brain wouldn't have let her get past that first night at the pub. Flashing red lights over a caution sign reading "DANGER Now Entering Fantasyland: WILL GET BURNED" would have stopped her in her tracks.

She turned to stare into his ice blue eyes. The lights from the house were reflected in them, like flames. He was holding his breath.

He wanted to reach out and touch her, but he was afraid she would turn and march straight back to the cottage, incapable of forgiving him for misleading her. He'd known it from their first meeting. Truth was important to Elizabeth, maybe more important than anything else.

"Please. Say something." He enunciated his words, trying to make her understand how serious he was taking this. He couldn't let her walk away from him. "I only misled you about this. I swear. There's nothing else. This isn't a symptom of some larger issue. Y'aren't going to be hit by any more surprises, one after the other. This is it. You can ask me anything. Please, just don't close yourself off from me." He reached out to cup her face, stroking her cheek with his thumb.

"Elizabeth?" he whispered.

He'd said what she needed to hear. It was true, she wouldn't have let things get this far. But now that she had made the decision to let this gorgeous man in, there was no going back. She'd forgive his deception, on the grounds that he wasn't hiding anything else.

"This is it?" The lightness of her voice surprised them both.

"Yes." He was firm.

"OK," she said simply with a shrug. It came out sounding very laid back. She was too overwhelmed to respond in any other way.

"Really." It wasn't a question. His other hand came up to her face so she couldn't look away. "No coddin'?" He searched her eyes.

"That means joking, right? No, I'm not joking. If that's all there is and that's the reason you didn't tell me, then fine."

Her laid-back disposition gave way to the fire that always lived inside of her, waiting to be put to use. "If you're anything other than *completely* honest with me from here on out, technicalities or not, I won't even give you the opportunity to explain. Got it?" She gave him a genuine smile, colored by something else. A look that said *don't fuck with me or I'll cut off your balls*. It was effective.

"Yeah, no, that's fair." He shook his head like a child who was expecting a much harsher punishment, but understood the consequence of a repeat offense.

"OK, then. Show me your castle, Mr. Knightly." She let him lead her.

"Knightly?" he asked quizzically.

"It's a Jane Austen thing." She smiled to herself, thinking of Austen's most perfect suitor. Darcy was her favorite, but Knightly was the only suitor who never faltered throughout the course of *Emma*. She was suddenly glad Connor hadn't asked about her *second* favorite book. Answering *Pride & Prejudice* would have cemented her as a romantic in his eyes—and that would have given far too much away. Just because she'd never allowed anyone to get close enough to really see her, to love her, it didn't mean that deep, deep, down Elizabeth Lara wasn't a true romantic at heart.

She turned to stare at a hedge, biting her lip to keep herself from laughing. The absurdity of her situation was not lost on her. She'd definitely crossed over into Fantasyland.

"Good evening, Lord Bannon, Miss." A thin older man bowed to them as they entered into a large foyer.

"Hi," she said awkwardly.

"I've told you, Declan, none of that rubbish, please. I thought we had an understanding." He gave the man a stern look.

"Sorry, sir, I mean Connor, sir. It's just, you've never had a lady here. I wanted to err on the side of caution."

"Declan, this is Elizabeth Lara from California. Elizabeth, this is Declan Daniels. He keeps the house in order, especially when I'm away. He was so excited to have something to do tonight." He looked at Declan. "Is the wine out?"

Declan answered with a small nod.

"Nice to meet you." Beth stepped forward to shake Declan's hand. He was taken aback, but pleased by her warmth.

Declan excused himself.

"This way." Connor took her hand, leading her past a large staircase and into one of the front rooms while Declan disappeared.

The room was large, but comfortable. In place of stuffy antique pieces stood modern leather furniture around a fireplace flanked by several enormous windows. A pool table stood near the opposite wall, completely surrounded by floor-to-ceiling bookcases containing thousands of titles. The style could have been rich modern bachelor or updated lounge at Cambridge. The dark wood floor creaked as they walked in.

"So Lord, huh? You mentioned a title? Time to get it all out there, Bannon."

"Yes, well. . . ." He hesitated.

She narrowed her eyes, weary again. "No more holding back, remember?"

"Oh, I'm not holding back, Luv. I just think it's all complete rubbish. Kind of embarrassing for me to talk about, you see."

Embarrassing? That was unexpected.

"So, in Gaelic nobility," he poured her a glass of white wine and brought her to sit on the large tufted couch, "there are those called *flatha*. Which means we are descended from at least one historical grade of *Rí*, or king. There were *rí túaithe*, which were local petty kings. There were *Ruiri*, which were regional kings. And *rí ruirech*, who were kings of overkings."

"And which type of king are you descended from?"

"An *ard rí*, a high king."

"So that's above a *rí ruirech*?" Her pronunciation was terrible.

"Precisely." He took a sip of his wine.

"Which makes your title. . . ?"

He turned bright red. "I'm a *flaith*, or prince of the old Gaelic nobility."

Beth almost laughed. *Hello. My name is Connor Bannon. Nothing embarrasses me. Except the fact that I am a prince and I sometimes confuse The Muppets with Sesame Street.*

"The whole thing is ludicrous. It doesn't mean anything, really. I inherited this place which dates back to the seventeenth century and loads of money from family holdings that date back quite a ways, but otherwise it's just an honorary title. I'm not into the power kick that some *flaith* thrive on. Like the old man.

"People around here like to call me 'Lord' and sometimes attribute an unnatural level of respect just because I share some genes with someone who died a really long time ago. It's absurd." He took a long drink from his glass.

She thought he was going to continue his mini-rant. When he didn't, she prodded, "So there aren't any other responsibilities?"

"Well, I get called upon to judge things or present things when I'm here. Like the dessert tasting. They wanted me to do more, but I declined. I usually decline. I only really agreed to the dessert tasting because I hoped your sweet tooth would persuade you to come with me." He gave her a lopsided smile. "An extra enticement, if you will. The promise of sugar."

What an odd connection to make. He'd tried to lure her to go with him through the promise of dessert? She considered her love of cake and chocolate. On second thought . . . maybe that wasn't such a crazy plan. "But how did you know I had a sweet tooth?"

"When Mona and I were leaving food, I noticed all the packages of Hobnobs and other biscuits. I guessed." He touched her nose with a finger. "I wasn't sure you would be well by then, but I hoped. And then I ran into Mona and she told me you were on the mend."

"You put a lot of thought into that night." She was flattered, but unsure. It didn't make sense to her. "Why would you bother? I mean, I get you found me mildly interesting because I wasn't afraid to yell at you, but then I completely fell apart on you at the Cliffs and then was out of it for almost a month." She shook her head. What was attractive about any of *that*?

She needed to understand. "I know you said that seeing and hearing me grieve affected you and that you waited for me to be OK so you'd know that you would be OK, but why would you be attracted to me romantically after witnessing it all?"

He moved to tip her chin up, holding her gaze. "You were exactly who you needed to be every second that we were together. You are a beautiful woman, but I could see your scars, I could see through your armor, and that made me care for you instantly."

"Like I said, *hero* complex," Beth said lightly.

"No, Luv. I didn't want to save you. It was because I could see past the face you put out to the world, to your scars, that I thought you could save me." There was deep emotion in his voice.

He held her in his gaze. Beth stopped breathing.

"Should people be in relationships to be saved? Shouldn't we save ourselves?"

"Sometimes we need a little help." He brought his lips down softly, using his tongue to trace her lower lip and then spreading her mouth open. She could feel her heart in her ears. It was a long kiss. Achingly slow and deliberate. He tasted like California.

She pulled away before she lost all ability to think. "So how exactly did I save you?"

"Well, in addition to being yourself, polite or not, you experienced so much grief at losing Mags. It just crushed you. Seeing it happen like that, I couldn't ignore my own feelings anymore. Then I did whatever I could to help and that forced me to be home.

"To sit by the lake. To look at my mum's statue. And then there was the overwhelming pull to be near you. I cut my business trip short because I felt like I *had* to see you again."

He didn't say anything else as she processed his words. He waited for her response. To say or do something that would tell him that they were on the same page.

His declaration softened her. It finally made sense. She snuggled into his shoulder.

Beth didn't see the huge smile that transformed his features; he was pleased by her affectionate gesture. He leaned his head into hers. "Can I ask you something?"

She nodded.

"What changed today? At lunch I had to kiss you into submission, to get you to say yes to another date. I could tell that you wanted to, yet still something held you back. But tonight when I picked you up, there was something different. You were unguarded, more open to me from the start. Like you'd made up your mind about something."

"That's probably because I did." Her voice was soft against his shoulder. "I decided to let this be whatever it is meant to be. I was so focused on it being a one-time thing because I didn't want to get hurt. I mean this," she pulled away and motioned with her finger, "can't possibly lead anywhere, and honestly, I've never really wanted a relationship to lead anywhere.

"I thought that it wasn't worth opening myself up further. Wasn't worth the eventual sting."

He spoke softly. "Why does there have to be pain?"

Beth gave him her *isn't it obvious* look. She listed the roadblocks she'd thought about after the picnic.

"OK, the distance thing is something, I'll give you that. But you don't really know where your future lies right now, so why should that get in our way? The serial bachelor thing, I've already explained that I'm just a guy who knows what he wants and doesn't lead women on.

"Your commitment-phobe thing, well, I think it's a good sign that you've decided to open yourself up to me. And that this," he looked around them, "didn't scare you off."

"I know. I agree to all of that. That's why I'm here." Her response was short, matter-of-fact. She was hungry. Reading Mags' letter, processing her feelings, and then stepping through to Fantasyland burned a lot of calories. "Now I do remember you promised me some food. Or does dinner mean something different in Ireland?"

He gave her his dazzling smile. "Yes, Miss Lara."

Chapter 16: The Castle

They ate in a long dining room, complete with chandelier. After having a flashback to Kim Basinger and Michael Keaton in *Batman*, she moved to sit next to him. Declan looked a little put out by their new seating arrangements, like someone had taken away his candy. He quickly rearranged his features and served their next course.

They had French onion soup, filet mignon with garlic potatoes, and a rich chocolate cake. Connor was absolutely delighted by the unfiltered sounds coming from Beth as she'd eaten the cake. They resembled her enjoyment of the burger that first night at the pub.

Afterwards, he led her down a wide hallway to the library. Floor-to-ceiling dark shelves, complete with rolling ladders, flanked a large wooden desk and several display cabinets.

He was visibly excited. "I want to show you some of the pieces I've collected through my work."

Oh, good. She was glad he was finally going to explain what he did for a living. She'd kept the American in her successfully at bay and hadn't asked. "You mentioned you work in acquisitions?"

"Yes, I travel the globe looking for rare items. Pieces that have great value to certain collectors. Then I sell them at one of my two auction houses in London and Rome."

"So you're like Sotheby's?"

"No, my houses are smaller and more geared towards rare finds, historic pieces, and nostalgic items."

"What is your auction house called?"

"Bannon's."

Of course.

He handed her an old round tube. "Take a look at this."

It was a kaleidoscope. She pointed it towards a lamp. The red, blue and green triangles moved as she turned the dial.

"This one was part of the very first series Sir David Brewster created when he was conducting experiments on light polarization. He made it in 1815, two years before the word 'kaleidoscope' was even born. I tracked it down at an estate in Austria."

He walked over to a sword mounted on a wall. "This supposedly belonged to Niall McGrail, a high king in the fifth century, and the one I'm related to." His voice was full of reverence.

"You sound quite proud to have it."

His back straightened. "I am."

She tried to work out the contradiction. "How can you be proud of it, but feel embarrassed to be related to him?"

He looked at her, taking a moment to think. "I'm not embarrassed to be related to him. I'm embarrassed that because he lived sixteen hundred years ago, people want to call me 'Lord.' That's just completely mental." He turned to look at the heirloom. "I like the sword, though. It's a piece of history. As a history major, you can appreciate that, right?" Connor kept his eyes trained on the piece as he registered the slip. Beth didn't notice.

"Uh, yeah. I totally get it." It was a beautiful piece of worn metal, with a simple handle. "What was this castle named before you changed it to Bannon?"

"Castle Grail. My father's name was Keanan Grail."

His energy turned black as soon as he uttered the name.

She wanted to chase the darkness away. "What's this?" She looked through a glass table at an old piece of parchment.

"That," his voice rose with childlike excitement, "is a map thought to be drawn by one of Captain Kidd's crew. The markings are very faded, but you can still see the outlines of the New England colonies, Europe, the oceans. . . ."

He extended a magnifying glass mounted to the wall so that she could examine the markings. "I picked it up from a private collector in New York. The man was an old recluse. He was a hoarder with entire rooms full of old documents, maps, photographs—odds and ends that he inherited or that people brought to him."

Something clicked for Beth. "This is what you do? Connect with people, places, and estates that might have hidden treasures?"

"Exactly." He beamed.

"And I bet you love the Indiana Jones films. . . ."

He shrugged. "Who doesn't?" Obviously.

Her face transformed with a slow smile. "Ha! You are still living out that weekend when your mom drew a treasure map. You've just found a way to make a living at it."

"Well, I don't really need to *make* a living, but, yes, I suppose in a way I do."

She watched as his eyes scrunched together. He was thinking hard about what she'd just said. Like he'd never made the connection before.

"And how did you spend your time as a wee one?" He turned the tables.

"I took pictures." Her eyes found one of the windows. The night had swallowed whatever view lay beyond. "I begged Mags for a camera for Christmas. She got me my first one when I was seven. I thought I was so good." She shook her head at the memory. "I didn't stop taking pictures until school started taking up more time. I could never have made a living at it. . . ." She trailed off as she remembered how much she'd loved to look through a lens.

She'd stopped taking anything more serious than snapshots with friends by the time she was sixteen.

He wrapped his arms around her waist from behind and whispered, "You could do."

"No, I'm a lawyer," she protested.

His chest pressed into her back. His breath tickled her neck.

"No, you were a lawyer. You could choose to continue being a lawyer, or you could set off on an entirely new career."

Turning in his arms, she looked up into his face. "Maybe, but I don't want to think about that right now." She kissed him slowly, suggestively. He didn't need her to tell him twice. She spread her lips further apart, letting him dive deep inside of her.

"I think it's time I showed you where I sleep." He kissed down to her neck.

"What an excellent idea," she agreed.

Connor led Beth up the stairs, down another long hall, and into a massive room. A king-sized bed with a padded leather tufted headboard stood opposite the double doors. A long window seat lined one wall. The room was dark except for the light that spilled through the ten-foot-tall leaded windows; it was a dreamy kind of light emanating from the grounds below. She started to walk towards the glass, curious about what she might see. He didn't allow her to make it that far.

He kissed her neck from behind and moved his hands over her breasts, massaging them through the thin blue fabric. She let her head fall back against his shoulder. After a few seconds, he released her to move his hands to the zipper at the back and undid it slowly.

He removed the dress from her shoulders and pushed it down her body until it was pooled at her feet. She stepped out of it, her back still facing him. His lips continued to caress her neck while his fingers undid her bra. He brought one arm forward across her breasts, squeezing as he went. His other hand went down into her panties. Finding her entrance, he slipped two fingers inside. The delicious invasion caused her to arch back into him.

She moaned with pleasure as he continued to explore.

Her voice was low, full of unhindered desire. "Connor." It was a verbal caress.

In one movement, he turned her to face him, while still inside of her. She cried out.

Her fingers unbuttoned his white linen shirt easily, making their way to his pants. He released her for a moment to remove the rest of his clothing while she removed the rest of hers, including her boots.

When they were both free, he brought her in to his chest, kissing her with all the desire he'd been saving since lunch by the lough. Her breasts were crushed against his chest, her hips aligned with his. He could feel every line of her. He moved them to the bed without breaking the kiss.

There was the sound of a wrapper as he hoisted her against the headboard into a standing position with one arm. He kneeled on the bed in front of her, taking one breast into his mouth and then the other.

"You're so beautiful." He looked up at her like he was under some spell. The look melted her insides further. He kissed her stomach, moved down to her thighs, and then his mouth was on her. Her knees buckled as the intensity of his tongue threatened to unhinge her. Her body shuddered.

He stopped, looking up at her again. He wanted to devour her any which way he could have her. "Come 'ere." It was a growl.

He brought her down so she was straddling him, back against the headboard, and then he plunged into her. Pushing deeper into the inner recesses of her body. Her head fell backwards, relishing in the feel of him. She wrapped her legs more tightly around his back, meeting him thrust for thrust.

He kept his mouth on her while driving his hips in to greater depths. She found his mouth with hers and they joined their tongues, suppressing her screams and the groans escaping his chest as they both climbed together.

They rose higher and higher until they both found an exquisite release. Neither had control of their limbs as they fell into each other and onto the bed.

"That was . . . unbelievable," Connor breathed. "Is it just me? Or was that unbelievable?"

"No, it was." Beth gasped for air like she'd been holding her breath. "It really, really was. Even better than last night."

His voice was full of wonder. "I could feel you open up to me. Like whatever you decided earlier, freed you. You let me in." She expected him to break into a mischievous grin or make a joke after the words "let me in." He remained serious, intense.

He turned onto his side to look at her. His hand caressed her cheek; his fingertips outlined her lips. "What changed your mind, really? There had to be something that changed."

Every cell in her body was relaxed, satiated. Turning onto her back, she looked up. There was some ornate pattern all across the white ceiling. She couldn't make it out in the dark.

In that moment, she knew she was ready to tell him. "Mags left me a series of letters. I got them the day after the funeral." She took in another breath, eyes fixed on the ceiling. "She was always really honest with me when she was alive, but apparently there were things she couldn't say to me before or things she had already said, but I couldn't hear."

She paused, remembering each letter in turn. He waited for her to continue, stroking down her arm until he reached her hand, lacing his fingers through hers.

"They jarred me. To my core. That's why I hopped on a plane and came here without much forethought."

"What does she say in them?" he asked gently.

"Things about my job, about my life choices." She remembered the words of her second letter. "One said, and this is a direct quote: 'You are too goddamned uptight! For fuck's sake, have a drink. Let your hair down. Open yourself up to new people and experiences.'" She changed her voice for effect.

He laughed with his entire body. "I like your Mags."

"Yeah, you would have." She smiled at him.

When he didn't stop laughing, she protested, "Hey, come on, it isn't *that* funny!"

"Oh, yes it is. She had you pegged, didn't she? And so did I. That's why you decided to come out to the pub that night, isn't it?"

She moved her head into his shoulder so he couldn't see how red she'd become. She didn't enjoy being so predictable, but the feeling quickly subsided as she nestled into him. Sensing her vulnerability, he stopped teasing her, bringing his arms in to circle her body, drawing her closer.

"And you opened another letter after the picnic?" He wanted her to keep talking openly. Keep letting him in.

"Yes."

"Well?" he prodded.

"She told me a story about a man she loved. The father of her daughter Elsa. They didn't spend much time together, but she never regretted their love affair. She encouraged me to . . . fall often." She chose her words carefully. She didn't want to say *fall in love.* "To let relationships be what they are meant to be. So here I am."

He moved his head away from her so she could see his eyes. "I love your Mags." He said it like he was swearing an oath. The look that followed made her heart stop and the butterflies dance. "And for the record, I've already fallen."

"Come on, Luv. Stay," he pleaded with her as she got dressed two rounds and several hours later.

"No, I want to sleep in my bed. Plus, I'd really rather avoid the walk of shame. What will Declan think?"

"Declan? Why would he be here in the morning?"

"He doesn't live here?" It was such a big house. Big *castle*.

He shook his head. "All the staff live in their own homes. Even though they're full-time, they only come here when I've requested them or when I'm away and I need them to care for the house."

Looking over at his naked body sprawled on top of the bed, she wanted to return to him, but didn't want to walk back in the morning. She couldn't fall asleep in Fantasyland— she'd never wake up. "No, it's OK. I'll just see you tomorrow."

She leaned down to kiss him one last time, pulling away to find her shoes. She heard him get up and move around as she zipped each boot. When she turned to look, she found him completely dressed.

He took in her surprise, then looked unsure. "Is it all right if I come with you?"

She smiled; she didn't try to hide her pleasure. "If you want to."

Flashing her a boyish grin that made her go weak at the knees again, he said, "Yes. I want to."

They walked down the stairs. Connor grabbed a remote located on a table in the foyer next to the giant doors. He touched a button and all the lights in the house went dark. He locked the door and led her down the curved path, back out through the trees with only the light of the moon to guide them.

They reached the cottage quickly. She changed into her pajamas while he stripped to his boxer-briefs. He reached into one of the drawers in the bathroom to unearth a wrapped toothbrush as she got ready for bed. They fell into an easy rhythm until finally she curled up on her side and he wrapped his arms around her, both nestling into each other blissfully.

CHAPTER 17: FUNGIE

She was still wrapped in Connor's arms when she woke. He felt her shift and opened his eyes.

"Good mornin', gorgeous." He leaned in to kiss her.

He withdrew an inch so their noses touched, moving his head back and forth to give her an Eskimo kiss.

He released her to stretch his arms and take in the time. Almost eleven in the morning.

"I'd better be off. I've got a few errands to run before our big outing."

"It's very presumptuous of you to think I'm free," she scolded.

He gave her a look that said, *please, darlin', I know you're free.*

She relented. "Oh, all right. What big outing?"

"I'm taking you to meet Fungie." He said it like it was the most obvious thing in the world. Of course that's what they'd be doing today.

"And who or what is Fungie?"

"You'll see." He smiled and jumped out of bed, getting dressed at lightning speed. "Just wear comfortable clothing and shoes. Stuff you wouldn't mind getting wet, and sunscreen. I'll pick you up at one." He bent down to kiss her quickly before he was out the door.

Blood flowed through her veins as she stretched. She felt like blasting music and jumping on the bed. It had felt so good to surrender, to let herself feel, to not judge, not analyze, and just be open to him. She dug out her iPod and connected it to the stereo in the living room, blasting eighties rock as she fixed herself an omelet.

By one she was ready, dressed in spandex yoga tights, a loose-fitting cotton shirt, water-resistant Ugg boots, and a classic Yale hoodie. She tied the sweater around her waist as she waited. Ten minutes later there was a knock at the front door.

"Sorry, Luv, I had to take an unexpected business call." He was annoyed. He threw an arm around her shoulder, kissing her cheek. He wore black gym pants and that same gray hoodie, cut off at the sleeves. It was the look he'd sported on their "first date." She hadn't seen his green Celtic cross in daylight since the day they'd met.

"Is everything OK?" she asked as they got in his car.

"It's fine. I just have to leave for a few days." He reached over, interlacing their fingers.

Her stomach fell a little. She was just getting the hang of this intimacy thing. She didn't want him to leave.

"I'll miss you." He squeezed her hand. "Will you miss me?" He looked over at her.

"Yes." There was no point in hiding it.

He was unusually pleased as he examined her disappointment. "I'm glad. I shouldn't be gone for more than five days." His own displeasure rose up at the idea of being away from her for any measure of time. "Maybe just three," he said hopefully.

"When do you leave?"

He sighed. "Tonight."

They were silent the rest of the way.

"OK, so Fungie is a bottlenose dolphin. He's known as the Dingle Dolphin because he's been hanging out in Dingle Harbour since 1983?" She summed up the story he'd told her about Fungie as they walked to the boats.

"And he's been my friend ever since. I was one of the first people to notice that he was actually sticking around the harbour. I used to get one of the fisherman to take me out to see him. Later, when the tourist boats started showing up to capitalize, I'd beg my mum to let me go. I managed to get out a couple times a month. More if I'd managed to earn some money doing odd jobs for people in the village or as a special treat."

She was excited. Really excited. Beth loved dolphins, and growing up she'd secretly longed to have a special relationship with one, just like Connor described. "Does he recognize you?"

"Oh yeah, I've been getting in to swim with him since the eighties."

She was delighted. "Can anyone swim with him?"

231

"No, only experienced swimmers. Every boat has one guy or gal who regularly gets in. The tourists have to be introduced by one of the swimmers he knows, and even then they make sure that Fungie's mood allows it."

"Is he temperamental?"

"No, no. He just gets really excited. Loves to play. Easily scares the tourists when he's especially lively."

They reached a boat and stopped. There was a line of tourists already waiting. It was chilly near the water. Beth pulled her sweater on and crossed her arms over her chest. A second later she heard a familiar voice.

"Hey, Bannon!" Kilian called from behind them. He clapped him on the shoulder. "Elizabeth." He took her hand and kissed it with a wink.

"All right, all right." Connor reclaimed her hand.

"Right, here's that thing you requested. Fully charged, card ready to go." Kilian handed Connor a bag and then walked to the front of the line.

"Sorry, folks, I've been booked for a private tour. Feel free to grab lunch at one of our fine dining establishments just up the main street and come back at three. Thank you very much." He sounded even more Irish to Beth's ears, like he was playing a character for the crowd.

The tourists whined and protested as Kilian waved them away.

"This is for you." Connor handed Beth the bag Kilian had brought with him. "I had Kil pick it up in Killarney for me."

She unzipped the bag and took out its contents. It was a Canon 5D Mark III, complete with a 50mm 1.2 prime lens. Even though Beth didn't shoot anymore, she still kept up with the latest gadgets. Always intending to buy them, but never having enough spare time to actually do it.

"Connor, I can't accept this!" She caressed the camera with her fingertips, marveling at the smooth, new feeling. And the weight. It felt perfect in her hands. "This is a three-thousand-dollar camera! And the lens must be another fifteen hundred." She was still staring at the camera while Connor stared at her.

He was happy, like someone had given him a gift. "You can. It isn't about the money. Think of it as a partial refund on the exorbitant rent you paid for the cottage, if you like."

Her fingertips traced the ridges in the lens.

"Obviously you could afford it yourself, but be honest—you wouldn't have gone out to buy it. Think of it as a sign from the Universe that you should start taking photos again." He beamed at her.

She kissed his cheek in thanks.

"Which reminds me, you do not have to pay rent. It feels strange now that we're . . . *involved.*" He gave her a rakish wink to match.

She gave him a serious look. "Uhhh, *no* to the free cottage. Thank you, but . . . no. That would feel really wrong to me."

When he protested, she agreed to a reduction in the price to match other comparable rentals.

"Now come on, we're boarding." He was a little put out as he helped her onto Kilian's small vessel, *The Starship*.

Beth sat at the front of the boat, getting acquainted with the camera, changing settings and snapping pictures of the harbour as they went. Connor had gone below deck to change into his wet suit.

"You've done wonders for him, ya know?" Kilian yelled over the roar of the engine as he steered. His mop of brown curls swirled wildly around his head with the wind. "I've never seen him this happy."

"Since his mother?" Beth yelled back.

"Since ever."

Wow. She was pleased and somehow terrified.

He studied her face. "He's good for you too, isn't he? You're much changed since that first night at the pub."

She looked at him. "I guess so." It was as simple as that.

Connor emerged just then. She grabbed a picture of him flashing a smile and a thumbs-up in his dark blue wet suit.

They stopped a few minutes later in one of Fungie's known play zones. With no sign of the dolphin, Connor jumped into the Atlantic. His pale skin turned bright red as the cold water hit him. He blew a whistle at his neck.

"Is that a dolphin whistle?" she asked him, still looking through the lens of her camera.

He scrunched his eyes together as he looked up at her from the water. "I don't know if it's what trainers use. Picked it up when I was a kid. It's what I've always used to call him if he wasn't around."

Just then something to Connor's left caught her eye. It was moving fast.

She pointed. "Is this him?"

"I don't know; I can't see him yet." He hadn't finished speaking when Fungie jumped out of the water right over his head.

The dolphin swam back around to face him, his mouth, open squeaking at Connor animatedly. "Hi, buddy!" He stroked his head. Suddenly Beth didn't need to imagine what Connor must have looked like as a boy. With Fungie he was ten years old again.

Beth looked through the lens and took several pictures. No two creatures had ever been happier to see each other.

"Watch this." Connor took his hand and treaded water in a circle. Fungie followed his hand.

Connor got him to flip in the air right by the boat, splashing Beth. She'd had just enough time to shield the camera.

"Fancy a swim?" He grinned up at her.

The dark water unnerved her a degree. Water had always scared her. She'd become an avid swimmer because she'd hated that shaky feeling she always got. The rippling, distorted view from beneath the surface made her feel like an elephant was sitting on her chest. As a child, she found the emotion was so overpowering that she'd felt certain she could imagine what it was like to drown. She'd long since conquered her fear, but contemplating a dive into the ocean always took her back for an instant.

Connor's red skin took her thoughts in another direction altogether. "Isn't it freezing?"

"Awww, now don't be a city gurl." His accent was thicker in the water. "It's only freezin' to let you know that you're alive."

Her expression dropped as she heard Mags speak through him.

He was alarmed at how quickly her smile faded. "I'm only coddin'. You don't have to get in."

She recovered, taking her cue from the Universe, "No, no. I'll try it," she told him. Her brain was filled to the brim with his comment. She wondered if Mags could see her, could whisper into Connor's ear. Disappearing below deck to change into the suit he'd brought for her, she went through the motions in some altered state. She was topside a few minutes later.

She climbed onto the boat ladder that brought her closer to the water. "I can hear you, Mags," she said under her breath as she twisted her body and let go of the rail to dive head first into the cold Atlantic water.

It felt like a thousand needles pricking her through the suit. "Oh, geez . . . it's cooold!"

"Swim a little, get your blood movin'," Connor suggested.

She did and got her teeth to stop chattering. Connor brought Fungie over to her. She reached out to stroke his head, tracing the arrow pattern on his melon. He opened his mouth and squeaked at her.

"He approves." Connor came up from behind to hug her.

Something about the gorgeous wild animal made her feel dauntless. Adrenaline pumped through her veins as she moved away from Connor. "I want to try that circle motion you did with your hand." She extended her arm, placing her palm to Fungie's nose and moved in a circle. He followed her. She was beyond excited.

She swam a little farther out, wanting to get him to flip like Connor had done, but she didn't want him so close to the boat that he might hit it. He'd probably done it thousands of times before, but she didn't want to be the cause of his getting hurt regardless.

She mimicked Connor's arm gesture and Fungie flipped his body twice in the air. She clapped her hands in appreciation. Feeling empowered, she made up a hand movement and watched as he jumped out of the water in three consecutive arcs.

Connor motioned to her to come back. "Watch out; he's getting really playful, Luv."

She started to swim back, her legs kicking behind her. Just then she felt Fungie's nose at her feet. Instinctively, she brought her legs together and straightened them. Fungie propelled her forward at record speed, lifting her out of the water. She extended her arms to the side like she was flying and giggled like a little girl.

She'd always, *always* wanted to do that. Fungie's last push lifted her completely out of the water. She brought her arms around to her head, diving back in like the dolphin had done. She landed a couple of feet from Connor, still giggling as her head reemerged from the water.

She'd never in her life felt that kind of joy.

"You OK?" Connor reached for her.

Her only response was to keep giggling.

"It took me years to be able to do that with him," he admitted, impressed. "How'd you know to do that when he came up behind you?"

"I love dolphins," she finally managed, trying to stop laughing. "I've been to *a lot* of marine parks and dolphin shows." She could only keep the laughter at bay for so long; her giggles bubbled up again. "And I've *always* wanted to do that."

He was still shocked that she'd been able to sync with Fungie so soon after meeting him. "But you've never gone swimming with dolphins before?"

She shook her head. "Another thing I've always wanted to do, but never got around to doing." She reached for him, locking her arms around his neck and kissing him quickly. He tasted like the ocean. "Ahh, that was amazing!" She let him go to stare at Fungie behind her.

"Thank you." She hugged the dolphin. He moved his head up and down, giving her a sort of side Eskimo kiss. "Thank you, Mags," she whispered so only Fungie could hear.

They stayed in the water for another half an hour, playing like a pair of little kids with their dolphin. They cheered for Fungie as he played alongside the boat, flipping and twisting as they made their way back to shore.

Beth's face hurt from smiling. She talked like a ten-year-old the entire drive back. Connor mostly listened, a huge grin plastered on his face. He loved that she had enjoyed Fungie so thoroughly.

Their buoyancy faltered as they reached the cottage. They were suddenly aware that they wouldn't be spending the night together or seeing each other the following day. He hugged her tightly and kissed her fiercely before he left.

Chapter 18: Kait, Kil, & Shaun

The morning flew by on her laptop. It had gone largely ignored since her arrival in Ireland, but now there were online tutorials to go through for her camera and post-editing software she'd always wanted to try.

She walked around the lake, framing small flowers in the viewfinder, and mastering the light settings. Photography had taken her back, like an old flame welcoming her home.

It was nearly seven by the time her brain registered the light fading from the sky. Her stomach growled, angry that she'd gone the entire day without eating. She packed the camera in its bag and headed for her rental car. It was time for more exploring.

She was eager to speak to more locals and make new friends. O'Leary's Pub seemed like a good place to start. It was like the camera had reignited her need to be social and hear people's stories. That was what a picture was, after all. A story.

Apparently, Thursday nights were very busy at O'Leary's. The wave of sound hit her as soon as she cracked the door open. Every table was taken. She looked over at the bar. There was an empty stool next to two twenty-something guys dressed in head-to-toe preppy douchebag chic. Tourists, no doubt.

The one facing the door wore a pink shirt; it was probably called salmon. His hair was shaggy brown and unwashed, like a frat boy who couldn't be bothered to take a shower between all-night ragers. He was holding two fingers up to form a V at his face, forcing his tongue between them in a crude gesture. It only took a second for her to recognize him as the boy who'd wanted to "slip it to her." Ugh.

His bloodshot eyes caught hers just then. Dropping his hand, he licked his lips suggestively. Beth was overcome by an urge to kick him in the nads. She had nearly resolved to leave when a mop of curly brown hair and a handsome face intercepted her.

"Well hallo!" Kilian was suddenly there, bringing her into a bear hug.

She stepped back and looked at him. He was almost as gorgeous as Connor, with his chocolate eyes and full lips.

Relieved to see a familiar face, she smiled up at him. "Hey, Kilian!"

He led her to the table he was sharing with a thirty-something couple holding hands. "Elizabeth Lara, this is Shaun Morgan and his fiancée, Kaitlin Massey. Elizabeth is stayin' at Rhia's old place."

"Yes, I know. Very pleased to meet you, Elizabeth." Shaun extended a hand. "And eh, sorry for the mix-up there.

It was rather unusual for Connor to be home like that," he said timidly.

Shaun had a kindly face, not handsome like Kilian or Connor, but nice enough. He was a tad chubby and had straight brown hair.

"Nice to meet you as well." She smiled at him, trying to put him at ease. "It all worked out." She waved off the incident like it was nothing.

"Hi Elizabeth, I'm Kait." They shook hands. Kait was pretty. Her long, curly hair was reddish and slightly frizzy. Her freckles made her look like an attractive grown-up Annie.

"Elizabeth. Hmmm. . . ." Kilian sat opposite her, holding his chin and thinking. "No. That's just too long. What do your friends call you?"

"Beth."

"You don't *feel* like a Beth to me. Got anything else?"

"My great-aunt used to call me Lizzie, but I'd rather she remained the only one," she said, trying to play along.

He turned to Shaun and Kait. "Guys, what do we think?"

"Lisbeth?" Kait offered.

"Liz?" Kilian tried. "You could be a Liz. It's very sexy and powerful. Like Kil." He squinted, a clumsy attempt at bedroom eyes.

"You can call me Liz," she agreed, laughing. "What's your last name, *Kil*?"

"O'Grady."

"Well, thanks again for taking us out to see Fungie on your boat, Kilian O'Grady."

"You are most welcome, Liz." He moved in closer to her, conspiratorially. "But it isn't my boat."

She leaned in too. "Well, then whose boat is it?"

"Connor's." He shrugged. "He bought it so he could go see Fungie whenever he wanted. When I moved back from Dublin after failing with my latest band, he offered it to me so I could get in on the tourists. It's my day job while I regroup, write some music, and find a new sound. I gig here and there, like that other night." Kil looked down at his glass. "He's a good mate. Always tryin' to help out wherever he can."

"Oh, so that's your story. You're out there trying to make music full-time. Niice." She nodded appreciatively.

He was down on himself. "Hardly. It's a rough road."

She waited until he looked up at her. "But Kil, you're out there, trying to make it happen. It's brave and bold and badass." She gave him a big smile and nodded. She'd always admired anyone who went after their dreams. Crazy and big and beautiful dreams.

He perked up. "I guess it is a little, isn't it?" And just like that, Kilian started to regain his swagger.

Kaitlin and Shaun had been listening intently, especially Kait.

"Connor took you to see Fungie?" She was shocked.

Beth looked over at them. Even Shaun was taken aback. She nodded.

Kaitlin was all admiration. "Wow! You've landed the whale! I've never even seen him with anyone—well, except for, you know, the odd picture in the tabloids. An actress here, a supermodel there, but you never see him with anyone more than once." She looked over at the boys for confirmation. They raised their eyebrows in unison, the men had never thought about it, but supposed her to be right.

Tabloids? Supermodels? She remembered seeing his face on the rag in the chocolate shop. Her stomach dropped twice, once at the idea of him dating supermodels and once at the thought of her *landing* him. It bothered her. She didn't want anyone to think she was trying to take him off the market. She was a realist. And a commitment-phobe.

Everyone was looking to her for a response. She thought of Julia Roberts in *Pretty Woman*. What she wanted to say was, "Well I'm not trying to land him; I'm just using him for sex." She almost laughed at the idea of saying that to Kaitlin, but she was still an outsider. She didn't want to offend and it wouldn't have been true.

It had gone beyond the physical. Instead she said, "We're spending time together." Quickly followed by, "Did you guys order already? I'm starving!"

It was a fun night. They ate, they drank, they told stories, and she took pictures. She looked through the images on her computer the next day. A lot of them were blurry because they spent so much time laughing. As the night went on, Beth felt more and more herself with her new friends.

Although she was new to them, the feeling she'd come away with was familiar. It felt very much like the group of Irish kids she'd befriended in France all those years ago.

They'd invited her out to dinner again. Tonight's exploration would take her to a group dance of some kind. She wasn't really clear on the details. Kait and Kil were pretty far gone by the time they'd tried to explain it.

She grabbed Fozzie Bear and sat down on the couch to read Mags' next letter. Letter five came in a plain white envelope. It was much thicker than the others. She opened it to find a large Post-it.

Lizzie,

You are a very creative person. You always were. How do you think you're able to win all the time? You think outside the box. Here is my personal prescription for you.

Lizzie's Rx for a Happy Life:
Step 1: Color
Step 2: Create
Step 3: Drink
Step 4: Dance
Step 5: Love

Love You,
Mags

Okay. Apparently, it was that easy. Beth didn't know what to think about the Post-it. It was attached to another envelope. Inside were several photographs.

There were pictures of her sticking her tongue out at the camera at a dance recital when she was six. They'd danced to "Under the Sea" from *The Little Mermaid.* Piano recital photographs where she'd insisted on teasing her hair like a mad scientist when playing Mozart.

Pictures of science projects where she'd determined which Madonna song was best to dance to for an ideal heart rate. The teacher had laughed at the idea. She'd gotten her revenge by making it to the California State Science Fair.

Pictures that Beth had taken with her first camera. Some were landscapes, and others were abstracts with butterflies and painted light.

Pictures of crazy Halloween costumes she'd made with her friends in junior high when they'd gone as the Spice Girls, which wouldn't have been very interesting, except she was the only girl in the group and her guy friends had been very straight. It had taken some convincing, but when it was all over they'd been the talk of the eighth grade.

She laughed. Whether it had been Mags' influence or her own sensibilities, she'd definitely spent most of her life coloring outside the lines. She wasn't sure she really understood this particular message, but she had a sneaking suspicion she was on the right track with her photography. And with that, she went outside to play with her camera.

Chapter 19: Gangnam Style

Friday nights in Dingle meant the appearance of several food trucks along the harbour where the vendors had set up for the festival. Beth met Kait, Kil, and Shaun in front of a Moroccan truck at eight. They bought crêpes from the French truck, named Escar-to-Go, and several meat dishes from the English truck, Brits on Wheels.

They walked past most of the long picnic tables nearest the trucks where a younger crowd had gathered, including the shaggy-haired frat boy and his friend from the night before. There were more of them now, all hitting on a group of scantily clad girls. They were in fine form, humping the air and making the gestures to match, clearly drunk and high on something. The girls exchanged disgusted looks and tried to ignore them.

Beth's group found a round table by the water near a single street lamp. The waves crashed on the rocks, blocking out most of the noise from the other locals and tourists who'd flocked to the trucks.

Kait turned to Beth, her gossip face on and ready. "So did you represent any celebrities in Cali-fornia?"

Oh no. She wanted dirt. "A few."

Kait lowered her voice, like it would just be between the girls. "Which ones?" Her eyes glittered with mischief or possibly with the soft light of the street lamp. Or both.

"I can't talk about it, Kait. Sorry."

She looked like someone had stolen her piece of cake, but then she recovered enthusiastically. "Well, tell us about some of your more *mental* clients, then." Kait wrapped her tongue around the word "mental" like it was something delicious to eat.

Beth glanced at the guys; they seemed interested in her answer, so she relented.

"Everyone can get a little crazy in a divorce, but there are a few that stand out." She tapped her finger to her lips. "Let's see . . . I once had a couple fight over a two-hundred-dollar blender even though they were both millionaires."

Shaun let out a low chuckle. "Whaaa. . . ? Was it made of gold or somethin'?"

"No, she bought it on a day where everything was going really well. She'd gotten a promotion, her best friend was moving into town, she got all the green lights on her way home . . . you know, that sort of thing.

"It was her one perfect day and the blender reminded her of it. And all *he* could think about was the annoying noise it made when she made her smoothies at six a.m., every single day. She refused to give it up. He wanted it just to take away some of her happiness as punishment for sleeping with his

250

best friend—even though he had a flight attendant on the side for years."

Kilian shook his head. "Eejits!"

They were all into it now. Shaun prodded her. "And? Who won?"

"I represented the wife. I got them to agree to sell it and split the proceeds, which of course meant nothing when they were splitting up ten million. What he *didn't* know is that they sold it to me for one dollar and I just gave it back to her when the final papers were signed."

Kait erupted in a giggle. Shaun slapped the table with a, "Ha!"

Kilian gave her a devilish smile of approval. "Brilliant." It reminded her of Connor.

The dance was held in an old town hall off the harbour.

"Will someone please explain how this is supposed to work?" Beth asked, tired of not understanding what they were going to and what she was supposed to do once they got there.

"OK, the band will play traditional jigs and you can just jump around with your partner. Like you did that night at O'Leary's," Kait responded.

"You were there?"

She smiled, "Oh, yes." Her face transformed into the same look the other locals had given Beth on that first night at the pub.

Of course.

Kait continued, "They'll alternate jigs with music played by the DJ. The DJ will play anything and everything, including group dances like the Macarena or Gangnam Style or there could be line dancing. He'll mix it up, too, playing current songs and stuff from any decade."

"And this happens every Friday?"

"No, about once every three months. It's just a night when we get to dance to any song you can think of. It can be a big mess of music that doesn't work at all and no one dances to or the best mix of songs you'll ever hear. Bit of a toss-up."

Beth looked around at the large space. There were tables along the sides and a stage at the front. There were older people and teenagers. People in jeans, like the group she was with, and people who had dressed up. At Kait's instruction she had worn jeans, boots, and a form-fitting tank top. Kait was dressed the same.

She fingered the Celtic cross at her neck, missing Connor. He'd sent her a text on the new Irish cell he'd given her. She'd enjoyed not being tethered to a phone and wasn't thrilled to be presented with another one, but so far only he had the number. The text had informed her that he might be able to make it back by tomorrow.

"Seems like everybody comes out for this," Beth observed.

Kait followed her eyes around the room. "Yeah, everybody is right. That's the judge over there." She pointed towards a happy-looking woman in her sixties. Beth recognized her as one of her co-judges on the dessert panel. "And that there is the head of the Garda." She nodded to a large, but mostly round man at the same table.

"The whole community comes together. Just watch out for the tourists; they come in from Cork and sometimes even Dublin. They can be as thick as a cow's arse. If any of them bother you, just tell them to bite the back of your bollox," Kait commanded.

They grabbed shots at the makeshift bar set up by the entrance as the music began. She watched as the band played a jig and people rose from their seats whooping and hollering.

The shaggy-haired tourist came up behind Shaun and Kilian, clapping them on the shoulders like they were old buddies. From the look on their faces, they weren't. They shook him off. He was already plastered. "Hey, lads! How's the talent?" His eyes roamed up and down Beth's body. "Oh, not bad, I see. *Definitely* worth a poke."

Kilian moved to stand beside her. "Easy now, she's taken." He put an arm around her shoulders. From far away it looked like a protective gesture. Like he was protecting her from the tourist. What he was really doing was applying pressure to her arms, keeping her from moving closer to the guy who thought it was OK to tell women they were *worth a poke.*

Beth gritted her teeth, straining against Kilian.

"We'll see." The guy gave her a creepy wink and walked off with the equally obnoxious group of young men he'd come in with.

Beth stared daggers at his back. "Friend of yours?"

Kilian released her. "No, never seen him before. Clearly part of the tourist set. They get piss drunk beforehand and then usually have to be thrown out for this or that." He was very Zen about the whole thing. "He's not worth it." She didn't bother mentioning the incident from the week before.

"Ignore them!" The music was making Kait bounce. Her features were playful. "Come on!"

Beth watched as Shaun took Kait out to the dance floor.

"What d'ya think, Liz? Shall we give it a go?" Kilian extended a hand.

She took it. They walked to the edge of the floor, waiting for a space to clear, and then threw themselves straight into the beat like they were jumping rope and only had one chance at it.

Kaitlin had been right: it was the strangest mix of music she'd ever heard. Two jigs were followed by Lady Gaga's "Bad Romance," followed by the Electric Slide, followed by more traditional music and then into a group hustle. They went back to the bar often. Liquor seemed to be the key to going with the bizarre flow of music.

When "Gangnam Style" came on, there was a general cry of excitement. Apparently, it was a favorite. Beth hadn't even known "Gangnam Style" could become a group dance. She and Kilian were in one of the back lines. From what she could tell, it just required performing six or seven of the moves from the video in sequence. It was one of the only music videos she'd seen in the last several years.

She was sure she looked ridiculous, but so did everyone else. The people towards the front were mostly teenagers and had every move down cold. Like they practiced in their bedrooms. The older adults just sat on the sidelines and laughed.

One move required her to square her feet and thrust her pelvis backwards and forwards. By the third time around, she thought she'd gotten the hang of it. That was when she felt someone grab her from behind.

"What the. . . ?" She turned as the man continued to paw at her hips.

It happened quickly. Kilian shoved the shaggy-haired tourist off of her, but the asshole grabbed her arm as he went, pulling her forward. She grabbed him by the shoulders and kneed him in the balls, forcing him to release her. She'd had lots of practice putting jerks in their place and this guy was half the size of others she'd taken on.

He crumpled to the floor, hands coverings his privates as he winced in pain. And then Connor was there advancing on the kid as he lay on the floor.

The music stopped. She didn't have space in her brain to register that Connor was suddenly there in front of her. He looked murderous. All the darkness rushed back and swallowed his features.

Beth got between them, stopping Connor from going any further. Kilian and Shaun held his arms.

"Crazy bitch!" the guy yelled, stumbling to his feet and lunging at her. She wasn't sure what he had hoped to accomplish with the sloppy advance, but she reacted instinctively, grabbing his wrist and twisting. In one lithe movement she flipped him on his back.

He hit the ground, hard. The entire town looked on as he squirmed on the floor.

Elizabeth heard Mona's voice from somewhere behind her, chatting up her friends in a low whisper. "That's Elizabeth from Cali-fornia. She knows all sorts of martial arts and things. We should take a class, gurls!"

The boy continued to writhe. He was full of venom. "You can't do that!" He didn't quite reach a yell because the wind had been knocked out of him. His beady eyes darted from Beth to Connor and back again.

She felt sorry for him. He was clearly addicted to something. Whatever baggage he carried through life, it was eating him alive. In her experience, even spoiled rich douchebags had their reasons for being awful.

Connor turned to the table Kait had pointed to earlier. "Judge? Garda?" His voice was strained. She could hear everything he was holding back.

"Self-defense. Completely justified," the judge declared, waving a dismissive hand. She was used to the fracas the thick tourists brought with them. "Show the maggot out," she said with some pleasure, smiling at Beth.

They made eye contact and the judge nodded appreciatively. She was pleased to see a woman finally stepping up.

Several burly-looking men dragged the creep off the floor. His tourist friends followed, looking beet red. Some even hid their faces as several people had taken their cell phones out to snap pictures.

A few people clapped as they left and several whistled at Beth. The music started again. Kilian took her hand, kissing it with his signature wink. "Liz." He clapped Connor on the shoulder and walked off to say hello to some of the musicians taking a break at the bar.

The look on Connor's face was some combination of admiration, anger, desire, and concern. "I would ask you if you are OK, but I think you're probably a right spell better than me." His face relaxed a degree, the corners of his mouth turning up.

The urge to hug him was strong, but the sea of eyes on them kept her rooted in place. "How are you here? I thought you'd be back tomorrow, at the earliest." She hoped her expression held the correct amount of pleasure and decorum for the situation.

He wasn't hampered by the same concerns. Reaching for her, he curved one arm around her waist, drawing her in to him, and spoke at her ear. "I missed you." He kissed her cheek. "I wanted to surprise you. Kilian told me you were coming out with them." He took her hand, leading her off the floor.

Once he'd cleared them of the dancers, he spun around to face her. With an ominous look and a strained voice, he instructed, "Wait right here," before turning on his heel to go outside.

He maneuvered around a woman with shoulder-length black hair and an older gentleman in a suit to get to the door. Elizabeth didn't notice when the woman whirled around to stare at her.

Connor didn't return right away.

Elizabeth ventured over to the bar for a cocktail. She was annoyed Connor had just left. Looking around, she tried to find Kilian. Kait and Shaun were still on the floor having a ball. With no sign of either Kil or Connor, she'd made up her mind to ask Kait if she could borrow Shaun for a jig at the next opportunity.

She wasn't going to stay on the sidelines waiting; even Mona was out on the dance floor, moving with impressive agility in her pink dress and pinned curls. Impatient for the song to end, she ventured to the bathroom near the back of the hall. When she emerged a few minutes later, she found Connor searching for her.

Elizabeth didn't need to say anything. As they walked towards each other, he could see that she wasn't pleased with him.

She was about to ask where he'd disappeared to when she caught the remnants of that black energy. He was trying to hide it.

He fixed his eyes on her, visibly lightening. "Sorry, Luv. I'm back." He kissed her briefly. She was less than enthusiastic. "That was something else. Remind me not to cross you." He ran his fingers through his hair, trying to ease the tension.

She shrugged, still thinking about where he'd gone. "I've spent time in some of the sketchiest neighborhoods in the country. You should see San Francisco's Tenderloin District. Or parts of New Haven."

The music changed, taking her thoughts with it. "Be prepared or learn to regret it," she said absently, wanting to get back out there.

"Forget the gossip column; you'll be lucky if you don't make the front page." He leaned down, obstructing her view of the floor, trying to make amends with an apologetic expression. When that did little to wipe the frown from her face, he captured her lips in one feral movement and wrapped his arms around her. The embrace had the intended effect. He had her attention.

It was a raw kiss. Wild. Full of tension and something else . . . gratitude?

Their public display smoldered. Many eyes turned to watch the famous Connor Bannon kiss the unknown, gutsy American. Beth was aware of their small audience. Some vague thought about impropriety flew into her brain and back out again.

Chapter 20: A Lady?

"What do you think, Lara? The green éclairs or the green tartes?"

Beth looked at the colorful display case. The glass case held a mountain of green pastries and treats of all shapes and sizes.

Almost a week and a half had passed since the dance. With all the planning and anticipation, the day before St. Patrick's Day was a busy time in the village.

The town was abuzz with excitement. She didn't know if it was the promise of a good time, the prospect of liquor flowing like water, or something else entirely. The spirit of the Irish. The knowledge that everyone in the world could, for one day, be Irish with them.

People vibrated at some higher frequency. They were all riding some magic radio wave. Beth half-expected to run into a leprechaun by the time the festivities were over.

"Why do we have to play favorites?" She smiled up at Connor. "Let's invite both the éclairs *and* the tartes to the party." The lightness in her voice gave rise to a roguish half-smile on his face. He had a special soft spot for her enjoyment of good food, especially sugary confections. She transformed into a light-hearted soul with every bite. It pleased him to no end.

He laced his fingers through hers and turned to the round woman with puffy red cheeks behind the counter. "We'll take the small Guinness cakes, the éclairs, the tartes au citron, the Luck o' the Irish Brownies, and some of those biscuits," he said, pointing to a tray of shamrock cookies with a thick fluffy frosting. Green, of course.

"Three dozen of each, please. And could you have them delivered up to the house at around four tomorrow?"

The woman's answering smile reminded Beth of Mrs. Claus. "Yes, of course, Mr. Connor, sir."

He winked. "Thanks, Ida. You're a peach."

Ida gave him a girlish giggle.

That was a lot of sugar. "How many people did you say you invited?" Beth asked.

He shrugged, showing no emotion. "Ten."

She tried to remember all of the friends he'd mentioned. There would be many familiar faces, like Kil, Kait, and Shaun, but there were several new people she'd never met. "And how many have told you they're coming?"

He kept the same expression on his face. "Ten."

She raised an eyebrow. "Perfect turnout. I guess you're a good draw, then."

"Eh." He carried on in that same absent way. "They probably just want to see the castle. I'm not exactly known for throwing parties."

262

"That's surprising. It's such a big space." Her thoughts trailed off to the large "house" he called home.

Connor continued explaining something. His indifference morphed into something more bashful; his features transformed as he admitted something to her. Lost in a memory, she could no longer hear the gorgeous man standing next to her in the pastry shop.

They'd been inseparable for the last week and a half. Since the night of the dance. Afterwards, they'd gone back to his house. She remembered.

He'd just finished giving her a tour of the first floor. They'd explored the grand lounge, which was so opulent it reminded her of the Great Lounge at The Ahwahnee Hotel in Yosemite. They'd visited the kitchens, two more parlor areas, a music room, and the gym. He'd saved the solarium for last.

Its tall leaded windows were at least twenty feet high, an oversized triangular bay window. A little light spilled in from the outside, but not enough for her to clearly make out the contents of the room. He maneuvered her into place in front of the centerpiece of glass.

She felt his lips at her ear. "Wait here for just one second, Luv." He kissed her cheek before leaving the room.

She heard one door close and then another. She looked out the windows. The darkness cloaked whatever was out there. She squinted to find the faint outlines of trees and then she imagined she could see something moving.

All at once, the scene before her came to life. There was a long rectangular pool lit from beneath the water. It was an electric blue. The tall trees that framed the area were covered in elegant white lights. There was a gazebo off to the right. No, a grotto. The ancient pillars and old stone were gently lit by a magical blue light. She couldn't tell where it was coming from.

And then there was Connor. Standing next to the pool. Beaming. The beautiful display couldn't compare to him. Her insides melted all over again. No one had the right to look that gorgeous. He took her breath away.

He walked off. Presumably to rejoin her. She stood there gazing out. It was like Disneyland. A fairytale. It was hard not to feel overwhelmed.

Back in the solarium, he stood a few feet away. "Do you like it?"

She didn't turn. The word came involuntarily. "Spectacular." It was a whisper.

There was nothing else she could say. None of it felt real; it was all too heartbreakingly beautiful to comment on.

He moved to stand behind her. She felt his fingertips run down her bare arms, sending a shiver up her spine. Slowly, he moved one hand down to her hip to find the hem of her tank top. He lifted it one degree at a time until his hand was gliding across her stomach.

He stopped there, drawing light circles with his thumb. The other hand followed. He held her against him, both hands splayed against her stomach.

Beth's mouth watered as his hands started to move in opposite directions. One came up to the area beneath her bra, moving his index finger along the line where her breast met her abdomen. And then he moved underneath the wire. The other hand had undone her jeans and was inching its way downward.

"Do you know how beautiful you are?" he whispered at her neck.

And then both hands possessed her. He grabbed her breast and sent two fingers to explore her at the same time. He was intense. Rough. It had felt like a continuation of their raw kiss from earlier at the dance.

Her head fell back against his shoulder as he continued his feral assault on her. Her body pulsed with desire. Throbbed with the intensity he was bathing her in.

His voice was wild. "Do you know how *mental* I felt when that—that *fuckhole* grabbed you?" His fingers increased their pressure. Everywhere.

A moan escaped her chest. She wanted him to take her completely. She surrendered to her senses as he pulled her clothes off in the same wild manner.

Now naked, her skin glowed from the fairytale lights. Even his eyes possessed her as they roamed over her body.

Removing his clothing in record speed, he moved her to stand behind the tufted couch set opposite the solarium windows. She heard the wrapper. With one hand at her shoulder and the other at her hip he bent her over, shoving her down in one movement.

But he didn't take her. He moved his hands down her back, over her hips and back up to her breasts. She thought she would pass out—sensory overload. Her need had never been greater.

Her hair spilled over one shoulder. Looking behind her at him, she found his eyes. They burned with a desire that matched her own. She mouthed a single word: "Please." She held his gaze.

And then he was inside her. Filling her to the brim. Her mouth fell open. There was nothing gradual about his possession. He flexed his hips, going further and further. His hands bit into her hips, using them to bind her to him.

The feeling was exquisite. She surrendered to him. Fell further and further down into some higher plane of existence. With each thrust, their bodies and souls melded together. The pounding rhythm threatened to unhinge her completely. Her screams reverberated off the ancient walls. The paintings bore witness to her ecstasy.

"Lara. Eh . . . Lara. Beth!" She felt someone squeeze her hand. "Hello? Earth to Lara." Connor waved a hand in front of her eyes. She was back in the pastry shop. The blood rose to her face as she realized the memory had sent her to some other dimension. Her lips turned up involuntarily.

It was a shy smile. The kind Elizabeth no longer thought she had in her. "Sorry."

His knowing grin was all mischief. He could guess. The hunger appeared in his eyes before the words had escaped his lips. "Where did you go?"

"Nowhere. It's nothing. Really. What were you saying?"

He narrowed his eyes. "Uh-huh. I was saying I have to go to the offie around the corner to confirm their delivery time for tomorrow."

"Offie?"

"Liquor store. So do you want to pick up your pictures and meet me in ten minutes?"

"Oh. That sounds fine." She was grateful to have some time away from him. Give her a chance to regain her composure. If she kept looking so red, he'd keep asking her to tell him what she was thinking. The way he always did when she blushed, which had happened more often in the last ten days than in the previous three decades.

He kissed her quickly before heading out. She thought she heard Ida let out a girlish giggle behind them.

The pictures varied wildly, from sunsets over the Atlantic to friends holding up pints at the pub. There were pictures of Connor walking ahead of her on one of his favorite paths through the woods surrounding Lough Rhiannon. They'd spent time walking together under the sun and through the shade. To the grove of oak trees he used to lie beneath when he wanted to look at the stars. To his favorite climbing trees. He'd even shared the route from Rhia's treasure map with her.

She was familiar with every shot, of course, having spent much of her free time learning to use all the latest photography software, but she found she still needed prints. Still needed the images to be brought into tangible form.

She flipped through the pictures. Remembering. There was a snapshot of Connor taking a bite of the two-week-old enchiladas he'd made for her during the hibernation, as they'd come to call it. His eyes were closed, his mouth contorted in disgust. He thought they were awful. She didn't get a chance to see if he was right.

They had many lazy days at the cottage, going from the kitchen to the bed, and back again. They watched TV on the new flat screen he had installed. Going from the movie channels to the sports channels. Taking turns explaining rugby and gymnastics to each other.

They'd spent time at the castle as well, watching movies in the state-of-the-art theatre on the second floor. *The Godfather*, *The Breakfast Club*, and *Far and Away* all made an appearance. She'd insisted on watching *Far and Away* because secretly she'd always wanted to watch it in Ireland.

The John Williams score boomed through Connor's thirty-seat theatre. He loved how much pleasure she took in the little things. She'd shake her head, a look of pure disbelieving delight as her favorite Williams melodies filled the speakers and shot through her body. He couldn't take his eyes off of her.

She came upon a black and white photograph she'd processed through one of her new favorite editing programs. Connor was in bed, shirtless. His ripped model physique looked photoshopped. A white sheet came up just below the cut of his hips. One arm was bent behind him to support his head. The other lay at his side, the Celtic cross tattoo on full display.

He had been sleeping. She wanted to take the picture with his eyes closed, but at the last second he opened them and the resulting look was primal. A second later he'd seized her by the waist in one lithe movement, throwing her down on the bed.

They'd grown together in that short time, existing in their own bubble. A bubble full of comfort and glamour, lust and purity. She'd shown him the pictures that came with letter five. There was adoration and curiosity and love in his expression as he caught a glimpse into her formative years. Beth had taken note of the first two, but didn't recognize the third.

He'd responded to her gesture by taking her up the spiral staircase next to the kitchen nook. She'd gone up there, but hadn't spent time in the empty space, which spanned the length of the first floor and shared the top part of the glass wall overlooking the lake. She didn't think there was anything to see.

"What are we doing? There's nothing up here." She turned towards the windows. "Although the view is amazing."

"You'll see." He walked over to the far wall.

The big, open wood floor invited her to dance. She did a few practice turns and ended with a pirouette, using the lake as a spot. How quickly it all came rushing back; the moves were written in her muscle memory.

Connor pried open a floorboard against the wall. The snap of the wood piece clattered to the floor, bringing her attention back to him.

He reached down and extracted something. It was a blue tin box about a foot long. He set it down in front of him and then sat on the floor next to it. She joined him.

His breathing had changed. He moved his hand to open it and then stopped, letting his hand fall back to his lap. Pain registered in his eyes.

She was on high alert.

The air was still, full of raw emotion. She could feel him building towards something. Running towards a precipice. Some unknown demon he had to slay. She watched as his masculine shoulders transformed into those of a little boy, rising and falling rapidly. He hunched over.

She put a hand on his knee. He responded to her touch, looking at her with a sadness so pure, it felt like she'd been stabbed. His eyes watered, turning his cool blues into shimmering sapphires.

Slowly, he reached out to open it again, lifting the lid to reveal a box filled with small treasures—the items from his treasure hunt—and photographs. A young woman carried a newborn in her arms. Her smile dazzled. The woman from the statue. Rhia.

A boy of around ten in a rugby uniform held a trophy over his head triumphantly.

A boy of seven gave the camera a joyous grin as his mother wrapped an arm around his shoulders and kissed him on the cheek.

It was this last photo that broke him. The sobs tore from his chest like a violent storm that threatened to drown him. Beth reached for him just as he collapsed into her. She held him as the storm threw him into the riptide. She rocked him as he rode a wave, until finally he could swim to shore.

They lay together on the floor. No words passed between them, but relief and gratitude radiated from their bodies. She was grateful the Universe had brought her to that moment so she could be there to save the gorgeous man and beautiful soul lying next to her. He was grateful the Universe had finally brought him his *síorghrá*.

He'd explained later that he had renovated the cottage from top to bottom, leaving nothing of the life he'd shared with his mother behind, save the box he'd buried in the floor filled with the memories he cherished most. The ones he'd been unable to relive since his mother's passing.

She looked at the clock on the wall of the photo lab; it had been almost ten minutes. She quickly went through the remaining photographs in the envelope, remembering all the nights they had shared. They always stayed at the cottage, even if they'd spent the day at the castle. Connor continually tried his best to get her to stay with him there, but she refused.

Their bubble felt too much like a dream and she knew that sooner or later she'd have to wake up to reality. Always returning to her bed at the cottage was the only lifeline she had to the real world as she drifted deeper and deeper into Fantasyland.

She thanked Derek, the printer behind the counter, and stepped out into the fresh air. All at once a shiver ran down her spine. A feeling of alarm, of intuition. She felt like she was being watched. Beverly's Irish Treasures stood across the street. For a second, Beth thought she caught a glimpse of a ragged mop of dark hair behind the crystals and dragons in the display.

Just then a familiar voice broke through her thoughts. "Elizabeth, dear! How are ya?" Mona launched into a bone-crushing hug. "I'm so glad about you and Connor." She smiled and then turned somber. "Now don't go believin' everything you read. The people who work at the papers are a conniving lot; pack of maggots they can be." She was forceful, willing Elizabeth to believe her.

"You mustn't let it get to you. Don't worry about what they say. You're good for him." She nodded wisely and then bustled up the street, waving behind her as she went.

Mona could be like a tornado. Always going somewhere. Eager to talk, but sometimes when you met her on the street she'd leave you wondering where exactly the tornado had dropped your house. This was one of those times. Elizabeth watched the little woman go, puzzled by what she'd said. What fresh line of gossip had she inspired now?

Beth shook her head and walked back down the street to meet Connor. She passed the newsstand on her way, glimpsing something from the corner of her eye that made her stop in her tracks.

A photo of her standing over the creepy tourist as he lay flat on his back made her mouth fall open. A second tabloid showed she and Connor wrapped in a passionate embrace in the corner of the hall. A third rag held a picture of the tourist being dragged out, his friends in tow, hiding their faces. Every photograph was from that night.

The only attention Elizabeth ever enjoyed was the kind that came by way of a major accomplishment, or for the things she wasn't expected to do, like drink a group of frat boys under the table. Her stomach dropped as she read the headlines: *Audacious American and her Assets Snag Irish Noble* and *Don't Mess With Her: Elizabeth Lara, Ready to Be a Lady?*

The bold print made her stomach churn. She bought a copy of each and quickly tore through the pages.

It was a lot of fluff. She was allegedly an L.A.-based lawyer who was in Ireland to get over her divorce when she ensnared the gorgeous Bannon. She'd brought the creepy tourist, whose name was allegedly Stephen, to his knees and then Connor and his friend, *Kyle*, had taken him down.

They followed the account by summarizing Connor's status in the press. Apparently he was known throughout the UK and Europe as a playboy who changed women as often as he changed clothes. There was talk of supermodels, and actresses, and business women . . . and even a princess. Kait's words came back to her. She knew which bits about her were true, but she wondered how much of the Connor summary could be true. The account confirmed what he'd said about not leading women on, not going on many second dates . . . ugh. The whole affair zapped her of her buoyant mood.

Her brain was racing, filled with anger and confusion. The sinking sensation felt a little like showing up for a test she didn't know existed, had never studied for, and didn't know the answers to.

The lies made her feel better and worse at the same time. It helped that it was rubbish, but it pissed her off that they'd published it.

The articles that ran opposite the cover story mentioned politicians who'd been cloned and discussed the secret love children of celebrities who'd cheated on their celebrity spouses with other celebrities.

She relaxed a little. Clearly none of the tabloids were *The New York Times*. Still, it made her feel sick. Like their bubble had been exposed to a needle.

"Hey, Luv, we're all set." Connor appeared, kissing her cheek and wrapping an arm around her waist. "Whatcha got there?" He looked down at what she was reading.

Words failed her.

Alarm crept into his expression and then his eyes hooded over. When she still didn't respond, he took the papers, closing them to reveal the covers one at a time.

He looked at her then, fear in his eyes. He hadn't warned her about this part. Fear turned into resignation, his expression sad. Like he'd just lost something precious.

His voice was gentle. "It isn't a big deal, Lara." He'd called her Miss Lara so often in jest, it had become a term of endearment, until finally he just called her Lara. He took her hand, squeezing it reassuringly, willing her to be OK.

Why wasn't he angry? "You don't look surprised."

He shrugged helplessly. "I've had to put up with this drivel before. It doesn't happen all that often, but I have made the papers throughout Europe for this or that over the years. It's always a pack of lies. Chalk it up to a slow news day. If I have a business lunch with a woman, we're suddenly an item." He tried to laugh it off and then stopped abruptly when her feverish look didn't fade.

"I'm a small fish, really. Tiny, in fact. I'm not one of those poor sods who gets followed around everywhere, a stream of paps in tow. There's never anything to tell so they mostly put me on the cover for my pretty face." His joking bravado tried and failed to have an effect.

"But it isn't *your* face on the cover," she spat angrily. She knew it wasn't his fault, but he should have warned her. It was a whole lot more than she had bargained for. How could he think it was funny?

She did a quick mental analysis of all the international attorneys she knew well, forming a plan to wade through the rights of the press in Europe and any remedies available for printing lies.

Connor saw the change immediately, recognizing the old energy, the one he'd encountered on that first day. Although, on that day the raw power of the legal shark had been diluted by exhaustion and grief.

This version of his Lara was darker, more potent. He was taken aback. He dropped her hand and stepped away; she was literally expelling him from her personal space as the law took over.

She felt him move away and looked up. He looked confused and something else . . . intimidated? Scared? She shook her head, trying to let the anger pass through her, the poison drain out.

She didn't notice when Connor's features changed from fear to an iron resolve. He wouldn't let her push him away. Determination and love colored his expression. Beth couldn't appreciate either as she closed her eyes, seeing only red. She took a deep breath. And then another. Until finally the law seeped out.

She hadn't been harmed by the stories. At worst, the papers had colored her as a heartbroken temptress who could beat people up. She was sure her opponents had thought worse after she'd annihilated them in court or at the negotiation table.

One last breath. She opened her eyes, able to see the green again. A chill ran up her spine as she realized how quickly it had all come rushing back. How it had consumed her so completely, obliterated everything she'd come to like about herself . . . *again*.

Connor spoke then. "I'm sorry. I should have said something. But," he hesitated, "it honestly didn't even cross my mind."

She was calm now. "What else do you have to deal with?" She needed to know what she'd gotten into.

"Just what I've mentioned before about people wanting things. There's the occasional obsessive who fancies herself in love with me even though I show no interest whatsoever. The papers. The expectations."

He sighed, running his fingers through his hair. "I'm not the feckin' Prince of Wales, but I didn't grow up expecting to inherit all of this either, so it feels a bit much for me sometimes as well."

He looped his fingers into the front pocket of her jeans, pulling her in to him bit by bit. "Bear with me, Luv. It's strange for me too. Don't shut off." He buried his face in her hair.

She hugged him back. There was no way to tell what she'd gotten herself into. A romance with Connor couldn't just be a romance with Connor. There were levels that didn't exist in normal relationships. She hadn't considered the effect on her life. Considered what falling for him would mean.

What else came with the territory? She tightened her arms around him, feeling uneasy.

Chapter 21: St. Patrick's Day

Their little setup, which was actually rather extravagant, looked odd in the grand lounge. Practically puny, next to the *twenty* or so couches and tables with as many areas for socializing, under the *three* old-world chandeliers and enclosed by the *two* human-sized fireplaces on either side of the long rectangular room.

"Will that be all, Connor, Miss?" Declan had been delighted to set out the catered food, treats, and bar area.

"Yes, thank you, Declan. It's almost five; our guests should be arriving soon. Go out to the pub or wherever you plan to wet your shamrock. *Lá fhéile Pádraig sona dhuit!*" He extended a hand cheerfully.

"And to you, Connor, sir!" Declan shook Connor's hand with a proud smile and left them to their party.

They had food from O'Leary's and another pub, The Shamrock, delivered. It was set out on two long tables so that their guests could help themselves. They had stew, Guinness-battered fish, salads, burgers, soda bread, three different types of fries, and grilled chicken with a Guinness sauce, all set on serving trays. It was enough to feed fifty.

The dessert area was equally impressive—when you didn't take the opulence of the grand lounge into consideration. When all was said and done, they'd purchased nearly two hundred treats, all covered in green.

The requisite St. Patrick's drinking area was a portable bar, with Guinness and three other locally-brewed beers on tap. Several whiskies and other choices lined the table next to it.

Beth sat down on one of the large tufted couches nearest Connor's smorgasbord.

"That is *a lot* of food." She nodded slowly, wondering how they could possibly consume it all. She turned towards the bar. "And even more liquor."

She crossed her arms. Looking down, she wondered whether or not she should have gone with something more loose-fitting instead of the tight green tank top and blue skinny jeans she'd worn.

The tall black boots she'd taken off earlier were on the floor next to her. She reached for them, extending her leg like she was putting on a pair of stockings. She'd only meant to stretch her legs out, but Connor had noticed the gesture.

His eyes hooded over. His stride was all masculine power. It was a walk she'd come to recognize as his "you've just made me so hungry I'm going to devour you" walk. His muscles constricted, on full display under the tight green shirt that showed half of his Celtic cross tattoo.

His jeans hugged him in all the right places. He looked effortlessly beautiful. Her mouth watered. The energy in the room changed in an instant; it was thick with delicious tension.

He reached her then, pulling her across his lap and positioning her knees on either side of his hips. His arms wrapped around her waist, crushing her to him. He slid down so his neck rested on the top portion of the couch and grabbed her face with both hands.

Their lips tangled in a dance of quick hungry pecks and long moan-inducing kisses.

She placed her hands on his forearms, just beneath his elbows, and then pushed down so he would release her. They were both panting.

"We cannot do this right now. People will be here any minute." She tried to reach the rational part of her brain, but her body wanted to surrender. His lips turned up into a smile; he could read the thoughts as they crossed her face.

He seized her around the waist before she had the chance to cool down and threw her down on the couch, resting his weight on top of her, kissing her even more fervently.

"You're right." He pulled away as quickly as he'd thrown her onto her back.

"What? No, no, come here." She reached for him.

"No, no, Luv." He took her hand and kissed her palm. "I won't be able to stop." He moved off of her, sitting back on his knees. "Eh . . . I'm going to go to the cellar where it's . . . *cool*. I'll bring some more whiskey up. OK?"

He didn't wait for a response. He got up and almost sprinted away, before he changed his mind, leaving her to steady her breathing on the big leather couch.

His decision to go to the cellar didn't help steady her. The last time they'd been in the large, cool room with the dark stone walls, he'd shown her his expansive collection. She'd walked around on her own taking notice of the dusty old bottles under the ancient arches and the cobwebbed corners; it had felt like the Pirates of the Caribbean ride at Disneyland and Mr. Darcy's Pemberley all in one.

Her stomach had tightened then as the fantasy hit her with renewed force, causing her brain to fog over and her body to ache for him.

Connor had sensed the change in her energy almost immediately. He'd stalked her from behind as she continued to look, but not see the bottles around her. Her walk slowed and her breathing shallowed. She could feel his eyes devour her from behind. She knew he was giving her *that* look. The one that said, *I crave your body*.

They'd turned towards each other at the same time. He'd placed his hands underneath her dress and fondled her backside before picking her up and taking her to a stainless-steel table near the entrance of the cellar. She had been glad he'd been as eager to get to the point as she had. He quickly dropped his pants and pushed his fingers through her delicate lace panties, taking her hard and fast.

Beth shook her head, forcing her thoughts back into the grand lounge, trying not to think about the rest. They just couldn't keep their hands off of each other. She was grateful her shot had been scheduled for the week before she'd left for Ireland. Taking a few deep breaths, she sat up and then walked to a window. She threw it open and let the coolness wash over her.

A few minutes later Connor returned with a crate of bottles and a wooden box. From the look on his face, the cellar hadn't done much to cool him off either.

Just then the doorbell rang. Five clear bells chimed. She'd never heard it before. He extended a hand to her from across the room, beckoning her to come with him. "Our guests are here." He smiled.

"*Your* guests," she corrected. She crossed the distance, taking his hand.

"*Our*," he persisted, kissing her quickly and leading her down the hall out to the foyer and finally to the gargantuan front doors.

They were a party of ten, including Beth and Connor. Two guests, a couple named John and Emily, had sent their regrets at the last minute owing to John's inebriation the night before. That left Kilian, Kait, Shaun, Bram, Bree, Rowe, Mollie, and Fintan.

There were "*Lá 'le Pádraig sona dhuit!*" greetings all around. It sounded like *lah leh PAH-drig SUN-uh gwitch* to Beth's ears.

"Elizabeth Lara, meet my mates from Dublin. Rowe and Mollie Watson," he indicated the blond couple to her right, "and Fintan Malloney." He motioned to an attractive man with light brown hair that came to his shoulders. He could have been a model.

Apparently, gorgeous men traveled in packs. Between Connor, Kilian, Bram, and Fintan it was a smorgasbord of a different kind.

She shook hands with Rowe, Mollie hugged her warmly, and Fintan kissed her hand.

"Lovely to meet you, Elizabeth." His lips lingered on her skin, and his voice was silky smooth. He looked up at her, giving her *actual* bedroom eyes.

"All right, all right, enough of that!" Connor reclaimed her hand the way he had when Kilian had done the same thing at the harbour. "Jaysus, I never thought so many of my best mates would be trying to sleep with my woman!" He threw up his hands in jest.

They all laughed, except Beth, who turned a Ferrari red.

Bram turned their attention to the matter at hand. "Ban, let's eat, eh? I'd ate—"

Beth cut him off, wanting to guess at the phrase she'd heard so often. "The arse off of a baby elephant?!" she finished, pointing at him with an *am I right?* expression.

"No, Luv," he said calmly, gravely, and then he broke, "I'd ate an oul wan's arse through a blackthorn bush!" He threw his head back and howled.

She'd have to remember that one. Although she hadn't been able to recognize the majority of words escaping from his mouth. Just when she thought she was getting a handle on Irish sayings. . . .

They settled into the grand lounge, piling their plates with food and filling their pint glasses with Guinness.

"Everyone, may I please have your attention." Connor moved to stand between the sitting area and the food so he could be seen by everyone. "Thank you for coming out to celebrate with Beth and myself." He looked to the couch where she was sitting with Bree and Kilian. "I'm grateful to have all my favorite people gathered together." He raised his glass. "*Sláinte!*"

"*Sláinte!*" they all agreed. The men made it sound more like a battle cry than a toast.

Beth had a feeling her first St. Patrick's Day in Ireland would be something to remember.

Connor continued, "And lads, it's a marathon, not a sprint. We've got all night to consume this feast."

Fintan came up to stand on Connor's right, clapping him on the shoulder. "Thanks for having us! *Finally.*"

Bree chimed in. "Seriously, Connor. You've been *a little* ridiculous." She gave him a very pointed look.

"Here! Here!" Bram and Rowe said together.

For a moment, Beth was uneasy. Did they mean he'd neglected all of them to spend time with her? She was suddenly self-conscious.

"What do you mean?" Beth asked Fintan.

Fin looked over at Connor without hiding his surprise. Connor looked down, looking a little guilty.

Oh God. What did they mean? Her stomach dropped suddenly. Should she be concerned? What were they talking about?

Fin looked back at Beth. "Connor doesn't invite people here. I've never seen Castle Bannon; I don't think Rowe and Mollie have either."

Bree nodded. "Bram and I came here as children a couple of times with our parents, but we haven't been since."

Weren't they all his closest friends?

"Same," Kait confirmed.

Beth looked at Connor, the question in her eyes.

He explained. "Yeah, I don't entertain here." He looked down into his glass. "Ever. Kilian's been here a few times and so has Shaun on business, but otherwise. . . ." He pressed his lips together and shrugged.

She could see behind his tight expression. It was because of his father. He may have changed the place from top to bottom when he took over, but it had still felt tainted somehow. Like a lingering poison.

He held her gaze. His eyes softened and his expression lightened as he read the understanding in her face. She smiled kindly and his features transformed into an earnest smile. Mischief danced in his eyes, like he knew something she didn't. "Until now." He looked back to their guests. "How about a quick tour of the first floor?" he asked them.

They all nodded eagerly, placing their food down and standing to follow Connor.

He turned to Elizabeth. "Lara, luv, will you take them?"

She flushed as he put her on the spot. Smiling tightly, she said, "Why don't you lead us?"

"Because I have had too much of the black." He had to go to the bathroom.

His true intentions were clear to her. He wanted her to feel at home here. Feel like the hostess.

By eight they were well on their way, having made a dent in the buffet and the bar.

Beth sat with Mollie and Bree on one of the larger couches. They were digging in to the desserts.

Beth let her head fall back. "Oh my God." She was eating a tarte au citron. The green food coloring tinted her lips a shade. "This is *divine.*" She didn't notice Bree giving her an appreciative smile.

Mollie agreed. "Have you tried the Luck o' the Irish Brownies?"

Beth picked up the inch-thick brownie drizzled in green frosting. After taking one bite, she couldn't speak. It was chocolaty with mint and Bailey's. She just groaned. It sounded like she was in pain.

Connor looked over at her quickly, alarmed. Then shook his head as he realized it was just another one of her food orgasms.

Mollie noticed Connor's reaction. She wrapped a finger around a long blonde strand. "You know, I've never seen him like this. And we've all been friends since Cambridge." She turned to Bree.

Beth stopped eating. Now on high alert. They were going to do that thing that girlfriends often did. They were going to analyze the relationship.

But she wasn't ready. Wasn't ready to think about the reality of the situation. All of their obstacles. He might appear to be open, welcoming her into his life, but she was wary. The realist in her was never far away.

Kait came to sit with them, sensing something sensational was happening.

Bree's eyes widened. She leaned in to them, hugging her arms and resting them on her knees. Her solid green tank dress hugged all of her curves. The position of her arms pushed her boobs up higher.

Her fire red curls fell forward over one shoulder. She lowered her voice conspiratorially. "Oh yeah, he's got it *bad*. I've never seen him go on more than one or two dates with anyone. Watch out, Beth, when someone like him falls . . . it's forever."

Her mouth went dry. The romantic in her was flying. The realist in her felt like she'd just recklessly flung herself off of a cliff without a parachute. *But it could never work.*

How had she gotten here?

And then Mollie dug in. "So are you stayin' in Ireland, then?"

Connor's head snapped towards them from across the room. His view of Elizabeth was blocked by Kait. The women had formed a tight circle.

Kait shielded her from the question. "Don't be nosy, Mollie, making her answer such questions. . . ." She shook her head reproachfully and then asked, "What will you do when he travels? I can't imagine he can stay in one place for very long; he's got articles and things to find for the auction houses, doesn't he? Will you go with him?"

"Don't be stupid!" Bree chimed in. "She's not just going to drop everything and follow him around the world. She's got a career, a life for Christ's sake. Maybe he should be the one to stay in one place for *her*! Or maybe they could go back to Cali-fornia." She caught Beth's free-falling expression. "Oh, sorry, Luv! I can't imagine it's been easy to think of such things."

It hadn't been easy. That's precisely why she hadn't done it. There was nothing beyond tomorrow with Connor. She couldn't think about it; she didn't want to think about it. To think about the loss of him. She'd chosen a state more faithful than denial—the perpetual present. The future simply didn't exist.

There was so much more to her time in Ireland. The women staring at her with curious eyes had no idea how much more there was for Beth. She'd come for Mags, for herself. There were the letters and the need to find herself again. The need to reconnect.

There was nothing more important than listening to that inner voice, the one that would tell her what to do next. Where to go next. She didn't know her path yet; she just knew that Connor was a part of it today, and that had to be enough.

She regained her composure and put her talent to use, once again understanding what it was that the women were after. They wanted the inside scoop, to weigh in, to know. She'd give them something to hold on to, appear to let them in so they would leave her be.

With all the glee of a young love-stricken girl, she clasped her hands in front of her and brought her shoulders to her ears. "You know," she began, "every day has been pretty great. I can't imagine it getting better than this, but you just never know what the future holds, right, ladies?" She gave them a hopeful, girly sort of smile like she believed their future was bright. Anointed by forever.

The women nodded predictably, happy with the temperature read they'd taken of the most talked-about new couple in Ireland.

Only Bree noticed the façade.

Beth knew they meant well, but if she forced herself to think about any of it, she would probably have to excuse herself and go back to the cottage before the sun had even set. She imagined it. Crawling into bed, drawing the curtains, curling up with a container full of the desserts she would inevitably pack away for herself before quietly leaving.

She was grateful the women didn't get the chance to renew their assault, although she had a sneaking suspicion that Bree would help her if they tried. While they were sharing insights, Connor had brought out the wooden box he'd fetched from the cellar, and placed it on the coffee table at the center of the couches and armchairs where they were all congrcgated.

The men saw it first, cutting their laughter abruptly. Bram took in an audible gasp. The sound distracted the women, forcing the close of their Connor and Beth discussion.

He opened the reddish box with a brass nameplate on the cover. Inside was a single bottle of whiskey set in wine velour on sponge padding.

"No! You didn't!" She'd only heard Shaun say a few things all evening. Now he was a ten-year-old who'd just been given a week-long pass to The Wizarding World of Harry Potter.

Connor's grin was no less affected. He was right there with the rest of them, only his grin said, *that's right, I'm going to share my coveted all-access pass with you, my best mates, because that's just the kind of guy I am.*

They all crowded around the table, settling themselves on the floor.

Kilian reached for the bottle. "May I?" His voice was full of reverence.

Connor nodded, moving away from them to bring over a tray of small specialty tasting glasses.

They passed the bottle down the line so everyone could get a good look. Beth was stumped by their reaction. Clearly this was a special whiskey.

When it was her turn she examined it. There was a drawing of a castle; Gothic black lettering beneath announced Knappogue Castle Whiskey. In elegant script, the label read:

A "Very Special Reserve" of
Unblended, Pot Still, Pure Malt
36 Years of Age
Put down in 1949
Bottled in bond in 1984
Bottle No. 117 Cask No. 8
Produced exclusively for the Hon.
Mark Edwin Andrews
Knappogue Castle, Co. Clare, Ireland

The numbers were all handwritten. The rich amber color reminded her of a strong Earl Grey. She handed it to Connor.

He explained, "You see, the Honorable Mark Andrews was a great lover of Irish whiskey. He purchased several casks and privately bottled his own collection. The 1949 is the rarest of rare whiskeys. Andrews gave some bottles away to his friends, but other than that it was never available at retail.

"It's rare for a bottle to pop up at auction and it usually only happens when a relative has passed and their estate is being sold off by their heirs. The Knappogue Castle 1951 is considered the oldest, rarest and most collectible Irish whiskey available. The key word there is *available*. If the 1951 is a shooting star, the 1949 is a comet."

Kilian took over. "They are worth thousands, but the real value is that you have to find one for sale to begin with and then be in the perfect position to buy. Connor's old man inherited several. He left him three bottles. He's never opened one."

A reverent silence fell upon the circle of friends as Connor held the bottle. Elizabeth could see the darkness seep into his eyes. He was conflicted about opening it, but he had made up his mind. He looked up at her, searching her eyes for something, or perhaps he was trying to convey something. Acceptance? Surrender?

He lightened. "So let's drink my inheritance!" With that, he popped the bottle open and poured them each a dram.

It smelled like dark flowers. It tasted of vanilla, lavender, and honeysuckle. It was the smoothest whiskey Beth had ever experienced, but it finished in her mouth with a subtle burn.

They each took their time with their dram, relishing in the feel of it. The men looked like they were in heaven. Their eyes had rolled back in their sockets; they'd turned into young, lovesick boys.

As they each came out of their reverie, the general raucous excitement of St. Patrick's Day manifested with a renewed fervor.

They moved on to Jameson Rarest Vintage Reserve, another costly rare whiskey. Connor had an endless supply.

By ten they were all sailing on a magic carpet ride of good food, excellent drinks, and even better company.

"How are youuu still standin'?" Bram slurred his words and extended his index finger at Elizabeth, clutching the glass with his other digits.

Fintan narrowed his eyes, sizing her up. "Somethin' is not quite right here. You're a tiny thiiing." His eyes were glazed over. "It's not physically possssible." He turned to the others.

Bree was lying next to the couch. She stifled a laugh.

Connor, Beth, Kilian, Fintan, Bram, and Bree were all sitting or lying on the floor. Mollie, Rowe, Kait, and Shaun sat at the food table coating their stomachs. Kilian raised his head to see what they were talking about. "No, no, lads. I've seen it for myself. She can hold her liquor. I think she might be more Irish than us."

Beth was sitting cross-legged next to the coffee table, her whiskey glass in hand. Connor was lying with his head in her lap. He looked up at her. "D'ya hear that, Luv? You and Ireland are meant to be."

Her tolerance was abnormal, but she had still hedged her bets. It was her first St. Patrick's Day in Ireland, after all. She wasn't sure how hard they would all go. The men hadn't noticed her continually filling her stomach with fries and bread. Or how often she got up to go to the bathroom, after which she'd stop in the kitchen to load up on water. The formula was really fairly simple. It was just math.

She was only tipsy. The boys were plastered. Connor had slowed down earlier so he was in good shape, but he was still far enough along that he stared up at her dreamily. Like she was a goddess and he was basking in her divinity.

"Let's play a drinking game!" Kait rejoined them after having sufficiently soaked up some of the alcohol. She was now ready to forge ahead. They all came back from the buffet table, joining the group on the floor.

"Which one, Luv?" Fintan prodded.

"Never Have I Ever."

Bree rolled her eyes. "God. I haven't played that in an age! We're not young twenty-somethings anymore, Kait." She was full of judgment.

"That's why it'll be so much fun!" Kait's eyes blazed with excitement and determination. Her curly red hair was frizzy and wild. She didn't wait for anyone to agree. "I'll start." She pressed her lips together like she was blending her lipstick. "Mmmmmm . . . never have I ever. . . ," she narrowed her eyes at Bree, determined to get her back for being judgmental, "had sex in front of other people," she retaliated.

Bree sat up, narrowed her eyes at Kait, and took a drink. "Oh, it's on, Massey!" Fintan also took a drink. "Never have I ever flashed a random stranger to get into a concert."

THE IRISH COTTAGE

Kait turned red enough to match her hair. She took a drink. Shaun gave her a questioning look. "We were eighteen and it was a dare!" She hid in her glass.

"Never have I ever had seexxx with someone more than twenty years older than meee," Fin declared and then raised his glass, taking a drink.

Connor sat up and looked at Rowe. They exchanged a look. "The Master's wife?" he asked. Fin nodded proudly. "Jaysus, Rowe and I always thought there was somethin' going on, the way you were always tryin' to charm her. But mate, she was as tight as a camel's arse in a sandstorm!"

Beth looked at Kait for a translation. "She was very mean," she explained.

"Yeah, but she was gorgeous. And the mean crazies are always the wildest between the sheeets." Fin smirked like a boy who'd been caught with his hand in the cookie jar and wasn't sorry.

They were all sitting up now, enlivened by the salacious conversation.

Shaun went next. "Never have I ever had sex outside." He took a drink, looking quite proud. Everyone drank except Kilian, Beth, and Connor.

Kait went again. "Never have I ever been terrified of turning into one of my parents." She took a drink, muttering, "God, I hope I don't get her hips," just loud enough for everyone to hear.

Only Connor followed. The air changed. They all looked at him. His jaw tightened as the darkness transformed his features. Only Kait was oblivious.

Beth was especially sensitive to him; his bitterness affected her. Before she could stop herself she blurted out, "Never have I ever been abandoned by both my parents." She was the only one to drink. She kept her eyes fixed on her hands.

Connor escaped his hole so quickly it was like hellhounds had chased him out. He squeezed her hand, wanting desperately to take her pain away.

The others glimpsed her scars for a fraction of a second before she took another turn with a statement that was guaranteed to take the attention off of her. "Never have I ever faked an orgasm with my current partner."

Kait and Mollie tried to stealthily drink, shocking their significant others.

Connor grinned widely.

The statements devolved from there.

Fin posed the final one. "Never have I ever bent over in front of a mirrrorrr…and looked at my own arsehole." He took a drink. Everyone gaped at him, even the men.

"What?" He looked genuinely stunned no one else followed. "I was eight and tryin' to confirm my theory that farttsss," he stalled on the word. They all leaned forward waiting for him to finish whatever ludicrous thought he'd had. And then he did, "…are pooop bubbles," Fin stated proudly.

Connor threw a piece of bread at his head. Bree sent a fry flying.

"Gross!"

"Ewww!"

But they were all laughing.

CHAPTER 22: TRAPPED

"I can't believe everyone bowed out by one," Beth said as she placed the food trays into the restaurant-sized refrigerator in the kitchen. They'd all called cabs, except Kilian and Fintan, who had both passed out on the couches in the grand lounge.

Connor came up beside her to deposit the leftover chicken. He leaned down to give her a quick kiss and then his eyes hooded over abruptly. "That suits me just fine. I want to bury myself in you."

Whoa.

"Stay here with me," he pleaded.

Her insides pulled; the warmth spread through her body. She shook her head in spite of the spell he'd just cast. No. No way. The cottage was her tether, her lifeline to reality. If she stayed, she would get lost in Fantasyland.

"Arrgggh, you are exasperating, you know that?" he said.

Beth shrugged innocently.

"Well, go on, then," he heaved. "I'll finish this, check on Kil and Fin, and be over in two shakes."

She reached up on her tippy toes and kissed him sweetly before grabbing her bag and heading for the door.

The March breeze blew around her as she walked, penetrating her jacket and jeans. The curved path leading up to the estate ended in the trees. The lake lay just beyond the woods.

Lough Rhiannon stopped her in her tracks. The magic of it hit her all at once; its beauty almost hurt. The moon was full; it cut the lake in half, like the sun setting on the ocean. The silver orb seemed bigger in Ireland, brighter. She looked towards the sky, bathing in the moonlight.

The breeze turned into a mild wind, lifting the leaves that had fallen in October, but had not yet been crushed by the elements. They rattled behind her.

Her scalp prickled. A shiver ran down her spine. She stared into the darkness, through the trees. For a moment the silver orb still appeared before her eyes, blinding her. One of the lights from the castle flickered. And then another. For a split second she thought she could make out movement.

She shook her head. Connor was probably right behind her. The night was making her paranoid. Still, she started walking to the cottage more deliberately, abandoning her leisurely stroll.

She unlocked the French doors, closing them behind her. Her fingers paused on the lock for a moment. Connor was right behind her; she let them fall from the bolt and reached for the curtains, drawing them closed.

She flung her purse onto the large couch and flipped on the lights, unzipping her shoes as she went. The package she had received earlier was waiting for her where she had left it on the small table outside her bedroom door. She had an overwhelming desire to open it and slip on the slinky nightgown as she waited for Connor, wanting to shock him as he came through the door. It was a delicious thought.

They'd been itching to get away all night, stealing touches here and there when they thought no one was looking. At one point they tried to sneak off upstairs before their friends had pulled them back so that Connor could help Kilian and Bram remember the name of the well-endowed girl they'd all liked when they were twelve. He had rolled his eyes and dragged Beth back with him.

She cut the box open with a knife and unwrapped the garment, moving the elegant red tissue aside. Her fingers caressed the smooth green satin, hooking her fingers in the thin straps to hold it up. It was gorgeous. The neckline plunged, and the hem would hit high on her thigh.

She would put away the mess on the small table later; in that moment all she wanted to do was feel the silky material against her skin.

But first, a shower.

After wiggling out of her skinny jeans, she connected her iPod to the stereo in the living area, blasting some Journey. The glee rose to the surface with the music. It had been a very good day. Almost perfect.

She sang out of tune to the band's signature songs and jumped around in her underwear for a minute. Her skin tingled with excitement. She felt like anything was possible, like the Universe had aligned so she could have this feeling of being connected to all things at once. Harmony. Balance.

Moving to her bedroom, she grabbed a towel and placed it on the hook beside the shower. Her fingers grazed the handle when she thought she heard the door. Oh no. He was back. She walked out to the bedroom in her green tank top and matching underwear.

"Ahhh, I was going to surprise you!" She was disappointed; the fantasy of hitting him with the lingerie had taken root. "Happy St. Patrick's, Bannon!" she said lightly, reaching the frame of the bedroom door.

It wasn't Connor. Standing in front of the glass wall was a thin man with dark eyes. His blue long-sleeved shirt was popped up at the collar, and his beige slacks looked dirty. Like his shaggy hair.

The boy the tabloids had called Stephen. His bloodshot eyes were blazing with an unhinged anger. He was holding a gun, pointed directly at Elizabeth's face.

CHAPTER 23: WEAPONS

Time stopped. Elizabeth froze.

His drunken loathing energy permeated the room, infecting it. Journey's upbeat songs of hope battled it, blaring through the speakers.

Her skin prickled everywhere. The adrenaline rose, heightening her senses. Holding up her hands, palms out, she said, "Let's just take a deep breath here!" The music was so loud she needed to shout.

He bared his teeth. "DON'T!" he spit at her. "Don't say anything unless you want to get your head fucking BLOWN OFF." His voice went from a yell to a deep boom that cut through the music.

His eyes searched the room wildly, taking in his surroundings for the first time. She did the same. Quickly, she calculated the distance between them. Fifteen feet. His entire body was vibrating, causing the gun in his right hand to shake.

How quickly could he adapt in his current state if she flung herself back into the bedroom and closed the door behind her? No. He would just shoot the lock; there would be no way out from there. She'd be trapped.

His eyes scrunched together like he was in physical pain. Was he? She scanned his body, looking for a physical weakness. Anything that could give her a clear picture of what she was up against. Nothing in her training had prepared her for this. There was no defense against a gun, especially at this range.

She thought she could make out a bruise on his neck, beneath the popped collar. He was also holding his left arm close to his body like he'd sustained an injury to his torso on that side.

"It wasn't enough, was it?" It was almost a cry. "Wasn't enough to humiliate me?!"

He moved to wipe his nose on the back of the hand holding the gun. She had to do something and this might be her only chance. Her body tensed, ready to spring towards the kitchen where she could get to the knives and get cover behind the counter.

He noticed, quickly moving the gun back into place, shaking violently as he did so. "Don't you *even try it you fucking bitch*!"

His chest heaved with the force of the scream. "You WILL listen!"

A ray of hope filled her body; maybe he wanted to talk. Maybe he just wanted to be heard, as was so often the case. It was lesson number one in negotiations.

She focused on relaxing her body, changing her energy from adrenaline-ridden cornered animal to Zen garden. If she could just make him feel safe. Make him believe she would listen to whatever he had to say without trying anything. Let him have his release so that he wouldn't feel the need to use the gun.

"Do you know how much *shite* I went through after that night? My fucking friends wanted nothin' to do with me. People posted photos of your assault on me everywhere—I was a laughing stock. All because of you and your tight cunt." He tried to control every word now, which made him feel more dangerous.

"But that wasn't enough for you, was it? Do you know who I am? My da is a very important man in Cork. He bows to no one, but then you ball-busting American princess come along and send your feckin' *flaith* boyfriend to fuck with me and my family?!" His trigger finger twitched; he was building himself up. What was he talking about? She needed to say something, bring him down before it was too late.

"Stephen?" She hesitated. "That's your name, right?" He grimaced and nodded. "I don't know what you're talking about. I didn't send Connor anywhere. Please tell me what happened; I'd like to know."

"Don't do that! Don't lie! I know you sent him—you must have! He came at us like a vengeful hound!"

She opened her mouth and shook her head, trying desperately to convey innocence. She had no idea what he was talking about and the only way to gain any ground was for him to understand that.

"I swear to God, I don't know what happened. I didn't send anyone after anyone." She didn't even know how that was possible; she and Connor had been inseparable since the dance. When could he have made the five-hour round trip to Cork?

He paused. Uncertainty crossed his face for the first time. She needed him to explain, get the poison out. And then he did. "That arsehole cunt tracked me down and told my da what happened, demanding I be punished—as if the photos and ridicule weren't enough! Just because I thought you were worth a poke—most women would have been flattered!"

Beth wasn't about to argue with the deluded man holding the gun.

"He told him he would use his power to bankrupt him if he didn't get me under control! The old man laid into me hard." He touched his ribs subconsciously with his left arm. His eyes watered. In that moment he looked like a boy in his teens, not a man in his twenties.

That didn't sound like the Connor she knew. It was so unlike him. She searched her memory. Did he have an opportunity to do this? She thought back to how he had led her off the dance floor and then quickly disappeared . . . after Stephen and his group had left. How she woke up at noon the next day, to a note on Connor's pillow telling her he'd see her that afternoon. She'd thought he'd just gone to have a shower at his house. He was back by two. And then she remembered the darkness. How scared he always was of becoming like his father. Using his power to strike out at others. . . .

She looked back at Stephen. He was broken. He'd probably learned to be a douchebag from his father. If his injuries were any indication, he'd probably been beaten before. He needed help. "Stephen, I am so sorry. I had no idea he had gone and done that. I agree the photos and the humiliation went far enough. Revenge is never a good idea. I'm sorry for your pain."

She imbued honesty into every word. It was all true. She never believed in revenge even when at her most lethal. She annihilated people in the courtroom, but she never acted in retaliation or revenge. It was a lower position to take. Irrational, even. Especially since it was so much easier to win from the high ground.

His eyes found a renewed fire at the word "revenge," turning crazed again. He put the gun to his own temple.

"Stephen, NO!" She raised her hands in his direction. "This isn't the way. Please…just put the gun down and we can talk." Her voice was still raised, trying to rise above the music.

His eyes darted down, up, to the side, and back again. She could tell he was crossing over into a state of mind where reason wouldn't reach him. Her eyes took in the items within arm's reach. Was there anything she could use to knock the gun out of his hand? Anything to stun him long enough for her to close the gap and wrestle it away from him herself?

And then she saw the glint of her pocketknife laying on the table, barely visible beneath the crumbled red tissue.

The mess she would clean up later. . . . If she could only distract him long enough to get her fingers on it.

Just then the door opened quietly. With the music blaring, Stephen hadn't heard it. Connor's eyes fixed on Stephen, taking a few silent steps towards him from behind. She needed to do something. Give him enough time to close the distance without Stephen hearing the approach. If he turned now, he could shoot Connor at point-blank range. There was no way he could survive a wound like that. He was still six feet away.

Stephen's eyes stabilized, a new clarity forming in them. It scared her more than any of his actions had done before. She knew she only had seconds left. "You're wrong. Revenge is the only thing I have left." He took the gun from his temple and pointed it at her again, hand completely steady. "I've got nothing left to lose. My parents disowned me. I don't have any friends left. Girls think I'm a pervert."

Beth thought about the way his eyes had roamed over her body. She had a weapon she hadn't used yet. She was standing there only in a tight tank top that showed off her boobs and a skimpy pair of underwear. Connor was now five feet away.

Beth kept her eyes squarely on Stephen and then deliberately changed her gaze. "I don't think you're a pervert," she said silkily. Lowering her voice just enough so it still cut through the music. She hugged her arms under her breasts, popping them further out of her bra, then looked down at them and back at him suggestively. She could see his features transform. It was working.

While his mouth went slack and he continued to stare at her breasts, she dropped her left arm, careful to keep his eyes fixed on her cleavage. Her left hand found the edge of the knife on top of the table; she closed her fingers around the blade and brought it to her side and then just behind her back. Her right hand had lightly traced the tops of her breasts at the same time, keeping his eyes on her.

The pocket knife wasn't weighted properly; she needed to get closer if she was going to hit him in the only place she knew of—the only place that was guaranteed to prevent the gun from accidentally going off—without killing him. She'd only practiced on dummies and that was a long time ago. But she knew that her life and maybe even Connor's depended on her hitting her target.

She took one step towards him. He hesitated, but his eyes remained on her breasts. She needed to keep going. She could probably do it from where she was standing, but if she could just gain five more feet on him, her odds would increase exponentially. Connor had frozen, trying to guess her game. He was still five feet away, trying to analyze how to tackle him without setting off the gun. It was now aimed at her heart as Stephen's focus had shifted.

The playlist stopped abruptly. It had reached the end. The last line of Journey's "Don't Stop Believin'" punctuated the air. Her first thought was that Connor wouldn't be able to get any closer without Stephen hearing. It was up to her.

"Do you want to play, Stephen?" Now that the music had stopped, she could use her sultry voice. She sounded nothing like herself; she was an actress playing a part. She was there now, ten feet away. Involuntarily, he moved closer to her, lowering the gun so it was pointed at her abdomen.

It happened all at once. Connor saw his opportunity and took a step towards Stephen. Stephen woke from the spell Beth had cast and whirled on Connor, turning the gun on him. And then she seized her one shot.

She brought the knife out from behind her back, switching it to her right hand, focusing on Stephen's wrist, just north of the center. She extended her arm and followed through with her hips, pivoting. The knife sunk into his wrist, severing the median nerve and tendons.

A bloodcurdling scream filled the room. Stephen's hand seized. The gun dropped to the floor. Connor lunged for him, pinning him to the ground and kicking the gun towards Beth. She bent down to grab it.

Stephen was writhing in pain. Connor kept his arms firmly behind his back, knife and all, his face against the floor. Elizabeth ran to the phone to call the authorities. Five minutes later, the Garda was there in full force with an ambulance.

CHAPTER 24: UNDER THE FULL MOON

It was two-thirty in the morning by the time the uniforms had cleared out. They'd already taken their statements, but Connor insisted on leaving with them to make sure Stephen was processed properly.

Beth caught hold of his hand just as he'd reached the front door. Waves of anger were rolling off of his body. He hadn't looked at her once, except to make sure that she was all right directly after the attack. He couldn't face her. He hesitated, pulling away.

She stroked his hand, drawing circles with her thumb, soothing him. Slowly he turned towards her. The anger in his eyes had been replaced by agony. She knew his face well enough to recognize the thoughts as they crossed his mind.

Rage at Stephen for nearly killing her, hatred for the father that had given him a vengeful side, self-loathing for his having given in to that side of himself, and finally agony at the thought of almost losing her. And it would have been his fault.

She hadn't stopped him to say it was all right. She didn't know if it was all right. Stephen might have gone after her without his interference, just for embarrassing him in front of the town and in the tabloids. He seemed unstable enough. There was no way to know.

Her hands found their way to his face, holding him in place so he couldn't look away from her. "No. More. Revenge." She gave each word its proper space. "I know you're angry. But this isn't the time for retaliation. That boy needs help; he needs a mental hospital, not a jail cell. We don't know what kind of abuse he endured at the hands of his father."

Connor's eyes widened. She could see the war that raged behind his eyes, between Rhia's blood and Keanan's. His anger gave rise to some basic level of understanding, of empathy. He nodded slowly and broke away from her.

Beth was exhausted. She lingered under the hot water of the shower, letting her muscles relax. The tension rose to the surface as the adrenaline left her body. She dried her hair and climbed into bed. Her body was tired, but her mind was wide awake.

Was she experiencing shock? No. The Zen-like calm felt true, not like a trick her body was playing on her. She played back the incident one step at a time. The truth was, she was happy with the way she'd handled herself, proud even. She'd been forced to use her wits and she came away from the situation unscathed. Yes. She was proud and *grateful*.

She turned to the clock: 4:00 a.m. Her body felt heavy, but she knew she wasn't going to get to sleep any time soon. She walked to the windows, throwing the curtains open. The lake was as beautiful as it had been three hours before. After throwing a thin blanket around her shoulders and grabbing a thicker fleece to lay on the grass, she headed outside.

She sat cross-legged and stared up at the moon, taking comfort in its familiarity. No matter where in the world she was or what she was going through in life, she knew she could always look up and the moon would be the same.

A deep warmth ran through her body. The blanket fell from her shoulders. She felt *good*. Like she was weathering the tide, keeping her head above water. Whatever the truth was about her parents, she could handle it. Whatever reason Mags had for lying, it was for the best. To lead her here. To this moment. This moment of clarity and self-assurance and peace. *Thank you, Mags, for guiding and protecting me.*

She smiled up at the moon, completely entranced, for an immeasurable period of time, until movement caught her eye. Connor was back. He walked confidently, with the raw power she had seen so often before, but there was something missing. The weight. It was gone.

As he drew closer she could see that he'd changed his shirt, which had been covered in Stephen's blood. But the pain had not left his face. He stopped as he reached the blanket, looking down on her, filled with regret. She didn't know what to say or do. She felt like the next move was his.

He collapsed to his knees in front of her. She knew he was putting himself at her mercy. That this was his way of apologizing. He didn't have the words. Not now. He only had this gesture. He could only surrender himself to her.

She reached out to touch his face. He closed his eyes and leaned his head into her caress. When he opened them again, all the emotions he'd felt in the last several hours condensed into one: desire. Thick and all-consuming.

The hunger set in her body as well, bringing all the excitement of the day and concentrating it low in her abdomen. The warmth spread farther south. She dropped her hand and slowly laid back on her elbows. Her chest heaved as her breathing changed, and her breasts struggled against the thin camisole. It rode up, revealing her smooth stomach.

He shifted his weight so he was now on his hands and knees, never taking his eyes off of her. Bending down to kiss her belly button, he moved his tongue lower, bringing his hands to her hips and digging his fingertips into the waistband of her pajama bottoms. She fell back against the blanket. Her skin felt overheated even though the night had turned cool.

Connor slid her bottoms and panties down, kissing as he went, until they were at her knees. He sat up and removed them completely. Coming back down to her abdomen, he kissed up to her breasts and then pulled her up so he could remove her tank top. He laid her back down carefully, sitting up to stare at her naked body.

Her skin glowed in the moonlight; she was luminous. The cool breeze felt like a hundred kisses against her bare skin, arousing her further. She'd never been naked outside.

He sat there worshiping her, devouring her with every look, until finally she sat up to undress him. She pulled his shirt off and brought him down to his boxer-briefs.

She laid back down with her arms overhead; she was now surrendering to him. Giving him permission to take her. Connor positioned himself on top of her, letting his hips bear down on her. She closed her eyes; her mouth fell open as she felt his need. He moved into her, letting her feel all of him. Slowly.

He bent down to kiss her neck, running his tongue down to her breast and taking her into his mouth. She squirmed beneath him. His fingers slid down to her sex, massaging her, making her moan into the night.

And then he slipped three fingers inside, possessing her. She opened her legs wider, inviting him in. She flexed her hips with his rhythm. Neither could wait any longer. Quickly he removed his boxers, retrieved the packet from his slacks, and positioned himself at her entrance.

Deliberately, he took her one agonizing degree at a time. She opened her legs wider, needing to feel him in the deepest parts of her body until finally he was buried in her. He supported his weight with his elbows, bringing his hands up to her face.

His fingertips lightly traced her cheeks, her eyes, her lips. He stayed there. Physically, it was as far as he could go.

His eyes bore into hers, willing her to see how much he adored her. How much he wanted her. How much he loved her.

A single tear fell from his eyes, rolling down her cheek. He closed the gap between their lips inch by inch, like he was asking for permission. Like it was their first kiss. Until finally he captured her lips with his, using his tongue to plow deeper into her mouth. A low moan escaped his chest. She moved her hips into him, and then he was moving too.

He took her hard, but not fast. Each thrust pounded into her, making her scream out, making her swear an oath to the heavens. She let him further and further in until their souls were joined under the divinity of the full moon.

They poured everything they had felt into their lovemaking. Into each thrust. Wanting desperately to melt into each other, as much as any two human beings could manage on an earthly plane.

Connor arched up, placing his hands on either side of her head to support his weight. He used his hips and his back to drive into her. She moved her hands to his back, feeling the muscles ripple just before each plunge, anticipating it, ready to scream out.

They climbed together. Bodies and souls united, crying out to the heavens as the stars looked down on them. Until finally they collapsed.

CHAPTER 25: CONFESSIONS

"Mornin', Lara," Connor whispered at her neck.

She opened her eyes; her vision was blurry. The sun poured in through the open curtains. She could tell it was already after noon. She registered Connor's body against her; he'd slept with his arms across her breasts, her back against his chest.

"Morning." She turned to face him, snuggling into his neck. He wrapped his arms around her tightly, protectively.

They hadn't spoken at all last night. They'd made love under the moon and then he'd carried her into the house where they had fallen asleep. But now it couldn't be avoided any longer. There were things to say. Things to know.

"It's time for explanations, Bannon," she said against his skin.

He sighed into her hair. "I know. Go ahead put me on the witness stand."

She brought her head up to stare into his eyes. The quickest way to the truth was to be direct, devoid of emotion. Get it out.

"Where did you disappear to after you pulled me off the dance floor that night?"

"Outside, to snag my own photo of the creep. I sent it to a private investigator I have on retainer. He worked through the night to prepare a file on him and his family."

"What happened the next morning?"

"I woke early. Seven, maybe. It was eating at me; I needed to know who this guy was and . . . and . . . how I could hurt him." He looked guiltily at her. He gulped. She didn't think she should have to ask him to continue.

"I checked my email; the file was waiting for me. His name is Stephen Devey; he's twenty-five. His father is Miles Devey. He owns a lot of property in Cork, but the file the PI emailed me also listed his investors. I know many of them directly or know the people they answer to. I'm also very well connected to the power players in Cork. Or rather, my father was."

He hesitated, but she wasn't about to make this easy. It had to come from him. Never underestimate the power of silence in any situation. "While I don't exercise whatever power I have as a flaith, I may have downplayed how much of it there is to seize if I so choose. I drove straight to Miles.

"Professionally, I threatened him with bankruptcy. Privately, I threatened to bring the scandal of his son, not to mention the scandal of his own series of mistresses, down on him so hard it would eradicate his good name and bring him to total ruin."

"How thorough." Beth's words were biting. She'd tried to remain neutral until he was finished, but it was all so ruthless.

He looked down at her, resigned to the whole of it. "I also used you. I explained who you were and, I think, correctly assumed that you would use your international law contacts to obliterate his son if he ever came near you again."

He was right, to an extent. She remembered how quickly she'd formed a plan to take on the tabloids for telling lies. "If he bothered me again, yes. But I wouldn't have gone after him in revenge." He had to understand that. It wasn't how she operated. It wasn't how anyone should operate.

He tightened his arms around her. "I know, and I'm sorry. You don't know *how* sorry. To think that my actions could have led to your getting hurt or worse—" His voice broke. The rest came out strangled. "I couldn't . . . bear it."

She rested her head on his chest, feeling it rise and fall. She thought about how much his own demons had affected him. How they were both a mess.

"Why didn't you want to obliterate him after he almost killed you?" he asked against her hair.

She was somewhere else as she answered, "In the process of trying to talk him down, I could see it. He was just a broken boy. His father kicked the crap out of him after your visit, and maybe he deserved everything he got, but he was not right last night. He needed help—you don't leave someone to die when you can try to save them."

"Even if they're pointing a gun at your head?"

"Well, priority number one is to save yourself, but once that goal is accomplished there's no reason to allow the person with the gun to die."

Connor kissed her forehead. "I suppose not."

"You've got some issues, Bannon."

He chose his words carefully. "In my defense, so far the only time I've used my position was to protect you. You bring that out in me. It's terrifying. I thought I was becoming like *him* after I did what I did in Cork, but part of me didn't care if it meant keeping you safe."

"Revenge is not a way to keep anyone safe. It comes from a place of fear and anger. You see that, right?" He had to see that; otherwise, she feared Keanan's blood would find a way to win, and then his pure Irish heart would be tainted, broken.

He released her and propped himself up on his elbow. "Yes. Believe me, I do."

"Do you?"

He wore his heart on his face, but she knew Keanan's blood was still in there.

He studied her as she studied him. "I have something else to tell you."

She was suddenly nervous.

Oh no.

What now?

"I'm leaving in two weeks." He watched her, trying to gauge her level of emotion. "To Egypt. It's a collections trip. I have a few leads on items I want for my auctions. When I make it to the African continent, I travel the region as much as possible and look for undiscovered treasures."

She could imagine it. Connor, an Irish Indiana Jones, traipsing through Africa looking for special pieces.

"It will take at least six weeks. I don't want to be away from you for that long." His fingers found hers, looking at them as he said the next part. "I know it's fast, but I don't see any other way . . . will you come with me?"

Oh. Fantasyland on another continent. The realist in her knew that it was impossible. Her inner voice was telling her it was wrong; that it wasn't her way, it was his. She was pleased that he'd asked. A fissure split her heart as she thought about the consequences, about what listening to her inner voice would mean for them. But ignoring it now would be tantamount to ignoring everything she had learned. To losing herself again, and she had just started on her path.

She didn't want him to hurt the way she was beginning to hurt. "I would just be in the way," she whispered. "It's your work. Your life. It's not my road," she said gently.

His jaw tightened, and his insides churned. He lay back against his pillow, one hand on his forehead. "Just think about it, Luv. Please." Even as he said the words he was calculating, devising his strategy. He knew what he wanted.

"I will," she lied.

She had sent Connor away on the premise that he needed to sort out his guests. Which he did. She needed some space to think. They'd made plans for dinner.

It was time to go further down her path. Time for another letter. Number six was purple.

Dearest Lizzie,

This letter is more a request on my part. I need your help. It's my unfinished business. You see, I mentioned Matthieu earlier to set up this particular letter. I told you that we came together three more times in my lifetime. What I didn't say then was that I never told him about Elsa.

He didn't know about the pregnancy because I had already moved to Spain and he to Rome. I found out later that he'd tried to track me down, but it wasn't like it is now. It was difficult to keep in touch with a nomad adventurer like me, so I never told him while Elsa was alive.

When we came together the next time, we were just so happy to have found each other again. It felt the same and new again all at once. But I was still not in a place where I could talk about her, so I said nothing.

The second time was much like the first, except we were middle-aged and more in need of each other's company than ever.

The final time we were both old and gray. I didn't know how long we would have together so I decided not to tell him. Decided not to burden him with the knowledge that he'd once had half of a precious little girl and lost her before he could know her. And I suppose I didn't want him to look at me differently for keeping it from him for forty years.

But as I am nearing the end, I know now that I was wrong. He deserved to know, even if it caused him pain. He deserved to see pictures of her and be told stories. I need you to find him and tell him for me. I've enclosed a memory card. I learned how to videotape myself (the power of YouTube)!

In the videos I explain to him what I explained to you and I tell him stories. I owe him that. I also went to a lab that digitized the few home videos I have of Elsa in Spain, and there are pictures for him too.

I know it is a lot to ask, but please do this for me, Lizzie. I trust that you will. The last I heard he was living in London; that was in 2010. He was a professor. I can't recall the name of the school, but he taught art. Remember, Matthieu Fleury. He should be about eighty-two now.

Thank you,
Mags

P.S. The next one is THAT letter. Thank you for following this mad old woman's plan for you. I love you, Lizzie.

Elizabeth turned the envelope upside down. A blue SD card fell into her palm. She placed it back inside with the letter. So Mags had unfinished business. Part of her was a little relieved. Mags was such a force of nature, so ballsy all the time, and nothing stopped her.

It was comforting to know that she was human. That she made choices and they weren't always right.

As soon as she'd read "London," her inner voice, her inner barometer had gone off. She'd always wanted to go back. It was a city so familiar to her old self that she knew it would be the best place to continue rediscovering herself and what she wanted out of life.

She had friends there, too. People she'd once been very close to, but the law had gotten in the way and she'd lost them all. It would be good for her to heal on that level.

It seemed her next stop would be London. She felt a sense of relief; she had a direction to follow, but she wasn't in a rush to leave Ireland. There was more to see, more to do, and her inner voice was telling her that she wasn't done here.

And then there was Connor. She bit the inside of her lip as something cut through her chest. Quickly, she focused on the task at hand.

She placed the letter back in the box and reached for *THAT* letter. It was a pitch black envelope, and the "7" was written in silver Sharpie. This was it. Finally. She felt like she was four years old again. Wondering where her father had gotten to and trying to will her mother to show up for her.

The envelope was light, like there was nothing inside. She tore it open; another blue SD card fell out. She reached for her laptop on the coffee table. Popping the card into the slot reader, she navigated to the only file it contained. A video. She leaned back onto the couch and pressed play.

Mags' weathered face appeared on her screen. Elizabeth's throat tightened. She didn't have any video of her. She never thought she would see her again. She clasped a hand to her mouth trying to keep her composure.

Mags fiddled with the camera and then sat back. She wore a bright red shirt. It looked like she'd had her hair done for the occasion. Her face was framed by elegant curls. "Hi, Lizzie!" She waved at the camera and then took a long, deep breath.

"Where do I start?" She rested her elbows on her knees, clasping her hands together and covering her mouth. "When you were three, your mother, Carolina, was brutally attacked on her way home from work one night. She wasn't raped, but the mugger punched her in the face. Her head hit the brick wall behind her."

She paused. "At the hospital we found out she had sustained a major head injury and that there was no way to tell how extensive the damage would be or if she would ever recover fully."

Beth didn't remember her mother being in the hospital at all.

"Something else happened in the hospital." She thought about how to say the next part. "Your mother, for reasons I will explain in a minute, had lied to her husband about her blood type. She lied and said she was B. But, Lizzie, she was A like her husband. They were both A. And you are AB."

Oh my God.

"I'm sure you understand what that means. Carolina's husband was not your father. He understood what it meant as well when the nurses approached him about giving blood and bringing in family members who were also A like her."

Mags' face became fierce, angry. "I don't care what truth comes out. When your wife, someone you claim to love, is lying in a hospital bed, unconscious, purple from all the swelling? You DO NOT do what that despicable man did." She took a breath to calm herself.

"I could have killed him. He took one look at her, one look at her chart to confirm her blood type, and left. He served her with divorce papers before she was even out of the hospital. She was in no position to fight back, and she was heartbroken. It wrecked her. That's why I moved in."

She took another breath to steady herself. "But you know, Lizzie, you're lucky. Lucky to not be genetically linked to that man. Truly. Your real father, whoever he may be, never knew you existed. I got that much from Carolina. She had broken up with the man whom she would later marry for several months. She came to visit me in Verneuil—I ended up going back in the seventies—and when she returned to the U.S. they got back together, but she was already pregnant with you. She knew he would never marry her if he found out you weren't his."

She waved a hand at the air beside her like she was saying good riddance to Beth's fake father. "I knew when I did it that it was wrong to promise Carolina that I would never tell you that he wasn't your father, but she was in such a miserable state. I thought she might die from the shame she wrongly carried on her shoulders."

"So in short, your father never abandoned you, Lizzie. The man you've always persecuted in your head, the man you've always fought against in court, he doesn't exist."

She looked straight into the camera. "I hope you can forgive me for keeping this promise. I'm sure Carolina wouldn't have wanted me to

326

keep it if she'd known how much the idea that your father had abandoned you would negatively affect your life choices. In your career and your issues with men.

"That's secret number one. Secret number two was based on another promise I made to Carolina." Nervously she bit her lip. "When Carolina got back from the hospital, she wasn't right. It was more than being heartbroken over losing that man. She wasn't as weak as you always thought her to be. She sustained some serious brain damage in the attack."

"It caused personality changes, mood swings. Anything could set her off into a screaming rant. You, my darling, got the worst of it. You kept trying to hug her, to make her better, but you couldn't and there were times when she couldn't be around you. She wasn't right in the head, do you understand?"

How could she not remember any of this? Some vague memory of her mother crumpled on the floor of her bedroom crying appeared before her eyes.

She stopped. Distress and agony colored her expression. "One day I came back from grocery shopping. I was only gone for twenty minutes. I announced I was making spaghetti for dinner. Spaghetti was your favorite back then; you'd always come running into the kitchen to hug my leg. When no one responded I went looking for you both."

Her eyes watered now. "You were in the bathtub. Carolina was over you, a hand on your chest, holding you beneath the water."

A sob escaped her chest as she relived the memory. "Your little arms were flailing all about; you kept trying to surface for air. But

Carolina, she was in some kind of trance. I grabbed her in a choke hold and threw her out of the bathroom, reaching you just as you'd stopped moving. I took you out and did CPR. After a minute you finally choked up the water. By then, Carolina had come to her senses. She was sitting outside the bathroom. Terrified."

The rippling, distorted view from beneath the surface made it feel like an elephant was sitting on her chest . . . the water . . . the dark figure above the surface . . . the pressure. The memory that had danced on the edges of her subconscious her entire life rose now, clear as day. She'd been so little, almost four. She didn't know what was happening until she found she couldn't breathe, and even then she'd never made the connection. Her mother's hand . . . her long dark hair grazing the surface. The reason she'd always felt certain she could imagine what it would be like to drown was because she *had* drowned.

Elizabeth felt ill. Like everything was underwater.

Mags breathed in and out, trying to steady her nerves. "Carolina looked like she wanted to die, but then something rose up in her. A fierceness that used to be a huge part of who she was before the attack, before her husband.

"She came into the bathroom. I was cradling you in my arms. She kissed your forehead and hugged us both. 'Auntie, I have to go. I can't be here. I have to go. Please take care of her. Tell her that I love her. Swear to me you won't tell her what happened here. Don't tell her

why I left. Tell her Momma loves her; make her understand how much I love her.'

"Sobs ripped through her body; she was determined to save you from herself. She kissed you again and then me. 'Swear to me, Magdalen.' I swore I wouldn't tell you why she left. She packed a bag and never came back to the house.

"You see, Lizzie, your mother didn't abandon you either. She saved you from herself, even though it killed her. She chose you over herself." Mags wiped the tears from her eyes.

"You were loved, mija. Very loved. I hope you will forgive me for honoring these promises. I am so sorry for hurting you. I hope the letters are helping you find your way. I love you, my Lizzie. I'll still be watching you from heaven or wherever the next adventure takes me." She gave her a tearful smile and stood up to turn off the camera.

Beth set the laptop on the coffee table and fell back against the couch. Sobs ripped through her body as she understood what it all meant. She didn't feel sick any longer. She'd never been abandoned. Her mother wasn't weak, she was strong, in spite of what had happened to her. She wouldn't risk her daughter's life again and so she chose to stay away.

Her real father didn't even know she existed. Like Matthieu and Elsa.

It was like Mags' video letter had ripped her apart and then put her back together in an order that finally made sense to her.

She reached for Fozzie Bear and hugged him to her chest. After several minutes of letting the emotions wash over her, she marched into her bedroom, opened the dresser, and found the cell she had buried. She hadn't turned it on in seven weeks and she never would again.

She walked out to the lake and flung the phone into Rhiannon. She had things to figure out. People to find. A path to divine. There was a lot of uncertainty in her future, but she did know it wouldn't include the law. No more punishing men as a way to stick it to her fake father. No more fear disguised as strength in an effort to not be weak like her mother. If she'd learned anything from last night, it was that she was strong. *Truly strong.*

She wasn't going back.

CHAPTER 26: ON THE ROAD

She didn't tell Connor about letters six and seven. It would mean admitting that she couldn't go with him, that she had her own path to follow. And she wanted to stay in Fantasyland a while longer. She wanted to enjoy their last two weeks together.

The days that followed were filled with joy and adventure. Every day he asked her to come with him. She managed to sidestep the question until three days before he was scheduled to leave.

He looked so torn that she felt compelled to tell him about the two letters. About how she had decided not to go back, about never having been abandoned, about Mags' unfinished business.

They were lying in bed. He'd remained silent as she told him everything. Finding out that she'd nearly drowned at the hands of her unwell mother had gutted him.

Hearing Mags' advice on following her inner voice made sense to him. He could see it in her eyes, that desperate desire to feel whole again, to like herself. He understood it because he had the same work ahead of him. They'd helped heal each other, but there was more to do . . . *alone.*

She deserved no less from him.

But even as she explained, as he felt the acute pain of their forthcoming separation, he devised a plan. He had work to do in the way of expelling his demons, to be a better man for her, but he knew what he wanted. He'd known it since that fateful day all those years ago. He knew that it would take some convincing—he could see what she couldn't—but he was determined.

They made the most of their remaining time. They alternated between staying in for lazy days and traveling. He'd taken her on a horse-drawn tour of Killarney National Park, his favorite restaurants in Galway and Limerick, and even an Irish dancing festival in Dublin. She'd captured it all with her camera.

Sometimes at night, she turned on her side so he couldn't see the tears fall. Sometimes at night, he watched her sleep and refined his plan.

And so the day finally came when it was time to go their separate ways.

"What will you do?" he asked. Even though he already knew the answer, he wanted to stay near her for as long as he could. He leaned against his car in front of the cottage. He was ready to drive to the airport. Declan would collect the car later.

"I'm going to take the next month and travel all across Ireland," she repeated for his benefit, nodding to herself, certain it was what her inner voice demanded of her.

"You don't need a month to do it." His voice was wistful.

"I know, but I'll take my time, take pictures, go where I feel like going, leave when I feel like leaving." She was excited by the simple freedom of her design.

"And then?"

"And then London for Mags' unfinished business. I was really happy there once, really knew who I was. I've always wanted to go back and spend some time there, and now I have an excuse."

He nodded.

A knot formed in her chest. It was time. A torrent of emotion hit her. Suddenly everything hurt. She had tried not to think about this part. She *couldn't* think about this part.

He hooked a finger through the belt loop of her jeans, bringing her closer. She pulled against him, not wanting to be drawn into his arms. It would mean the end of Fantasyland. No more gorgeous Connor. He pulled her the rest of the way, hugging her fiercely.

She could feel the tears falling down her cheeks and onto his gray shirt. He pulled away, grabbing her face between his hands. He wiped away her tears with his thumbs and kissed her with everything that he had, one last time.

"Thank you for helping to bring some color back into my life, Mr. Bannon," she whispered against his lips.

"It was a pleasure, Miss Lara." His ice blue eyes melted with emotion. He rested his forehead against hers. "Goodbye, *mo shíorghrá, chífidh mé i Londain thú*," he whispered and then released her. He opened the car door, stopping to look back. He gave her his dazzling smile, colored by something else. Like he knew something she didn't.

"What does that mean?" she asked, through her tears, letting the curiosity in so she wouldn't think about the pain.

His smile didn't falter. "I'll tell you one day." And with that he got in his car and drove away.

Her rental car was packed and ready to go on the following day. She would go south first and make her way through all the little towns. Meet whoever she was supposed to meet and take as many pictures as possible.

She went back inside one last time. Light from the evening sun spilled through the wall of windows. She closed the curtains and exited through the French doors, locking them behind her. She walked to the lake. The golden rays lit the water like they had on that very first day. Lighting it on fire. *Thank you, Mags. Thank you, Rhia.* She took one last picture of Lough Rhiannon and breathed in the special place that had brought her back to life.

Elizabeth got into the car and drove off to see the rest of Ireland, switching the GPS off as soon as she turned the key in the ignition, wondering if and when she would see Connor again.

A NOTE FROM JULES

If you enjoyed reading *The Irish Cottage,* then please leave a review. Reviews go a long way to helping a small fish like me. You have no idea the type of impact your words can make both on me personally and on the all-powerful online store algorithms that decide which authors to promote or keep visible.

Thanks in advance for helping me to stay in the game and keep writing for a living. It can be pretty scary out there sometimes, but the words you attach to *The Irish Cottage* (and the next book, *The London Flat*) are little pieces of gold.

Don't be shy—leave your thoughts and help others find me.

With my deepest gratitude and a whole lot of love, I thank you.

For information on upcoming titles, bonus content, and exclusive giveaways, join the Readers Group: www.julietgauvin.com.

Keep reading for an exclusive preview of the sequel to *The Irish Cottage*: *The London Flat. . . .*

The London Flat Preview

How was this happening?

"Yes, just there," the photographer instructed, as his assistant moved her an inch to her right. And again.

Elizabeth went reluctantly, feeling like an awkward teenager who'd missed the day on royal etiquette.

The tall, balding man in the dark suit behind the camera continued. "Make haste, Dorren."

The assistant named Dorren closed the distance between Elizabeth and the tiny woman next to her. Another Elizabeth.

Beth smiled nervously at her; Dorren's placement had brought her close enough to feel the woman's blue silk dress. The silver-haired lady smiled up at her kindly. The diamonds on her head caught the light from the elegant chandelier above.

"Lovely, we're there. On three. One . . . two. . . ." Beth turned to the camera. She held her smile, trying not to look disbelieving. "Three." The shutter clicked. "Thank you, Your Majesty."

With a wave of his hand, the photographer instructed Dorren to bring in the next group.

THREE DAYS BEFORE

"Cheers." Beth nodded to the cashier. Grabbing her strawberries with cream and picking up her shoulder bag, she moved to sit at a table in the outdoor square adjacent to the Covent Garden Market.

It was cool for mid-May in London. A rare spring.

The sun shone without the awful humidity.

She speared a strawberry and popped it into her mouth, delighting in the sweet, tangy blend of flavors. English strawberries were the best. Literally, the best.

She'd never tasted a bad strawberry in England—every single one was at least one hundred times better than any other strawberry she'd ever tasted in her life.

She opened the flap of her bag to extract the photos she'd just developed.

Digital photography had many perks—the instant gratification, the instant feedback, the freedom to play in post—but she found she still liked to hold the memories in her hands.

It had been weeks since she'd developed a new batch.

The first photo was taken at McGann's Pub in Doolin. The small band played at the front of the main room. Smiling faces looked on.

She scanned the rest of the pictures, remembering her month-long trek across Ireland. She'd gone everywhere, visiting pubs, tourist attractions, even hostels. While she no longer felt capable of enjoying a good night's sleep in a room full of bunk beds, she enjoyed dropping in during the evenings.

The most interesting people stayed in hostels. She'd met twenty-somethings from Sweden, thirty-somethings from Australia, and even forty-somethings from Belgium.

Nights were often spent around a fire pit or a dimly lit common area, everyone contributing something to drink, and someone always traveling with a guitar.

There was nothing so wonderful as firelight and the warm sounds of an acoustic guitar with new friends. Those moments always felt endless, like gifts from the Universe. No matter your age, those nights always made you feel sixteen again. The world was full of promise, and life could be anything at all. They were perfect.

Well, almost perfect. There had been one thing missing.

She resumed her examination of the stack of photos, finding one of Connor she'd had printed again. Her latest editing software provided a myriad of digital effects which she'd only just started to explore. The vintage rose-colored effect didn't print well, but Connor was beautiful.

It was a photo she found herself gravitating towards time and again: the black and white photograph of Connor in bed, shirtless. His ripped model physique looked photoshopped. A white sheet came up just below the cut of his hips. One arm was bent behind him to support his head. The other lay at his side, the Celtic cross tattoo on full display.

He had been sleeping. She'd wanted to take the picture with his eyes closed, but at the final moment he'd opened them. The resulting look was primal.

A second later he'd seized her by the waist in one lithe movement, and thrown her down onto the bed.

The memory flushed her cheeks and pulled at something inside of her. Spearing another strawberry, she placed the photographs back into her bag and took a lungful of London air.

"Elizabeth?" a deep male voice said from behind her. The British accent was thick and refined at the same time, typical of the posh London set. "*Elizabeth Lara?*"

Beth turned just as the man reached her side. She looked up into the green-gray eyes and handsome face of Wes Cartwright. His expertly coiffed dark hair came to his ears, his shoulders were broader than she remembered, and his full lips invited admiration. He belonged on a catwalk.

She was stunned to see him.

"Wes?!" She shook her head in disbelief, standing up quickly and flinging her arms around his neck. He swept her up into his arms; her feet dangled several inches above the ground.

They both laughed. She used his arms to steady herself as he set her down.

His simple white T-shirt hugged him well. "What are you doing here?" she blurted out.

He narrowed his eyes. "*Me?* I live here. This is where you last saw me, or have you forgotten?"

As she looked up into his gorgeous face, she remembered how young they'd been.

Twenty-one.

Spending the entire summer traipsing around London, the group of them. They'd been such good friends. But as was so often the case, they'd lost touch.

She tried not to think about how it was all her fault. How she'd allowed the law to wipe all of her meaningful friendships away. The fissure in her chest ached momentarily. Losing her friends was a wound she'd hoped to heal during her time in London . . . she just hadn't decided on her approach.

"Yeah, of course." She shook her head, her mouth still open in a wide smile. "I just . . . God, it's been almost fifteen years!"

"I know." His eyes searched her face and then moved down her body. "Good God, Liz! You look incredible. The years haven't just been good to you, they've preserved you in a time capsule. What have you been drinking and where can I get some?"

Her eyes mirrored his. "You're one to talk, *Mr. Runway*. You could be on a billboard somewhere."

His eyes flashed with excitement. "What are you doing here?"

Beth opened her mouth to explain, but where would she start? "I'm living here for a while." She kept it vague.

"Well, how long have you been back? And why haven't you rang?" he scolded.

She gave him an apologetic look. "A couple of weeks?" Her mouth turned up into an impish grin and then morphed into a frown. "It's . . . a long story. Just needed a change of sorts. I'd been meaning to look everyone up, but honestly," she considered her words, "I didn't know what to say since I was the one who failed to keep in touch."

His eyebrows drew together in surprise. He examined his beautiful friend. She looked embarrassed. He'd never seen her look embarrassed.

She waited for him to say something, but he just stood there, studying her. She didn't want to imagine what he saw—someone very different from the girl he'd known. He stood there trying to pinpoint the change in her; he wanted to understand.

Her back straightened. "Plus, you know, I've enjoyed rediscovering the city alone," she said, with a blasé bravado she didn't feel.

At that his expression finally shifted. He looked hurt. She remembered him well enough to know he was only acting.

"Just for a bit," she reassured him anyway.

He pursed his lips, trying to stifle a smile. She had changed, and yet she was still the same. Proud, but sensitive to the feelings of others. "Are you about done?" He shook his head, teasing her. "Or should I plan to bump into you in a fortnight?" He turned his body to leave.

She grabbed his arm to stop him. "No, no. This is good."

His features transformed into a bright smile as he sat down opposite her.

They slipped into conversation easily, each giving the other a paragraph-long synopsis of the last fifteen years.

She gave him the brief version. About law school and her career in San Francisco, Mags' death, fleeing to Ireland, coming back to London.

He'd apparently gone to graduate school to continue studying art. He'd curated a few galleries, but found that he didn't like working for other people.

Elizabeth wasn't the least bit shocked to hear it. Wes had always been a free spirit and a bit of a rebel. It was lucky for him that he was independently wealthy.

Apparently, he had been married to a Frenchwoman named Margaux in his late twenties. They'd met in Monaco and had some whirlwind romance. They'd met, married, and divorced within the span of six weeks.

It was *so* Wes.

They'd just been friends that London summer, but they were the type of friends who'd always been attracted to each other.

Always walking the line between flirtation and action. Their natural chemistry would have made it easy to fall into something more.

It was like nothing had changed.

Fifteen years gone in an instant.

They stood to hug each other goodbye.

Confirming their plans for dinner that night, he kissed her on the cheek and was off.

Enlivened by her reconnection with Wes, Beth walked back to her flat feeling twenty-one again.

For a moment she allowed herself to think about what it would be like, if they'd managed to find each other after all this time and do what they hadn't done all those years ago.

She fingered something absently at her neck, feeling the grooves of her tiny Celtic cross pendant.

Her symbol for Connor.

They hadn't spoken since that day outside the cottage when she'd chosen to listen to her inner voice instead of going with him. She'd felt the fissure in her chest rip open, but held firm because she *had* to. To follow him in spite of what she knew to be true would have been tantamount to spitting on the lessons it had taken her a decade to learn.

They'd planned to keep their distance while she traveled in Ireland and he in Africa.

Communication would be spotty at best while he was in the region, anyway. And she'd wanted desperately to live only in the moment without checking messages or connecting with anyone who wasn't directly in her path.

It had been very liberating, but she still felt it. The loss of him.

It surprised her how much she'd felt his absence at times. How he'd gone from a complete stranger to . . . whatever he had become, in such a short period.

He'd left Ireland six weeks ago. According to what he'd told her before leaving, it meant he was due back in Europe soon.

They didn't have any explicit understanding about what would happen when he was back. No actual plan to reconnect—she hadn't been able to think that far ahead. She just knew where the Universe was leading her next, and she trusted that the rest would work out just the way it should.

Now faced with the possibility of seeing him again, a delicious shiver roused her body and made the butterflies dance.

He had a hold over her. A hold the depths of which Elizabeth Lara couldn't bring herself to fully admit.

But she *did* know that even if things with Wes picked up right where they had left off, her past relationship with Connor would prevent her from exploring anything romantic with her old friend. No matter how well he knew her . . . or how much chemistry they shared.

Elizabeth walked down the busy London street, feeling more like a giddy schoolgirl than a grown woman as she evoked the Irishman's gorgeous face.

Connor.

The last six weeks had been an exercise in being present. In exploring the world, having fun, and feeling whole. She'd tried to keep thoughts of him safely behind a glass shield so she wouldn't fall into the trap of living in her memories, or create unrealistic expectations about the future. But now, with his return so near, the thoughts and emotions broke through the glass wall and tumbled out at her. Finally allowing herself to remember him fully made the random Tuesday in May feel a little like Christmas morning.

She stopped at a newsstand, nodding pleasantly at the round man with the cabbie hat behind the counter. The sugar from the strawberries and her conversation with Wes had made her thirsty. She smacked her lips as she considered her choices, finally grabbing a large blue water bottle with a red cap. Her eyes found the photography magazines off to the left. An interesting article on infrared pictures caught her attention.

She'd only recently begun thinking about infrared and alternate light photography.

It was then that she caught sight of a very special color. She swallowed and stopped moving abruptly. A pair of familiar eyes stared back at her.

Ice blue.

Her stomach plunged to her feet. He was back.

Acknowledgements

This book would not have been possible without the support, inspiration, and moxie of the YWLA Writers Group. Special thanks to Laura Brennan, Colette Sartor, Lisanne Sartor, Eileen Gibson Funke, Swati Pandey, Robinne Lee, Amanda Glassman, Deb Cohen, Danelle Davenport and Alex Napier.

Thanks to my family for all the support. I *heart* you.

Thanks also to Rudy at Starbucks for keeping me in Earl Grey.

Finally, thanks to my crew of Irish kids: Amy, Patrick, Dee . . . we'll always be eighteen and tipsy in Paris.

ABOUT THE AUTHOR

Juliet is originally from California. She is a true, hopeless, all-in romantic. Her first kiss was with a Frenchman in Paris, her first love was an Eagle Scout, and her first crash-and-burn was with someone from Harvard (Jules studied history at Yale—she should have known better). When she isn't writing she can be found photographing landscapes, binge-watching entire series on Netflix, or dancing the international cha-cha.

The Irish Cottage was inspired by her great love of all things Irish and the beautiful time she's spent traveling the Emerald Isle.

Titles by Juliet Gauvin

The Irish Heart Complete Series

The Irish Cottage: Finding Elizabeth (BOOK 1)

The London Flat: Second Chances (BOOK 2)

The Paris Apartment: Fated Journey (BOOK 3)

FOR RELEASE DATES, BONUS CONTENT & EXCLUSIVE GIVEAWAYS JOIN THE READERS GROUP

WWW.JULIETGAUVIN.COM

Manufactured by Amazon.com
Columbia, SC
08 April 2017